PHOENIX

J. V. SPEYER

For information contact:

Jessica Voloudakis
Writing as J. V. Speyer
138 Franklin Street, Braintree, MA 02184
857-212-6355
jvspeyer@gmail.com

Book and Cover design by Bad Doggie Designs
Edited by Quiethouse Editing
ISBN: 978-1-7355156-6-3

For Sophia.

CHAPTER ONE

Luis yawned and massaged his temples. He didn't want to be here. He wanted to be back at home in his bed, with his cat curled up by one side and Donovan on the other. The new chill to the weather, normal for Boston in October, made the scenario even more appealing. There was nothing better to ward against the odious autumn breeze than a lover beside him.

Well, nothing except actually doing his job. Luis had tried to prep for a trial that way once, bringing his notes and laptop home. His intentions had been pure. His actions hadn't, and he'd come perilously close to letting a serial rapist walk free.

He'd salvaged the situation. The guy was in the maximum security prison in Cranston, Rhode Island, where he belonged. He'd be there for the foreseeable future too. The fact that things had worked out once before didn't mean they'd turn out so well again. Luis wasn't going to take a chance like that with a defendant like this one.

He looked down at his screen again. In some ways, Santo Gelens wasn't anything to write home about. Luis had met hundreds of pedophiles over the course of his career. He'd met plenty of pornographers. He'd met hundreds of people who abducted children, and while they might have surface differences, they were exactly the same underneath it all.

Gelens had delivered Luis a first in his career though. He'd never met the guy who turned all those pathologies into a large-scale profitable career. Gelens abducted children, filmed himself abusing them, and produced and distributed the films that earned him the extra-special federal charges. Then he sold the children off to the highest bidder when he was done.

Or killed them. Whichever seemed easier at the time.

Kevin returned to his desk from wherever he'd been. He might get called to testify too. They'd worked the case together, after all. He'd seen everything Luis had.

"How are you holding up?" Kevin plopped a bottle of water down in front of Luis.

Luis toyed with the water bottle. He didn't think he was up to drinking it yet. "This guy has to know we've got him dead to rights. The only reason he's insisting on a full trial is to traumatize the jury."

"You're probably not wrong." Kevin sat down. "I mean you *are* the psychologist. That makes you the expert. I can't help but wonder if he's pleading not guilty because he truly doesn't see anything wrong with what he did though. Plenty of these guys just never do."

Luis considered that option for a moment. "Nah." He opened his eyes and sat up straight again, but he averted his eyes from the screen. There weren't any pictures, but the words were enough.

"His lawyer might try that, but Gelens made every effort to conceal his activities. That's consciousness of guilt right there—which means he knew it was wrong, even if he didn't necessarily agree with the law. And the ones he killed were the ones who resisted the most strongly—the ones who seem to have tried to escape. Again, it shows he knew what he was doing was wrong and he would face serious consequences if he was caught. Also, note how he avoided showing his face on camera and disguised his voice."

Kevin grinned. "Nice work. The lawyers won't trip you up there." Then he sighed, smile falling away. It hadn't reached his eyes anyway. It never did, on cases having to do with children. "I can't imagine what kind of defense he can offer other than insanity. Who defends someone like him?"

Luis shrugged. He couldn't quite get up the same passion Kevin did when it came to defense lawyers. "Someone has to. Everyone has the right to defense, right?" He squirmed. "I mean, yeah—this guy is guilty, there's no way he's not guilty, I'll go to my actual grave screaming his guilt. But we do fuck up sometimes, as a class. Remember Sacco and Vanzetti."

Kevin shuddered. "I know. I hate it, but you're right. I'm just complaining about it right now because I don't want to waste time sitting in the courthouse when I could be working on any of my actual open cases. It's not like Gelens is the only dirtbag ruining lives in New England."

"Tell me about it." Luis huffed out a little laugh. "At least this one's in Boston. Remember when we had to go testify up in Maine, every day, for weeks?"

"I've never eaten so much lobster in my life." Kevin chuckled. "The prosecutor thought he was making it up to us, but honestly I thought I was turning into a lobster by the end of it. I still have dreams where my hands have turned to claws."

Luis laughed. "Right? With any luck we can get through this quickly and get back to work. I know court testimony is part of the job. It's just one of the less fun parts."

"Could be paperwork."

Luis made a face. "I'd rather—" He stopped himself. "Wait. No. I wouldn't. Oh, hey, did I tell you my father asked for a new trial?"

"You've got to be kidding me." Kevin curled his lip. "On what basis?"

"On the basis of taxpayers having money to waste, I guess. I don't know. He didn't exactly call me to discuss his defense. The judge laughed in his face, which was nice of her." Luis cracked his knuckles. "Remind me to send her a fruit basket or something."

"Could look fishy." Kevin chuckled. He hadn't needed to tell Luis that, and Luis knew it. He was just messing with Luis. "Have your foster dad do it."

"Good point. You know he's thinking about retiring?" Luis smiled at the thought. "I have no idea what he'll do with his time, but good for him. He deserves it. He and Eduardo found each other so late in life, they should get to enjoy each other."

The old stab of guilt was there, just as it always would be. Jose had kept himself celibate while Luis had lived with him because he didn't want to create problems for either of them. Luis knew he was gay by the time Jose took him in, and Jose had been worried about the optics. Jose insisted he didn't mind, he was happy to make that choice, but Luis' gut still twisted every time he thought about the opportunities Jose had given up for his sake.

Kevin's smile turned soft. "It just proves we can find love at any age. Maybe there's someone for me out there." Then he barked out a laugh. "Of course, the way things have gone lately, they'll probably be a crook we have to arrest. Or worse, they'll work for the Organized Crime unit."

Luis laughed at that one. "Ugh. God forbid! You couldn't tolerate one of those jerks. You need someone intelligent." He shook his head. "Can you believe they tried to take a serial killer case out of my hands because the guy had an Italian name?"

"Of course they did." Kevin snorted. "I assume you smacked them down, right?"

"Yes, I did. Hard." He smirked. "The crime scene photos alone had the one guy, the one who's obsessed with clothes, running for the bathroom."

"I'll bet. Hey, how's Donovan doing with his promotion?" Kevin perked up.

A surge of pride threatened to burst through Luis' chest. He was amazed Kevin couldn't see it. He was all but lighting the office by himself. "It's only been a few months, but the closure rate is up by ten percent already. Statistically, it could just be the result of a shift in personnel or getting rid of dead weight like Porras, but I honestly think it's because of Donovan. He's so humble about it too, he's not bragging or anything. I found out about it from Alicia."

"Oh my God, look at you gushing." Kevin's smile grew fond. "When are you going to make an honest man out of him already?"

Luis' face burned. "I don't know. I mean it's something to think about." He reached into the drawer where he locked his gun when he was at the office. The small velvet-covered box was there, right where he kept it locked up so Donovan wouldn't find it. Now he pulled it out and tossed it to Kevin.

"I *have* been thinking about it. For a while now." He couldn't bring himself to look at Kevin's face. "I just don't know how to bring it up, or what to say. I mean we've only been living together since the spring. It's too early, isn't it? It's definitely too early. It's definitely rushing."

"Luis, you own a home together. You share a cat." Kevin cleared his throat. "It's not rushing. And the ring is beautiful. You have fantastic taste."

"It's too much. He's not a jewelry kind of guy. He'd never wear it. He'd tell me I'm being ridiculous, which I kind of am. And seriously, who needs a piece of paper to make their relationship real? Being married didn't make either of our parents particularly happy. Shit, my parents were married, and my father still murdered my mom." Luis' heart slammed against his ribcage, racing faster than it had when facing any suspect. "He'll probably say no on those grounds alone, right? I mean, like father like son, he'd turn me down out of self-preservation—"

"Luis, breathe." Kevin got out of his chair, came around the desks, and put his hands on Luis' shoulders. "It's not too early. If you want to marry him, and I think you must because you went out and bought a beautiful ring, you should ask him. Don't let your brain spin into a frenzy of doubt because both of your fathers are assholes."

Luis took a deep breath. Kevin was right, and Luis knew this on a mostly intellectual level. "I want to." He swallowed hard. "I just . . . I need to get my head straight first. He's kind of . . . you know?"

Look at you, all that book learning and still about as articulate as a baby. His father's voice mocked him from his prison cell.

"He can be touchy—he can be insecure, just like I can." Luis mentally flipped off the pathetic old man who still occupied too much space in his head. "My doubts don't have anything to do with him or with my love for him or with our relationship. They have everything to do with my own insecurities. If I show those doubts though, it's likely to hurt him and feed into his issues—which are also valid, and not something I want to feed."

"Well, you are the psychologist." Kevin huffed out a little laugh. "What are you going to do? Hoard the ring like Sméagol?"

Luis took the box back and hunched over it, petting it in imitation of the popular fantasy character. He locked it back in its drawer. "Maybe." Then he smiled. "I think I'll book a few appointments with Father Geoffrey. I know exactly why I'm freaking out, but it's not the kind of thing I can cure on my own."

Kevin patted him on the back. "Look at you, being all healthy and stuff! Who'd have thought, back when you two first reunited?"

Luis laughed, even though he was blushing. It felt good to be at a point where he could laugh at himself now. "Yeah, well, I wasn't in the best place back then. But I'm getting better, and so is he." He looked over at his computer. "And honestly, I think I'm as prepared as I'm going to be for tomorrow's testimony."

"Knowing you, you're going to be more prepared than the judge or either attorney." Kevin snorted. "I think you're good, Luis."

"It never hurts to be ready." He winked. "But now I'm going to go home and enjoy some time with the love of my life and our cat. It helps to remember why we're here, you know?"

Kevin headed back to his desk. "You're right. It does."

Donovan looked up when his office door opened for his five o'clock appointment. He'd barely gotten used to having an office, much less a door that opened. That was definitely one of the better perks of the job. The extra pay was nice too. Additional paperwork—that wasn't much fun at all.

When he saw the person disturbing the pristine quiet of his office, he grinned and rose. "Special Agent Morales." He got out from behind his desk and came around to shake Alex's hand.

Alex still had hair longer than regulation length, but he spent enough time undercover that no one complained. Today, he wore his full fed suit though, and professionalism looked good on him even with the hair.

"No one told me you were the agent assigned to this case. It's good to see you, man."

Alex laughed and gave Donovan a quick hug. "I told them not to tell you. I wanted it to be a surprise, just to see the look on your face. Nice new digs. Looks like they still squeak when you turn a corner too fast. Congratulations, Lieutenant Carey."

Donovan laughed and took his seat, more relaxed than he'd been all week. "Thanks. I won't pretend it was easy, but you knew that."

"Yeah." Alex looked away for a second. "We're still scouring Boston PD for some of the bad apples. Captain Power seems to be doing a good job all on his own around here."

Donovan winced. Captain Power wasn't taking any prisoners in his quest to root out conspirators who'd helped hide Fred Carey's murder of five protestors ten years before.

"Yeah, well, he's definitely a man on a mission. And the brass isn't going to get in his way, that's for damn sure. I try to stay out of it. It was bad enough when everyone thought I was the kind of guy who killed six people in cold blood, you know?"

"I can only imagine." Alex shuddered. "So what's it been like on this side of the desk?"

"Weird. I feel like I've been gaining weight every day. I haven't been, I make sure to work out and eat right, but I'm behind a desk and not out there chasing down bad guys. We've been doing a lot of good, and I'm proud of the work we've been doing, but it's an adjustment." He chuckled and shook his head. "You know, I always thought it was the kind of job a guy got when he was too old to work in the field anymore. But hey, I'm in my midthirties. When I thought that way, I thought my midthirties *was* too old to be in the field." He spread his hands wide. "What can I say?"

Alex's answering grin was impish. "Well, you know, I can see where you might think that . . ."

Donovan shook his fist. "Get off my lawn, young whippersnapper!"

They shared a laugh, and then Alex sobered. "So about this case. It's a little tricky, in terms of jurisdiction."

Donovan rolled his eyes. "That's because we're not sure whose jurisdiction it falls under yet. We know there's crime happening. State lines are probably being crossed, which means there's probably some federal involvement. That's not rocket science. The question is, who takes the lead and what's the protocol here?"

This was part of the reason Donovan hated working with federal agencies. Sure, he'd gotten the chance to reunite with the love of his life through working with the FBI. They'd still had to do this weird dance around who called the shots, and even then, it had been more clear-cut. The FBI had been asked to assist. Murder was a state crime, not federal.

This was a drug-trafficking operation, possibly including complications such as human trafficking, and it was happening in a part of the state that dipped right into Connecticut. The jurisdictional questions alone would keep an army of lawyers employed for decades.

Alex snorted. "Oddly enough, my superiors didn't feel compelled to call DC for this one. They 'trust you and Lieutenant Carey to deal with the crime first, and sort the paperwork out later.'"

Donovan stared at Alex for a moment. "You're kidding." He laughed then. "Good one. You almost had me."

"I'm not joking." Morales shrugged, supremely relaxed. "I know it sounds bizarre, but it's the truth. They know Justice is getting squirrelly right now. They'd rather take down this ring than have that bunch of—er, charming and dedicated souls swoop in and mess everything up to try to look like the heroes." Morales' grin twisted, becoming wry. "We know our reputation, and we know the limitations we're working under. All we want at the end of the day—most of us, anyway—is to make the country safer. From what it looks like, that's not happening out in Southwick."

Donovan shook his head and closed his eyes. "They tied a dude to a tree outside a bar and let him bleed out from a handful of cuts. That's not safe."

"Yikes. I didn't see that in our report."

"It only happened a couple of days ago. Considering the victim was suspected of snitching, I don't think we're going to get far in that specific investigation. Trace might give us something, but I don't want to push witnesses into getting themselves killed. I'm happy to have help with this one."

"And we're happy to have local help dealing with an organized crime ring. Er, did you tell Luis you were working with Organized Crime on this?" Alex bit his lip.

Donovan chuckled. "I did. And he cursed. In four languages. I love it when he does that."

Alex ducked his head, maybe a little sheepishly. Maybe Donovan was reading into it. Donovan never exactly forgot about Luis' past with Alex. He couldn't. He couldn't forget that he was the one Luis wanted, chose to spend his life with, either.

"So things are still going well for the two of you?"

Donovan couldn't read Alex's tone. He knew part of the barrier there was his own jealousy. Alex had been up-front about his own feelings regarding Luis back when he'd met Donovan. The term *hero worship* had come up a time or two, if Donovan remembered correctly. He didn't need to sit there and try to read for hidden meanings in Alex's tone or face. Luis loved him.

"Yeah. I mean who'd have thought, right? We've both got a ton of hang-ups and issues, but we're doing great. The house is in good shape; the family is doing well. Luis is actually coaching my nephew's soccer team. How grossly suburban is that?"

Alex burst out laughing. "That's . . . wild. That's just making my brain hurt. He goes from kicking the crap out of murderers all day to teaching kids to run around on a field."

"He's *good* at it too. I mean really good at it." Donovan found his whole mood softening as he remembered watching last night's game. "I remember for years he said, 'Oh, I don't do kids.' But yesterday, one of the boys got hurt, and you've never seen anyone be so gentle and soothing with a child before. The kid was even on the other team, and Luis was able to get him up and over to the sideline, got the knee wrapped, and even got him into the car so his parents could get him to the doctor. Kid didn't cry once Luis got to him, and even I could see it was bad."

"He's always had a way about him. You guys thinking about adopting?"

Donovan shook his head. "We haven't talked about it, but I don't know if either of us would ever really be up for it. It's one thing to be able to help a kid in an emergency. It's something else to be around a kid every minute, all the time. And considering the backgrounds we both have—I mean I'm not sure either of us has healthy parenting models in front of us."

Alex acknowledged this with a nod. "Your mom seems like she's got a pretty good head on her shoulders."

"She's evolved." Donovan kept his tone dry. "She's been great about welcoming Luis and basically being a mom to him. And he's not exactly alone. He's gotten closer to Jose now. Camila, one of the witnesses who helped exonerate me, has basically adopted him. But I'm not sure actually adopting would be a great idea.

"Plus, we'd probably have to be married first."

Alex smiled. "And that's not something you think is on the table?"

Donovan sighed. "We kind of talked about it, back in February when we worked on that human-trafficking case. Remember?"

Alex shuddered. "How could I forget? I watched a ghost try to drown him. And he fucking fried it, dude."

A bit of bile rose in Donovan's throat. "Yeah. Yeah, I missed that part. Probably for the best, even if I feel like crap about it. Anyway, the whole marriage . . . talk . . . didn't go well."

Alex scoffed. "What, you mean a discussion held while undercover, during extremely stressful circumstances, while rebuilding after a shock to your relationship, didn't turn out to be the most shining moment in your history? I'm shocked, man. Shocked." He pressed a hand to his chest. "You've been living together for a while, and you stayed together through a pretty big challenge if I remember correctly. If it's something you want . . ."

Alex raised an eyebrow then. "Is it something you want?"

Donovan reached into a drawer in his desk. If he remembered correctly, Captain Power used to keep a bottle of whiskey in this compartment back when it had been his desk. The only thing in there now was a small velvet-covered box. "Does that answer your question?"

Alex opened the box. "Christ, Carey. This is gorgeous! He's going to love it."

"Assuming I ever find the balls to give it to him." Donovan took the box back and sighed. "It's . . . I don't know. I keep thinking, *Oh, tonight. I'll do it tonight.* And then he winds up getting called to someplace weird, like Newport, to bust someone for something gross, and I'm like, *This is literally the worst time to propose. There is nothing less romantic than proposing in the middle of a serial killer investigation.* And so it sits there."

Alex grimaced. "I mean, yeah, dropping to one knee in a crime scene is a little gauche or whatever, but Luis is who and what he is. He's never going to not be on a crime scene or working on something grisly or wrapping up from something grisly. And you fell in love with the guy who does all that. Twice."

"I know." Donovan slumped in his chair. "I know it! I'd never dream of changing him. Well, that's not true. I'd love to give him a little more self-love, for him to see himself the way I see him. But that's different. He does what he does because he needs to do it, and he's damn good at it, and I love him. I don't want someone else in his body, you know? I want *Luis.* I wouldn't be out for anyone else, I wouldn't share my life this way with anyone else—the body is nice, but it's secondary to *him.*"

"Good. So propose." Alex sat up straighter. "You love him, I know he adores you. You want to make all this official, right? You want to make sure there aren't any complications if something happens to one of you? Then put a ring on it. Go home today. Don't wait."

Donovan closed his eyes. If he let himself, he

could picture himself doing just that. Luis would get home, Donovan would drop to one knee, and ask Luis to marry him. He'd be shocked, and he'd resist because it was Luis and he wouldn't think Donovan was sincere. But then he'd agree. They'd settle on a date and they'd be married and they'd live happily ever after.

"He starts testimony tomorrow in the Gelens case." Donovan shook his head. "He's a cloud of anxiety with legs right now. He's worried he'll flub his testimony and somehow that creep will get out on a technicality."

"That's never happened once in his career." Alex shook his head.

"No, but he's still worried about it. You know how he gets. I can't distract him like that right now, even for a good reason. We've got time, you know? I have to respect his needs here. I can't just trample all over how he does his job."

Alex grimaced. "I guess. You make a really good point, but I hate to think of something happening and you missing your window."

"I'll do it as soon as his testimony is finished. It's only a few days." Donovan grinned and pulled up his file on the Southwick drug ring. "Let's see what we can do about that drug ring in Southwick, shall we?"

CHAPTER TWO

Luis sat quietly on the benches in Judge Sullivan's courtroom. He didn't stand out much from any of the other people crowding the benches in the admittedly vast room, except maybe in the color of his skin. Even that didn't stand out as much as it often did. Gelens, unusual for his type, hadn't been particular in his appetites.

A wave of revulsion passed through Luis, and he fought to contain it. He'd testified before Judge Sullivan, more than once. He knew what he was dealing with. Sullivan had many strict rules, and more than one of them governed behavior that might prejudice the jury. Anyone convicted in his court would be convicted on the evidence alone, or there would be hell to pay.

Just breathe, Luis. In and out. For once, the voice in his head was his own, and it was helpful.

He glanced around the courtroom, both to assess the situation and to get control of himself. Gelens, the defendant, sat quietly at the defense table in the front of the room. He wore a suit and tie, like anyone else, and was not restrained while the jury was in the courtroom. The only outward sign of his guilt was the smug little sneer he turned toward every witness in the box, the jurors themselves, the prosecutor, and the press.

The witness currently on the stand was a tiny white woman, not even five feet tall. Bianca was one of the analysts from Quantico. She specialized in image analysis. She had a doctorate in one of the hard sciences—geospatial analysis, if Luis remembered correctly. Out of all the FBI's analysts, Bianca had turned out to have the strongest stomach for analyzing images in this type of case.

Right now, Gelens' attorney, Andrew Morello, was cross-examining Bianca. Bianca was a New Yorker by origin, and not the Fifth Avenue type. Someone had to defend people accused of even the most heinous crimes, and Morello might as well be the one to do it. He didn't know Bianca. He wasn't prepared for what she was going to do to him. Luis had just enough professional distance to pity Morello.

"Ms. Laterza—"

"Doctor."

"Excuse me?"

"Doctor Laterza." Bianca spoke slowly, as if

to someone just learning English. "I have doctorates in planetary geology and physics."

Morello tried. He really did. "I see. And now you look at men's sexual apparatus for a living."

Bianca raised an eyebrow at him. "I analyze images from a variety of sources to determine unique identifiers that would lead to a suspect. In cases where a sex crime is caught on camera, as discussed in my testimony for the prosecution, the penis is in fact a unique identifier."

"And how many penises have you seen in your lifetime?"

Luis rolled his eyes. If he had a dollar for every time some defense attorney thought he was clever and asked that question, he'd be able to retire. He wouldn't know what to do with himself, but he'd have the option.

"In the course of investigating sex crimes for the Federal Bureau of Investigation, I've seen over ten million unique penises."

"Out of how many in the world?"

"Approximately three and a half billion. The vast majority of those men don't show their faces on camera while committing crimes however."

"Objection." Morello looked over at Sullivan. "Witness is engaging in speculation."

"Overruled." Sullivan pursed his lips. "You walked into that one, Counsel."

Morello sighed, but picked himself up. "You're familiar with software that could alter images? Software that could, say, put one man's head over another's body?"

"Of course." Bianca didn't break a sweat.

"So it's possible someone digitally altered the films in which Mr. Gelens is said to have appeared to put his head on someone else's body."

"No. It isn't."

"Would you care to elaborate?"

"Well, since you asked so nicely." Bianca gave him her nastiest smile. "Mr. Gelens was accused—and convicted—of a prior sexual offense. Photographs were taken of the offending organ and entered into evidence at the time. Those were entered into evidence in this trial and made available to defense counsel as well. So not only do we have the films from his current offenses, we have a photo of the specific offending organ itself. It *is* him, and his dick, and no one else's."

Morello hunched his shoulders. "No further questions, Your Honor."

"I can send you more copies, if you want. I've got them on my phone." Bianca pulled her phone out of her pocket. "Here." She pushed a button, and Morello's phone went off.

The jury laughed.

Morello gaped. "How did you get my phone

number?"

"It's the FBI, Mr. Morello. We have *all* the phone numbers."

The whole courtroom erupted into laughter, with the exception of Morello and Gelens. Luis stifled his own chuckles and pinched the bridge of his nose. He foresaw several all-agency memos in his inbox about proper courtroom decorum in his future.

After a few seconds, Sullivan banged his gavel. "All right, all right. Dr. Laterza, thank you for your testimony. For future reference, unsolicited dick pics are not appropriate during court. You're dismissed. Do the People have any further witnesses?"

The prosecutor, Catherine Fahey, rose. "We do, Your Honor. The People call Special Agent Luis Gomes to the stand."

Luis got up and made his way to the witness stand. He could feel Gelens' cold gray eyes on him as he walked. He hated having his back to the predator. He knew he was far outside Gelens' age group of interest, but he still disliked the feeling of vulnerability. He wanted Gelens where he could see him.

The bailiff swore him in, Luis took his seat, and he got ready to testify. Fahey set the table by asking him about his credentials, which was pretty much par for the course. The jury needed to know why they should listen to him—to anyone in law enforcement, after everything that had gone on lately.

And Luis' career had given him a lot to be proud of.

Once Luis had established his authority, Fahey got to the point—the reason they were here in the first place. "Agent Gomes, you were the lead agent on this case, is that correct?"

Luis nodded. "That's correct. Once the task force in Quantico had identified the epicenter of the ring, my partner Agent Rourke and I were assigned to track the suspect down and bring him in."

"So you were not assigned to identify the suspect."

"No, ma'am." He glanced over at the listless jury, and almost cursed. They'd had them at the end of Bianca's testimony. Now they were going to have to work twice as hard to bring them back. "When we find evidence of child pornography, we kick the case to the Child Pornography Task Force in Quantico. It's specialized work, with a lot of fine details that are easy to miss if you don't know exactly what you're doing. They kick it back into the field when the time comes to make an arrest."

"Fair enough." Fahey gave him an encouraging smile. "But it happens that you were the one to kick the case to the task force in the first place, correct?"

Luis nodded again. "Yes, ma'am."

"Explain for the court how that happened, please."

Luis had to take a breath for that one. Cases involving children were always the hardest, for anyone in law enforcement. He hated having to think about them or remember them after the fact. He knew he'd never forget them.

"On April fourth, Agent Rourke and I were assigned to a missing child case with suspected foul play in Watertown. Nine-year-old Veronica Torosian and a friend were approached by someone dressed as an animal control officer under the guise of an issue with licensing for Veronica's dog, Casper. The 'officer' led her around a corner, with the dog. When the dog ran up to the friend a few minutes later, with the leash but alone, the friend sought help.

"It was too late. Veronica and the 'officer' were gone. Dog walkers found her body the next day in the Middlesex Fells Reservation." He glanced over at the jurors and winced. "I'll try not to be graphic.

"Her body was still on the warm side when she was found, indicating that she had been kept alive for several hours." He tugged at his collar as words failed him. Out of the corner of his eye, he saw Gelens laughing quietly.

He wouldn't lose his cool. He was more professional than that. Too much was riding on this case for him to let his anger get the better of him.

Fahey gave him a moment. "And that's when you kicked it to the task force?"

"No, ma'am. We suspected, of course, but that's part of the job." He managed a wry grin for the jurors and the press he saw at the back of the room. "After a while, your mind always goes to the worst-case scenario. You're not going to kick it to the task force until you have something for them to investigate though."

Fahey knew all of this. She'd prosecuted several of Luis' cases. These words were mostly for the jury. "And you got that *something* fairly quickly."

"We did. A film showed up within a week." He swallowed hard. "An informant was sufficiently disturbed that he didn't care about charges for his own stash of films. In his words, 'Porn is one thing, and I know it's disgusting and wrong. Snuff is something else.'"

Luis had to fight bile. He wasn't the only one. He couldn't make himself look at Gelens. To settle himself, he cast his gaze through the crowd again. Bianca's eyes blazed from next to the seat he'd vacated. She'd had to actually watch the whole video, so he didn't blame her for her rage.

Most of the jury looked green. The reporters had all worked disturbing cases before, but the informant's words made even them turn pale. Some witnesses shuddered visibly. Luis recognized Veronica's parents, weeping silently, and wished he could do something to soothe their pain. It must have been like being traumatized all over again.

Most people in the crowd showed some sign of being affected by the news, but everyone processed emotions differently. Luis knew that—he had a master's degree in that stuff. He was living proof. Hell, he'd spent most of his adult life "processing" his emotions with sex. He was in no position to judge how others coped.

The stone faces of a few other victims' parents weren't a surprise. Luis couldn't say how he'd react under similar circumstances, but he didn't think he'd want to display his grief or horror for the world to see. Some people were just private.

One woman, a white woman with a facial scar and peroxide-blonde hair, was grinning. Luis couldn't help but think of a hyena.

He snapped his gaze back to Fahey. He couldn't control the hyena lady. Maybe she was some kind of sick vulture. Maybe she was writing a true crime book and had just gotten the perfect quote. Maybe she'd had bad plastic surgery and couldn't move her face from that position. He couldn't focus on her right now. He had a job to do.

Fahey caught his eyes, rooting him in the present. "And that's when you kicked it upstairs."

"That's when we referred that aspect of the investigation to the task force, and it's a good thing we did. The assailant knew what he was doing. He left no useable evidence on the remains that we could use to trace him. We pursued him on our end and found the fake animal control van abandoned in Wilmington, but he'd cleaned himself out of it well."

Hyena Lady's expression hadn't changed. Luis again forced himself to ignore her.

"Agent Gomes, it took them six months to give you a suspect. Why is that?"

Luis focused on Fahey again. He had a ready answer. He'd prepped for this, spent ages going over his notes and the case timeline. The ground was solid beneath him here. He explained how thorough the task force had been, and how long it had taken him and Kevin to track Gelens down. "But we're positive we have our man, ma'am."

Hyena Lady's eyes bored into him.

Donovan glowered at the phone when it rang. It was four o'clock. He could leave in half an hour. Okay, technically, he could leave whenever he wanted; he was the boss. Still, he had to set a good example for the people reporting to him, even if he wanted to get home before Luis.

Still the phone was ringing, and he had to answer it. Especially when he saw the name associated with the obnoxious tone. Alex Morales wouldn't be bothering him during a case for anything trivial. For one thing, Alex had two detectives with him. If he was calling Donovan, and not Fitch or Nguyen, something must be wrong. Not that they weren't friendly, but Alex was outside his chain of command.

"Hey, Morales. What's going on?" Donovan kept his voice light. If by some chance things hadn't gone bad, he didn't want to tempt fate.

Sirens wailed in the background on the other end of the call. "Hey, Carey. Um, there was an ambush."

Morales' voice had a strain to it, one Donovan recognized all too well. "Shit." He stood up and grabbed his keys. "Both down?"

"Both breathing. Assailant is dead." Alex took a deep breath. "I couldn't—there wasn't an opportunity to take a nonlethal shot."

"I believe you. I'm on my way, Morales. Are you hurt?"

"Nothing a little duct tape won't fix—hey!"

Donovan heard the unmistakable sound of a phone being seized. "Are you Agent Morales' superior?"

Donovan paused in his mad dash for the door. "This is Lieutenant Donovan Carey, Major Crimes Unit, Massachusetts State Police. Who is this?"

The man on the other end cleared his throat. "Sergeant Robert Dupree, sir. Apologies. I'm one of the first officers to respond to Agent Morales' call for assistance. Detectives Nguyen and Fitch are on their way to Bay State Hospital. They're in bad shape but they're breathing. Agent Morales has a shoulder wound, through and through from what it looks like. He's refusing to get into the ambulance until the crime scene is 'secure.' Can you please explain to this man the scene won't be secure if he bleeds out onto the motel room carpet?"

Donovan huffed out a little laugh, in spite of the circumstances. It wasn't hard to see who'd mentored Alex. He rattled off Agent Holcombe's number from memory. "That's a supervisor at the FBI field office in Boston. She can actually give him orders. I can argue with Agent Morales all day, but I know exactly who put that idea in his head and

I've never convinced him to take care of himself either. Look, I'll be out there as soon as I can get there. You're in Southwick, right?"

"Starlight Lounge Motel, that's right. It won't be the first questionable stain on this carpet. I look forward to meeting you, sir." Sgt. Dupree passed the phone back to Alex.

"It's not that bad." Alex sighed. "Donovan, I'm sorry about Fitch and Nguyen."

"I know. It's part of the risk we all take. We'll talk about it in the hospital. Let them patch you up or the nice sergeant is going to sic Holcombe on you." Donovan closed and locked his office door behind him. "No time to waste. See you soon." He hung up and turned to the department admin.

"Two men down out in Southwick. I'm on my way out there. If you could let Captain Power and maybe Public Relations know, I'd appreciate it."

The admin sat up straight, face drained of all color. Donovan knew she'd do exactly what he'd asked of her. He didn't need to sit there and watch her do it.

He called Luis from the car. He didn't pick up, probably because he was still in court giving testimony. Donovan didn't mind. He left a voice mail as he pulled out onto the Mass Pike. "Hey, I was hoping to get home before you, but it looks like it's not going to happen. We've got two detectives down and one fed—Alex Morales. He's alive, it's a shoulder wound, but I'm going out there to handle things on the scene. If you get this message and you feel like it, give Morales a call and yell at him to let them take him to the hospital and fix him up. Love you."

Then he threw on the sirens and went full throttle all the way out to Southwick.

The media was already on the scene by the time he got there, lighting the place up like Boston Garden on game night. Donovan knew the main stations had just reached out to local affiliates in Springfield and Hartford to get people to the site, but it still bothered him. What ghoulish purpose did it serve to have bloody pictures of a motel room splashed all over people's screens without information to go with it?

Sgt. Dupree turned out to be a tall Black man, head shaved with a neat little beard, in his late twenties. He found Donovan easily. "Lieutenant Carey, thanks for coming out. I don't know what magic you used to get Agent Morales to finally get into the truck, but he got a phone call at around five and let them take him to the hospital."

Donovan grinned at that, although he kept his face away from the cameras when he did. One of the first rules of police work was to never smile at a crime scene. "I called his mentor. Agent Gomes knows just what buttons to push."

"That would be the Agent Gomes with the book? The one who found the Rabbit Tracks Killer?"

"Same guy." Donovan stuck his hands in his pockets.

"That's some pull you've got, Lieutenant." Dupree nodded appreciatively. "The scene is secure, although you'll want to put booties on."

Donovan accepted the shoe coverings that would keep him from tracking debris over the scene. "Are the feds on their way?"

"Some guy by the name of Wong started screaming at me about not moving anything." Dupree rolled his eyes. "I spoke to an Agent Borchard afterward. He apologized and told me 'Dr. Wong lacks chill and social graces.' That was putting it mildly, but whatever. We're not touching anything. Do you know these people?"

"Dr. Wong works for the State. I'm surprised you haven't had to deal with him yet. It's an experience." Donovan grimaced. "And yeah, Borchard is putting it mildly. Agent Borchard is probably the most mellow federal agent I've met. If he's on his way, he's likely got Agent Wragge with him. They're partners. They're decent guys, for feds."

Dupree gave him a suspicious look. "Do you work with a lot of feds?"

"Well, I live with one." Donovan led the way into the motel room. "I've had a few beers with both of these guys."

The crime scene didn't seem to hold a lot of information. It was a seedy motel room, like any number of other seedy motel rooms on the back roads of the Commonwealth. Donovan had lost count of how many there were and how many he'd had to go poking into over the years. Gunfire had shattered the curtain, which was old enough to be made from actual glass instead of plastic. The carpet probably hadn't been cleaned since sometime in the fifties. A body lay facedown in front of the bed, adding its own contribution to the stains. An AR-15 lay a short distance away.

"Christ." Donovan shuddered. "This really was an ambush, wasn't it?"

"Looks like it. You'd have to talk to your guys, but from what Agent Morales told me they were at least suspicious from the start. They were wearing their vests . . ."

"But standard-issue vests are only rated at level three. If he had an AR-15, they'd have had to go in with hard armor—level four." Donovan wiped a hand over his face. "Thanks, Sergeant. I appreciate your help. I'm going to give you a word of advice."

Dupree raised an eyebrow. "Oh yeah?"

"Yeah. Dr. Wong is the state medical examiner. He's going to come out here to handle the shooter. The FBI has their own evidence technician, a guy named Maxwell. He and Wong get along like a house on fire—if the house is filled with accelerant and gunpowder. Don't get in between them unless someone pulls a gun. It'll feel like you're banging your head against a wall, without the reprieve of the blackout afterward." He passed Dupree his card. "Let me know if there's anything I can do, any questions I can answer."

Donovan got away before he had to deal with Wong or any of the feds. He wanted an update on his people before he had to deal with any of the personality clashes involved.

By the time he got to Bay State Hospital, the emergency department was filled with cops. A lone camera crew, trying to make themselves inconspicuous, lurked in the back of the waiting room. Donovan almost felt bad for them. He'd hate to be the one to have to try to get answers out of state troopers after a shooting.

Reporters weren't his problem right now. He strode up to the triage desk and showed his credentials. "I'm Lieutenant Carey. I'm here about

Detectives Fitch and Nguyen."

The nurse behind the desk nodded and lowered her gaze. That wasn't a good sign, and a pit formed in the middle of Donovan's stomach. "Come on back, please." She pressed a button under her desk, and Donovan opened the door that suddenly unlocked itself for him.

The nurse let her colleague cover her station and guided Donovan back toward a long row of treatment bays. "I'll get Dr. Kumar. He's the trauma doctor in charge tonight. In the meantime, why don't you have a seat in here?" She gestured to a small conference room, with thick walls and low light.

A box of tissues sat on the table.

Donovan moved robotically toward the table, forcing himself to breathe. He could handle this. It was part of the job. His hands trembled, so he kept them in his pockets.

Dr. Kumar, a dark-skinned South Asian man in fresh, clean scrubs, entered the room. "Lieutenant Carey?" He closed the door behind him and sat down. "I understand you're the supervisor of the two detectives who were shot."

Donovan nodded. "I am. What's their status?"

Kumar nodded and glanced down at his tablet. "Detective Nguyen was hit twice, once in the leg and once in the abdomen. She's still in surgery to repair abdominal damage. You're aware of how we prioritize trauma damage, yes?"

Donovan bit down on his tongue. "Insides first, then extremities."

"Correct. I can tell you that her leg is severely damaged. I'm not able to tell you at this point if she'll be able to keep it." He took a deep breath. "But I have to confess, it's doubtful."

Donovan closed his eyes. "She's alive."

"She is. We're hopeful we'll be able to repair all the damage in her abdomen. The bullet damaged the large intestine and the kidney but didn't damage her spine. Everything else should be something that we can fix. She'll have a long road to recovery."

Donovan exhaled slowly. "Thankfully, she and her family will be well taken care of. What about Detective Fitch?"

Kumar looked away. "He was also hit twice. While he was still alive when he was put into the ambulance, he died en route to the hospital."

"Fuck." Donovan clenched his hands into fists. He wouldn't react worse than that. Not here, in front of a stranger. It wasn't his place. He had to think about the families. He had to think about the other officers, the rest of the team. He had to think about the other cops all over the state who would have to process this.

He looked back at Kumar. "Does Morales know?"

"The FBI agent who came in?" Kumar swallowed. "No. We were able to stabilize the bleeding and repair some of the damage to his shoulder. We'll get an orthopedist to look at the injury when the swelling has gone down and we've got a better view of what we're looking at, but right now he's resting in a room on the fifth floor." He managed a wry grimace. "For a given value of resting, I suppose. Am I correct in assuming you'd like to debrief him?"

"I would." Donovan rose. His stomach stayed where it was, weighted down by the two lives destroyed. He'd been the one to send them out. He'd given them this assignment. He couldn't get away from the facts.

"I'm sure I don't have to caution you about questioning him right now." Kumar rose and opened the door. "He's been given painkillers. You can't take anything he says too seriously."

"I know." Donovan pressed his lips together. "Alex Morales is more than some federal agent. He's a friend."

"Ah." Dr. Kumar led Donovan to the elevator and then personally guided him to Morales' room, all in silence. "You can give him the news, but don't let him get out of that bed. He's lost a lot of blood. While we've given him a transfusion, he's probably still pretty dizzy."

"Got it." Donovan shook Kumar's hand. "Thank you for your help, Doctor."

He entered the room and pulled the nearest chair over to Morales' bedside.

Morales blinked his eyes open. "Hey." He looked away. "You're not here with good news, are you?"

Donovan sighed. "Nguyen is still in surgery."

"And Fitch?"

"Didn't make it." Donovan took Alex's hand. "I'm so sorry."

"No—I am." Tears leaked out of Alex's dark eyes. "This is my fault."

"No." Donovan kept his voice firm. "The only person at fault is the son of a bitch who pulled the trigger. He made the choice. Not you."

Alex stared into space for a moment. Then he squeezed Donovan's hand. "Hey, Donovan?"

"Yeah?"

"Remember that conversation we had yesterday?"

"Yeah, of course."

"Don't wait. Everyone thinks they have time." He closed his eyes, and his hand went limp.

Donovan could see, based on the monitors attached to his friend, that he was asleep.

CHAPTER THREE

Luis kept his face neutral as he walked back into the courtroom, but he knew he didn't cut the most appealing figure. He'd been at the hospital out in West Bumblebutt, Massachusetts, until six in the morning, keeping a vigil by Alex's bedside. He'd only left when Brick Fontana showed up to relieve him, and even then he'd hesitated.

He knew Judge Sullivan wasn't going to cut him any slack, never mind who'd been shot in another part of the state. Nothing in Hampden County was Sullivan's problem, not until federal charges were filed. And as much as it sucked, Luis knew Sullivan was right.

He'd gotten to see Donovan a couple of times. He couldn't do much for him, not under the circumstances. Donovan didn't have time to be taken care of. He had to organize the hunt for the gang that had set his people up for death. Luis hugged him a few times, and he knew Donovan appreciated the support. There wasn't time for more right now.

Later, there would be. Later, Luis would hold the love of his life close and let him process his grief and his misplaced guilt in private.

For now, they both had work to do.

He forced thoughts of Donovan, and of Alex, from his mind. He was here to stop a serial predator. Fahey murmured her sympathy before starting her questioning. She knew about him and Donovan, of course. She probably knew Alex, for that matter. Even Morello stopped over to offer his condolences.

Fahey cleared her throat, and the jury was brought into the room. Luis looked them over and surveyed the room to see if anything stood out. Hyena Lady was there, the exact same expression on her face as she'd had yesterday. It had to be botched plastic surgery—no one could go twenty-four hours without her face moving. Most of the people in the gallery had been there yesterday, although maybe a few of the reporters had been exchanged for new ones.

Fahey was speaking. "Agent Gomes, you were the lead investigator on this case, as we discussed yesterday. You're also a profiler, is that correct?"

Luis nodded. "Yes, ma'am. I'm part of the Behavioral Analysis Unit."

"You coauthored a study about child pornography, didn't you?"

Luis had to smile a little bit at that one. He'd almost forgotten. It hadn't been his favorite project. "I did. It was probably four years ago. I worked on the project with the Child Pornography Task Force."

"So you're something of an expert on the subject."

Luis grimaced. "I'm more of an expert on criminal psychology, ma'am. It sounds like I'm splitting hairs, I'm sure, but I don't want to get up here and make it seem like I'm something I'm not. There are people out there who can testify about how these networks are built and how they operate in such detail it will make your head spin. That's not me. I take the clues they provide, and I hunt the perpetrators down, but I give full respect to their ability to dive deep into all that data. What I do is analyze the mind behind the behavior."

Fahey nodded, a little smile playing around the corners of her mouth. "Understood. In your expert opinion, would you say Mr. Gelens fits the profile of a typical child pornography distributor?"

Luis snorted. "Mr. Gelens exhibits behavior above and beyond the 'standard' profile of a typical distributor because he's not simply a distributor. He's also a producer." Luis launched into an explanation of Gelens' pathology that would make sense to a typical juror. He'd done this often enough that he could do it in his sleep.

It should have been enough. He just wanted to get back to Chelsea and throw himself into the hunt for whatever gang of freaks shot Alex and Donovan's detectives. The chair in the witness stand wasn't designed for comfort, and it wasn't designed for a tall man either.

Unfortunately for him, Fahey had more questions. She wanted to drive the nail into Gelens' coffin just as badly as he did, which meant leaving no room for him to try to escape his sentence.

"In your professional opinion, would you say Gelens was insane?"

Luis pressed his lips together. "I haven't given him a full psychological examination. I interviewed him upon his arrest, although not with a view toward a diagnosis. He does display traits consistent with a severely narcissistic personality, but that doesn't mean he can't differentiate between right and wrong or that he doesn't see the same reality as the rest of us. He knows the difference between right and wrong; he's simply not interested. He isn't suffering from delusions or hallucinations. He just views his victims as a means to an end—his own gratification and the augmentation of his own wealth."

Gelens' lawyer, Morello, leaped to his feet. "Objection! Your Honor, the witness is engaging in speculation."

Fahey whipped her gaze over to Judge Sullivan. "Your Honor, I refer you to the defendant's own statements during his interview after his arrest, previously entered into evidence in exhibit 14 and exhibits 324 through 459."

Luis and Sullivan shared a visible shudder. The second group of exhibits were the films in which Gelens had played a starring role.

"Overruled." Sullivan glowered at Morello. "Save it for cross, Counselor."

Gelens met Luis' eyes and smirked. Luis rolled his eyes and looked back at Fahey. What did Gelens have to smirk about anyway? He was going to federal prison for the rest of his life. Nothing could possibly save him.

Well, unless Luis screwed up. He'd have to screw up pretty badly, but anything was possible.

"Agent Gomes, what leads a person to behavior like Mr. Gelens'?" Fahey tilted her head to the side.

Prosecutors asked this question every time, and Luis always hated it. Someday, if he ever came across a case that didn't matter, he'd tell the truth. *They're just bad people.* Sure, it was more complicated than that, and it didn't apply to everyone, but Luis was too tired for complicated today. "Well, there are a number of factors that go into offenses such as Mr. Gelens'. Many pedophiles were themselves molested as children, but most survivors of child sexual abuse do not themselves go on to abuse. Many narcissists suffered some sort of trauma, some loss of the love and attention they needed as children. Most people who endure that type of trauma do not eventually go on to become narcissists or serial sexual sadists." He continued his explanation, watching the gallery and the jury carefully.

The jury seemed to be on board. Every pair of eyes in the jury box stayed fixed on him, even the fourth alternate juror who'd been nodding off throughout the trial. The spectators, some of whom were probably other witnesses, seemed to be interested as well. He knew some of them were victims' families. It had to be hard to listen to Luis speaking so clinically about someone who'd been so cruel to their loved ones, but they sat stoically and endured.

Luis had spoken to them before the trial, to make sure they were ready for everything that was to come.

At noon, a loud growl from Judge Sullivan's midsection prompted him to let them recess for lunch. Luis could have kissed him. He needed to get up and stretch his legs, or something.

He needed to stop talking, to stop thinking about a pervert serial killer, who had turned his deviance into a profitable business.

He wanted to find some quiet office somewhere, curl up into a little ball, and take a nap. It wouldn't take much. Twenty minutes would probably be enough to help him avoid biting someone's head off.

The nap was just as much of a fantasy as grabbing Donovan and running off to Bora-Bora. For one thing, there wasn't an office he could borrow. For another, he needed to put some food in his belly if he was going to survive more testimony, or cross-examination. And finally, he needed to check in with Donovan and with his own colleagues.

He pulled his phone out and dialed as he made his way over to the little burger place near the courthouse. He'd had to testify down here often enough that he knew this place, and he knew their menu. He got a seat and ordered a salad even as he struggled to get through to Donovan.

Donovan still sounded like a wreck, which meant he hadn't gone to bed either. "Hey. How's it going?"

Luis smiled and sat back. Even as bad as Donovan sounded, his voice still made the day better. "It's going. Just talking about this guy makes me want to bathe in bleach, but you know. How are you doing?"

"I'm alive. I had to talk to Fitch's parents."

"Yikes. I'm so sorry."

"Yeah. They took it as well as they could, but—well. You've done it before."

"Yeah." Luis couldn't say anything to that. They'd both had to notify families. It never got easier. "How's Nguyen?"

"Still out, I'm afraid. It's probably for the best. She's going to be in a lot of pain when she does wake up. Um, Morales checked out AMA, but you probably knew he would." Donovan chuckled. "It's what you would do."

"It's what I would have done before I had you to basically sit on me until I saw reason." Luis didn't look up as a server delivered his salad and a glass of water. He hadn't ordered water, but he probably sounded hoarse. He definitely needed it. He downed half of it before he continued. "If he winds up losing his job because he jumped the gun and lost the use of his arm—"

Donovan snorted. "Yeah, okay, Mr. I'm Going to Get Cut Up And Not Tell Anyone."

"He's supposed to learn from my mistakes." Luis' face got hot. "Not repeat them."

"Kevin's keeping an eye on him. And he'll

go to the orthopedist. He can't stay in the hospital, you know that. Not when he's the only one to walk away. You wouldn't be able to, I couldn't."

Luis nodded slowly, even though Donovan couldn't see him. "Yeah, you're right. I know. I just hate to think about it. Don't let him hurt himself worse, okay? He's going to be beating himself up something fierce."

"I know it." Someone in the background said something unintelligible, and Donovan cleared his throat. "Hey, I've got to get going. We've got a lead."

"Get 'em. Love you."

"Love you too."

Luis called Kevin next, just to check in. Kevin had a lot of sympathy for the long testimony he was going through, and promised he was keeping an eye on Alex. "He's staying with me and the kids for now. They sent him home with this amazing contraption that sends ice water through this cuff on his shoulder. Macha loves it. Can't refill it enough. I swear she's going to be an orthopedist when she grows up. She even wanted to see his X-rays."

"That's awesome." Luis had to grin at that. "She does like to take care of injured agents."

"Better than going off and trying to become one. Hopefully, you'll be able to come back to work soon. I think we're going to need you on this one. It's fine to get the middle managers from this gang, right? But we want the guys in charge. You're the best guy for that."

"Is Organized Crime getting out of the way?"

Kevin scoffed. "No. But you're the best guy to take care of that little problem too. I'm pretty sure their leader thinks you're the boogey man hiding under his bed at night."

A wave of nausea swept over Luis. "Ugh. I'm getting old. One all-nighter and I'm getting woozy. Look, I'm going to go walk it off. Nothing spells 'credible witness' like puking on the judge."

"Yikes. Grab some ginger or something."

"Good plan. I'll call and check on Alex later." Luis hung up, paid his bill, and shuffled toward the door.

The fresh seaport air should have helped clear Luis' head. It usually worked that way, but today, it just made his nausea worse. He staggered toward the courthouse. Had there been something in the salad, something spoiled? Food poisoning was all they needed.

He forced himself to straighten up, even though the landscape waved in front of him. He wasn't going to jeopardize this case. He was a professional. He'd ask Fahey for an antacid or something. Surely, she had something like that on hand.

He noticed an ambulance parked in front of the courthouse, just outside of the decorative and protective barrier.

A white guy in a pin-striped suit approached. At first, there wasn't anything where his face should have been, just a big black hole. Luis had seen a lot of terrifying things, especially since the arrival of Captain Lightfoot, but the faceless guy took the cake. He'd have screamed, but he was afraid he'd get sick.

Then Luis blinked, and he realized the stranger was Andrew Morello, Gelens' lawyer.

"Agent Gomes? You don't look so good." He put his hand on Luis' arm. "Do you need help?"

The world had already been spinning. Now it changed direction, whirling in the other direction like it had hit a wall. Luis couldn't keep his balance. He fell down, vision going black. The last thing he heard, before his hearing went too, was a woman's voice.

"It's okay, I'm an EMT. Just help me get him on this gurney."

Donovan yawned and tried to rub some feeling back into his face. Once upon a time, all-nighters hadn't bothered him. Of course, he'd been younger then, practically a child. And the all-nighters hadn't been quite so trauma centered. Staying up all night to cram for an exam, or even to stake out a suspect's home, was one thing.

Staying up all night because two of his detectives had been shot was something else entirely.

At least at the end of it all, there would be Luis. Talking to him on the phone had given him the burst of energy he'd needed to get a few hours further into his work, but even that could only get him so far. He was going to have to head home soon, but when he did, he'd have Luis in person. Luis would hold him, and remind him that he hadn't been the one to pull the trigger.

He was beyond lucky to have Luis in his life.

He pulled the ring out of his hiding place. Yeah, he was a lucky man. He'd be even luckier if Luis said yes. Maybe it was too soon. Maybe they weren't *there* yet, wherever *there* was supposed to be. If Donovan didn't ask, he'd spend the rest of his life regretting it.

The door to his office swung open. Donovan looked up, ready to bark at someone. His detectives knew better than to burst in on him without knocking—Captain Power wouldn't have stood for it, back before their promotions, and things hadn't changed.

When he saw Captain Power there instead of some hapless detective, the snarl died in his throat.

Donovan stood up, even though his legs felt shaky. "Sir. To what do I owe the pleasure?"

Alex Morales and Kevin Rourke followed him inside. Alex wore civilian attire and a sling. He looked like crap, which made sense given his injury. Kevin wore his standard-issue fed suit. His face had gone deathly pale.

"You're going to want to sit down, Carey." Captain Power closed the door behind the trio. "I'm afraid we're not here for a social call."

Donovan's blood ran cold. "What's happened?"

Kevin took a deep breath. "Luis disappeared from the courthouse. It looks like he's been abducted."

Donovan's whole world went white for a moment. He couldn't hear anything, see anything. No thoughts echoed through his head. There was only a blank emptiness.

The moment passed, and he chuckled. Feeling returned to his lower extremities. "Good one, guys. People don't just get kidnapped from a federal courthouse in broad daylight."

Captain Power sat down in one of the chairs on the other side of the desk. He gestured to the other one and gave Alex a meaningful stare. "Agent Morales, you look like you're about to pass out. Sit down. And maybe one of you can explain how this happened, since I'm not sure I understand it either."

Alex sat beside Power, moving like he was afraid he was going to fall over. His skin had a greenish cast to it, and he couldn't look up to meet Donovan's eyes. "He didn't make it back after court recessed from lunch. Defense counsel said he was staggering, looked unsteady and even drunk."

"Luis doesn't drink. Ever." Donovan scowled at him. "You know that."

"We all do." Kevin put a hand on Alex's good shoulder. "He's just the messenger, Donovan. Anyway, Morello—the lawyer—knew it too. He says he approached Luis just in time to see him fall over, because he knew just how odd it was. A woman in an EMT uniform approached, with a gurney, and asked for his help in getting Luis onto it. She loaded him into the ambulance, which was waiting nearby, and drove off with the sirens on."

Donovan jumped to his feet. "He never asked for ID?" He knew how absurd the demand was before he said it, but holding back when he was scared or in a rage (or both) had never been his strong suit.

"He was more concerned for Luis than anything else. When they got back into court, he soon realized no one from the FBI had contacted the court to let them know about Luis' medical emergency. He explained what he'd seen, the judge called us, and here we are." Kevin rubbed at his face, like he'd been out in the cold.

Captain Power cleared his throat. "They've taken the precaution of calling area hospitals, just in case the 'EMT' was on the up-and-up. Spoiler alert—she wasn't."

Fury rose in Donovan, a rage he couldn't remember ever having felt before. "Where is this Morello now?"

"With his therapist." Alex managed a small grin. "He's pretty horrified to find out he actually helped with abducting a federal officer, even if it was unwittingly."

"He'll never practice law again." Donovan collected his gun from his desk. "I'm going to make sure of it."

Kevin sighed. "Donovan, think about it for a second. Yeah, he probably could have checked the woman's ID, but he's not an investigator. He's *opposing counsel,* and he was still so concerned for Luis' health he stopped to help him. You're mad.

You should be mad. But maybe redirect that rage a little bit?"

Donovan opened his mouth to snarl at Kevin, but he shut it again. He took a deep breath and put his gun into his holster. "It's been a rough twenty-four hours. I'm probably not in the best emotional state to be making decisions right now." He closed his eyes. "There haven't been any demands, no one's claimed responsibility?"

"Not yet." Captain Power glanced over at Morales. "Obviously, the investigation is just beginning. Now, this is a federal investigation. The crime took place on federal property; the crime was against a federal agent during the course of his duties. There's not a lot of wiggle room here. That said . . ."

Alex cleared his throat. "The FBI is formally requesting the assistance of Lieutenant Donovan Carey for the duration of the search and rescue effort." He managed a wry grin. "Given that we're a little short-staffed right now, and given that you'd involve yourself anyway, it seemed prudent. And you're one of the best investigators we know, so we definitely would have wanted you involved anyway."

Donovan forced his body to relax. He couldn't help Luis if he was tearing everyone and everything around him down. And these folks wanted him to help.

He froze. "What about the Southwick shootings?"

Power cleared his throat. "I'll manage the day-to-day stuff for the department. We'll call you if we need to. Family's important, Donovan. You'll have the full cooperation and support of the state police in any capacity you need, of course." He stood up. "First things first though. We'll have someone drive your car home for you. I'm not putting you on the road right now."

Donovan opened his mouth to object, but he closed it again quickly. He'd do the same for anyone else in a similar situation. "Kevin, can you give me a ride back home?" He grabbed his jacket from the back of his chair. "We can talk on the way."

"Absolutely." Kevin helped Alex to his feet, and they made their way out into the bright sunshine of an early October afternoon.

Donovan didn't speak until he was in the car. "Okay." He buckled his seat belt. "I know you've got agents everywhere looking for him, right?"

Kevin grinned and pulled out onto the highway, cutting off a white woman driving a red Prius. She honked her horn at him but stopped when he flipped the sirens on for a second.

"Yeah. SSA Holcombe is down at the site reviewing security camera footage right now. Wragge and Borchard are working the case out in Western Mass. The ambulance was found at a golf course in Newton. Maxwell is processing it with all the care and attention you'd want." He took a breath. "We're going to find him."

"Newton." Donovan drummed his fingers on the dashboard. "Why Newton? Do you think it has anything to do with the Southwick case?"

Kevin shrugged. "We can't rule anything out right now. It's certainly possible, but I'd expect to see them just take him out instead of kidnap him. It's more their style."

Donovan barely got the window open in time to avoid being sick in the SUV. "Oh God." He wiped his mouth before sticking his head back into the car. "What if—"

"Don't finish that sentence." Pain slurred Alex's words. "Don't do it. You know better."

Donovan pushed the thought from his mind. He did know better. Neither he nor any other cop would ever admit to being superstitious, but finishing that sentence would make a horrifying possibility a reality. "Okay. So who else would have a motive for this? Someone involved with a case he's worked on, or is working on?"

"There's no shortage of those, I'm afraid."

Kevin sighed. His grip on the steering wheel was so tight Donovan thought he might break it. "We reopened a case last month where it turned out the wrong man had been convicted of murder. More than a few people were upset about that one."

"I remember him mentioning that. He hated having to put the families through all that pain again." Donovan ground his teeth. "What about his old man? Any chance Carlos could be reaching out from behind bars to pull a stunt like this?"

"It's certainly possible, but not probable. Carlos Gomes' correspondence is triple-checked, and he doesn't get visitors at all." Morales shifted in the back seat. "That part isn't mandated by the prosecutors. No one cares enough to go visit, or at least no one who cares enough has the freedom to visit. I hope you don't mind, but we do need to look into your father's potential involvement."

"I wouldn't put it past him." Donovan closed his eyes. "If this had happened six months ago, I'd have said Fred didn't have it in him to come up with a plan this detailed, but after what he did to me? Yeah, he's capable." They still didn't know the extent of the plan, but setting up the ambulance ahead of time showed a high degree of detail.

"Exactly. And considering how the fallout from all that is still ongoing, it's possible that some other cop decided to act on his own." Kevin shrugged. "It wouldn't surprise me at all if this *was* a law enforcement job actually. They knew where he'd be, for one thing."

Donovan fought down another wave of nausea. "Just what this town needs. Another law enforcement scandal."

"Right?" Kevin snorted. "We've got people scouring that golf course, but it looks like she transferred him to another vehicle. Unfortunately, there wasn't any security footage at the golf course, so we're out of luck in terms of the make or model. We do know it has to be big enough to fit the gurney because it's missing from the ambulance."

"The lawyer said he looked drunk. Do you think he was drugged?"

"I think he'd have to have been." Kevin swallowed hard. "I don't . . . I spoke with him—oh, it must have been right before the abduction. He told me he was feeling woozy. We both chalked it up to the all-nighter. He's in great shape, but he's in his midthirties now, you know?"

"I was just thinking about that before you guys came into the room." Donovan ran his hand through his short hair. "I just . . . I don't even know. I can't process this." He sat up straighter. He had to process it. Luis was out there somewhere, drugged, depending on him. "Okay. So we've got possible law enforcement involvement, possible suspects from prior cases, what else have we got?"

"The case he's working now involves a child porn ring." Alex cleared his throat. "They're not generally known for going after adults, so we can probably write that off."

"They don't usually go for adults, but they do kidnap people." Kevin glanced at the rearview mirror. "Gelens was making a lot of money with his ring. It's possible someone's mad enough about the loss of income to try to do something about it. It's not our most likely motive, but it's not one we should throw out just yet.

"First thing we need to do though? Both of you need to get some sleep."

"I can't sleep. Luis is in danger. You can't expect me to just curl up and snooze while he's going through God knows what." Donovan gaped at Kevin in outrage.

"You're no good to him if you pass out, Donovan. Get a couple of hours in and we'll regroup."

Donovan wanted to fight, but he knew his friend was right.

CHAPTER FOUR

Everything hurt. Even Luis' hair hurt, and he'd have sworn that was physically impossible before this moment. He didn't have to open his eyes to know he was in trouble either. He lay on some kind of stone or cement floor, bits of debris pressing into him. Grit smeared into his skin. The stink of dust mingled with vomit, puke that had to be a few hours old. After a second, he realized the stink was coming from him.

He wondered if he could force himself back into oblivion. The pain in his head was just about enough to do the job, and he wouldn't have to face whatever had sent him here. Then again, hiding from his problems hadn't ever gotten him anywhere good. His own self-preservation instincts wouldn't let him try to hide from whatever made him land face-first in a puddle of puke.

Neither would the voice making his headache worse.

"Aye, I know ye're awake. Ye're in a heap o' trouble now, lad, and I know that rank floor isn't anyplace ye want to be sleeping."

Luis groaned, but he sat up. His stomach lurched, and he had just enough time to bend over. The bile he brought up splashed onto the grimy, dusty floor, and not onto Luis himself.

It was a small mercy. His suit showed the evidence of prior sickness. No amount of dry cleaning would save it. *And I liked this suit too.*

He wasn't the only one who liked it. He'd chosen it that morning, or whenever he'd last been home, because it was Donovan's favorite. He'd wanted to give Donovan something pleasant to see when he got back from a day that could only be terrible.

He forced himself to look around. The suit was only fabric. He could cook Donovan a nice dinner or something after he'd showered.

He'd been left in a large room in a basement. Thick iron bars stood in front of windows leading to what looked like a wooded area. Some kind of wire mesh further protected the windows, but a passerby might never see inside. The light suggested it was maybe five o'clock—not yet dark, but it would be soon.

And sitting in front of Luis, further illuminating the room with the sickly glow of death, was Captain Lightfoot.

"Why does it make me feel better that you're here?" Luis cringed from his own fetid breath.

Lightfoot passed him his bottle of gin, the bottle Luis had given him in thanks for his help when they'd met. "Don't be swallowing this. Just swish it around in yer mouth, to clean it out. Ye've got nothing in ye, and if ye were to drink this, ye'd probably get to spewing again."

Luis cringed at the bottle, but the sour taste in his mouth was only increasing his nausea. He accepted the bottle, followed his ghostly friend's instructions, and spat the gin out into the dust.

At first, his entire being rebelled at the thought of even admitting the liquor into his mouth. Not only had he made a conscious choice not to consume alcohol because of his father's addiction, but Lightfoot had been swigging straight from the bottle for a year and a half. The liquid had to be at least half ghostly backwash by now.

After a second though, he had to admit he felt better. Not great, but better. "Thanks." He wiped his mouth again. "I don't suppose you know where we are?"

"Not specifically." Lightfoot shrugged. "I got pulled to you, when ye were choking on your own sick. It looks like we're in one of those madhouses they built and then abandoned, but that doesn't tell me much. They've got such places all over the state, for all the good it does them."

Luis blinked at him. "How would I have gotten here?" He scratched at his head. "Why would I come here? Was it for a case?"

Lightfoot tilted his head. "Ye dinna remember?" He tapped Luis in the forehead.

Pain surged as memories flooded back. "I was testifying. We broke for lunch, and I got sick." He frowned. "I was feeling fine before lunch. Was it—" He made the connection. "The water. I didn't order it. It must have been drugged."

"Aye. Slipped ye a mickey and ye were too wrapped up in everything going on to notice." Lightfoot shook his head. "After that, it would have been short work to get you out of there."

"The ambulance." Luis closed his eyes again. "It was right there, waiting."

"Ah. Must be it, then." Lightfoot rose to his feet and held out a hand to Luis.

Luis took it, despite the risk of frostbite. He couldn't afford to sit around and wait for rescue, even if every cell in his body screamed in agony.

It was only pain, after all.

He let Lightfoot help him to his feet and waited for the world to stop spinning. "I'm dehydrated."

"She left ye a bottle of water, but it's been opened." Lightfoot raised an eyebrow. "Fool me once, shame on ye. Fool me twice . . ."

"Yeah." Luis surveyed the room. There was, indeed, a bottle of water in the center of the room. He ignored it. Unfortunately, everything else had been cleared from the space. He could see footprints in the dust, showing where someone with small feet had done the work to remove whatever had been stored in here.

"This was premeditated." He looked over at the door. "Think it's locked?"

"Sure as you're born." Lightfoot snorted. "Ye're in no shape to be crawling around in the basement of an ancient madhouse anyway. There's stairs over yon." He nodded toward another door. "Likely locked, but since when has that been a problem for a man like me?"

Luis managed to laugh, even though his abdomen ached. "Valid. Your lack of boundaries has never been more helpful."

"Got that right." Lightfoot grinned, a hideous rictus of bone and decay, and disappeared.

He reappeared seconds later. "The stairs are steep, lad. Work on regaining your strength. We don't know who or what we'll find at the top."

Luis nodded. He shuffled over to the wall, intending to sit down. When he saw the trail of rodent feces along the floor, up against the wall, he moved away.

Despair washed over him. He'd been stupid enough to get kidnapped by someone with an unknown agenda, and now, he was locked in the basement of an abandoned mental hospital. These old places were full of ghosts. They were known for it. The fact that Luis hadn't found any but Lightfoot yet was sheer luck, and while Luis had generally met with good and helpful spirits, these old hospitals were mired in trauma and pain. Darker spirits would almost have to be in residence.

And he was too sick to do anything about it.

He wasn't going to get any better anytime soon without water. He could chance the water his abductor—identified by Lightfoot as a woman—had left for him, but he'd just be knocked out again. The familiar weight of his gun was gone from its holster. His phone had been removed from his pocket. He had no way to defend himself, unless bile could be considered an offensive weapon.

He had Lightfoot.

"You said you were drawn to me." He caught the ghost's eyes, or his eye sockets anyway. "Why?"

Lightfoot chuckled. "Lad, if I knew that I'd be able to solve so much more than I can now. I find I'm pulled to ye when ye're in danger. Maybe it's me penance for all the evil I did in my life. Maybe it's the universe's way of giving ye a wee bit of help. I don't know, and it doesn't bother me. Ye get into the most interesting scrapes as it is."

Luis smiled ruefully at that. "Got that right. As far as I know I'm the only federal agent to get kidnapped from the front of a federal courthouse in broad daylight. At least I'm unique!"

"Ye're the only lawman I've met who's a medium as well. Gives ye an unfair advantage, I say. But life isn't fair, I suppose, and neither is death." Lightfoot swigged from his gin.

Luis watched carefully for backwash. As always, the bottle stayed perfectly full.

"So here's the question. You're not always with me. We know that."

"Do ye though?" A worm dropped from beneath Lightfoot's battered hat. "Ye're right though. I do have my own life to lead, such as it is. There's a delightful wee bar downtown that mixes the most delicious cocktails. They'd be wasted on ye, of course, but I do love sneaking in and stealing them from the barmaid's station."

"Of course you do." Luis couldn't even be mad about it. "Hey—would they be open now?"

"Are ye craving yer first drink? Because I don't think a goblet full of gin and absinthe is a smart idea in yer condition, but ye're an adult."

Luis stared at his friend. "Er, no. But a bar is going to have water, right?"

Lightfoot laughed in delight, a dry rattling sound. "Ye're a smart one." He winked out of existence, returning moments later with three glasses of water. "Drink slow. Can't have ye getting sicker."

Luis hugged Lightfoot. "This is twice in one day you've saved my life. Thank you."

Lightfoot seemed to gain a little more flesh, enough to look astonished at least. "Think nothing of it. I'm your friend."

Luis took small sips of the cooling water. He could feel it caressing his throat all the way down, soothing his tortured esophagus and steadying the room. It wasn't a trick they were going to be able to use often—or was it?

"How much does it take out of you to do that?" Luis ignored the skittering he heard around the edges of the room. He'd been in worse situations. It was just rats.

"Well, I'm not about to steal you a steak dinner, that's not sane, man." Lightfoot looked at him askance. "Someone's bound to notice a steak dinner floating through the air, yeah?"

Luis snickered. "I wouldn't dream of it. And I couldn't keep it down anyway. What are the chances you could, say, leave a note for Donovan and tell him I'm alive?"

"Oh, aye. He's probably turning his poor stomach into knots, isn't he?" Lightfoot tapped his jaw. "What else can I tell him? I've no clue where we are, so I can't tell him that. He can't see me, so it has to be something I can write in a quick note where he can see it."

Luis considered. "You saw the woman who nabbed me, right?"

"Aye. She was an odd one. Face looked like a mask, like it were frozen."

Luis almost dropped his glass. "Hyena Lady? She's the one who did it?"

"Aye, that's exactly what she looked like."

"Perfect. Tell him the kidnapper was at the trial, watching. It's a good clue."

"Aye, if you say so. I'll return." Lightfoot disappeared again.

Luis was alone once more. Outside, the light had essentially disappeared from the sky. Now Luis was alone, in the dark, with the rats.

He hoped Donovan got the message quickly.

Donovan hadn't thought he would be able to sleep when he lay down in his bed, but exhaustion had such a hold on him he went under right away. He didn't even dream, so no time at all seemed to pass for him between closing his eyes and reopening them to Kevin's shouted, "What the flying fuck?" from the guest bathroom.

He jumped to his feet, gun at the ready, and raced toward his friend's voice.

The first thing he noticed about the bathroom was the stench. He'd smelled this foul odor before. It was the stink of the grave, of corpses left out in the midday sun.

The second thing Donovan noticed was the bottle of high-end gin, sitting on the granite counter.

The third was the message, scrawled on the mirror in what looked like lipstick.

LUIS IS ALIVE.

Kevin had just finished a shower. He'd wrapped a towel around his waist and covered his mouth. What little color he had had drained from his face as he stared at the mirror.

Alex ran up behind Donovan, still shirtless from his own forced nap. He gagged at the stink, but otherwise held it together. "Did some ghost seriously just show up to . . . pass on a message?"

Donovan did a double take. "You knew?" For a second, jealousy reared its ugly head again.

"Well, I did watch him fry one in the pool

during that mess in Boston. It was hard to miss. I think he'd rather not have told me." Alex pointed at the message on the mirror. "Why don't the ghost stories we tell ourselves around campfires ever warn us about the stink?"

The first message disappeared. More words showed up. BECAUSE THE REAL DEAD AREN'T PACKAGED UP ALL SWEET FOR WEE CHILDREN.

It took Donovan a second to parse out the language. "Captain Lightfoot?"

AYE.

It was the first, and only, good news Donovan had received since Alex showed up with the case in Southwick. "You've seen Luis, then. How is he?"

HE'S IN BAD SHAPE. THE KIDNAPPER GAVE HIM SOMETHING TO KNOCK HIM OUT AND HE RESPONDED POORLY TO IT, POOR LAD. HE SAID TO TELL YOU IT WAS SOMEONE IN THE CROWD AT THE TRIAL.

Donovan almost sobbed with relief. Leave it to Luis to find a way to pass on a message.

"Er . . ." Kevin gulped. His skin turned a greenish color, indicating he wished he hadn't. "Where is he?"

IN A BASEMENT.

Alex scowled. "That's less than helpful,

Captain."

The gin bottle rose and tipped, as if someone was taking a swig from it. Words disappeared and appeared again.

IT'S NOT AS IF THESE PLACES COME WITH A LOCATION PAINTED ON THE WALLS, YE DAFT BUFFOON. 'TIS WELL YE'VE GOT YER ABS, AS YER BRAINS BE FIT FOR WORMS.

Donovan grimaced. Luis had mentioned that Lightfoot could be impatient, but he hadn't been all that specific. "Er. Forgive us. We're a little new to this whole . . . bathroom séance thing. You don't see the location, you just go to a person?"

I UNDERSTAND WHAT HE SEES IN YE. YES. IF I HAPPEN TO KNOW THE PLACE, IT'S WELL AND GOOD. HE SEEMS TO BE IN AN OLD MADHOUSE.

Kevin did the math. "The state's littered with abandoned asylums."

AYE.

Alex swayed a little on his feet. "Could you hear anything in the background that could help us narrow the location down? Trains, cars, cows—I'd take it."

NOTHING BUT RATS. I WISH IT WERE DIFFERENT.

Donovan nodded, heart sinking. It was too much to hope for, he supposed. "Thanks for bringing us the message. Is there anything he needs? Anything you can bring back?"

I CAN'T BRING ANYTHING LARGE. OR IRON.

Alex perked up. "Can you bring a phone?"

Donovan tried to ignore the hope swelling in his chest. It couldn't be that easy, could it?

AYE.

Alex staggered back to the guest room. A moment later, he returned with a phone. It didn't look like his standard-issue phone. Maybe it was his personal phone or some extra item he carried around for fun. Tech geeks were like that sometimes. Alex had that geeky aura about him.

Kevin gave him a funny look. "How the hell are we going to explain that to a judge?"

Alex shrugged. "I don't mind admitting we used to date if that's what it takes to get him back. Captain? If you can tell him that's the cover story?"

"And that I love him?" Donovan added quickly.

DO I LOOK LIKE A PAGE TO YE? Then, HE LOVES YE TOO.

The phone disappeared, along with the bottle of gin and all but a lingering hint of the graveyard stench Lightfoot brought with him.

Alex leaned against the wall. "So that's what it's like to be Luis these days. I feel like I need to start going back to church or something."

Donovan managed a grin. "At least we're all wearing clothes this time. Lightfoot's not always careful about boundaries."

Kevin cleared his throat and looked down at his towel. "All of us?"

"I'll let you get some pants on. Then maybe we can talk about this?" Donovan blushed. Kevin might have twenty years on him and Luis, but he was still in great shape. Not that Donovan would go there, he was faithful, but he had eyes.

Five minutes later, all three were gathered in the living room, with their laptops and their pants, to discuss the search for Luis.

Kevin had dressed in jeans and a white Henley. Donovan wasn't used to seeing him in anything but the standard fed suit, so the sight was a little jarring, but they were in this for the long haul. They should all be as comfortable as they could.

Donovan glanced at his watch. Eight o'clock. What was Luis doing now? Was he cold? Scared? Fighting off some kind of terrorist?

Kevin cleared his throat. "All right. So I've been getting updates while the two of you were sleeping. Here's what we knew before we got a visit from Captain McCreepypants. Morello, the lawyer, has mostly been ruled out as a suspect. It's possible that he might have been involved, I guess, but SSA Holcombe has spoken with him extensively and says he seems genuinely concerned about Luis' welfare. Morello's defended other clients in cases Luis has worked, so if he was going to do something he'd probably have done it before now."

"Valid." Donovan clenched his jaw so hard it hurt. He'd been counting on that lead. "Was he able to give us any direction to look?"

"Too many and not enough, I guess. He has four clients being defended in upcoming trials that Luis has worked, and he's also cocounsel on Carlos Gomes' appeal."

"You're kidding." Donovan recoiled. "That's a state charge. I thought Morello specialized in federal crimes."

"Oh, who knows why he's on this case?" Kevin threw up his hands in disgust. "The problem is, none of the four federal clients are facing the kind of time that would make pulling a stunt like this a smart idea. Granted, some people are so scared of jail they'll do anything to avoid it, none of this makes sense."

"Could it have something to do with Fred?" Donovan swallowed past his nausea at the mere thought. "Fred's in jail, but he's got plenty of supporters. It's possible one of them's involved.

And someone in law enforcement would absolutely be able to get the testimony schedule, which would explain that message we got."

Alex shuddered, which had to hurt considering the condition of his shoulder. "Yeah, I hope I never get another clue that way again. It was definitely helpful though. What are the odds we can ID everyone in that courtroom?"

"Pretty high, now that you mention it." Kevin's fingers flew across the keyboard. "Security for the Gelens trial is tight. Given the accusations against him, there's some concern that a victim or relative of a victim will take matters into their own hands. Some people are concerned that a client might be afraid Gelens will share too much information about his little black book, so to speak, and decide to clean up the mess. They've been logging everyone who goes in or out, and making sure they're disarmed as well."

"So you'll be able to get a list of spectators?" Donovan leaned closer, as if proximity to Kevin's laptop could somehow speed things up.

"Hopefully. It might not be for a couple of hours, or even till morning. It depends on the techs." Kevin ran a hand through his hair, hit send, and leaned back. "So. Let's work with Lightfoot's information. Alex, your phone—I assume you sent it with the GPS enabled."

"Yeah, and it can't be disabled unless the phone is destroyed." Alex sagged in his chair. "This dead guy said Luis is in an old abandoned insane asylum, right?"

"There's tons of them in Massachusetts." Donovan ran through a list in his head. "Thirty-five, I think. They're all kind of hot spots for crap. When I used to be out on patrol it was just one more thing to look out for—kids sneaking out to go break into the abandoned buildings and party or hunt for ghosts or whatever. Which—sure, I was a kid once too. You always want to explore.

"And then you get bit by a rat and need a round of rabies shots. Or you fall through a rotten floor and have to be evacuated. Or someone who's camped out there for whatever reason takes exception to you intruding on 'their' space and comes after you." He rolled his eyes. "All nothing but trouble, but there's so many of them all over the state it's impossible to narrow them down."

"We know the 'EMT' transferred him to another vehicle." Kevin pulled up a map on his laptop screen. "Here. We may not know the make or model, but we know it happened in Newton."

"Doesn't really help." Alex pointed to the pinned location on Kevin's map. "The golf club is close to both I-90, I-95, and Route 20. She could have gone anywhere."

"True." Donovan pushed the image of Luis, unconscious and strapped to a gurney in the back of a van, from his mind. He could only function if he took the personal aspect out of it. "And Massachusetts isn't so big she couldn't have gotten to most of those locations by the time we saw Captain Lightfoot. That said, this woman wouldn't have kept him alive if she didn't have an agenda. And that agenda probably involves keeping him relatively close to Boston, right?"

Alex and Kevin seemed to consider that for a moment, and then Alex nodded. "Looks like it, anyway. She's not going to go kidnapping federal agents for fun. This isn't a comic book. We can probably eliminate any of the facilities in the western part of the state."

"Let's eliminate the ones still in partial use too, and the ones still patrolled on a regular basis. She's not going to risk getting caught by some rent-a-cop or local guy." Donovan pulled up a list, readily available on the internet, of the state's abandoned hospitals.

"What about all these places that say they were demolished?" Kevin pointed to the list on Donovan's screen. "They're probably useless."

"Not necessarily. A lot of old buildings are supposedly demolished, but when you visit the sites, you still find huge parts of the buildings remaining. And the cellars would be the most likely parts still there. That's why I'm not ruling out places like Metropolitan State Hospital or Danvers State Hospital, which they turned into condos. There are still pretty extensive grounds around the buildings that are mostly reclaimed by nature, where you can find indicators of what used to be there. I literally tripped over a cemetery by Metropolitan State Hospital once, after they 'demolished' the site. It's still there. We're going to have to figure out a way to search all of them."

"Leave that to us." Kevin set his jaw grimly. "If Luis is in one of these places, we'll find him. Hey, Alex, are you getting anything from that phone?"

Alex shook his head. "Nothing yet. If he's in underground, in one of these old buildings, in the woods? We might not. The signal might be too weak. He'll find a way, if he can."

Donovan had to hope Alex was right.

CHAPTER FIVE

Luis' stomach settled once it had processed the water Lightfoot brought him. It was a small mercy, considering how close the rats were getting. His logical brain told him not to focus on the rats since he couldn't control them, but the emptiness of the room and the darkness surrounding him made it difficult to concentrate on much else.

He forced himself to think about what he knew. As near as he could tell without testing or observing the patient—himself—the kidnapper had dosed him with some kind of sedative. He suspected ketamine, but again, he couldn't be sure. His explosive reaction was a common side effect, especially since the attacker hadn't been able to calculate an appropriate dose.

Was there an appropriate dose? Luis couldn't imagine that there was.

Skitter skitter skitter.

The rats were getting closer. He closed his eyes, since they weren't doing him any good anyway, and it helped him to focus on his other senses. Yes, now that he wasn't devoting so much energy to trying to see, he could hear one of the little rodents closer than the others.

Something brushed against the cuff of his dress pants.

He lashed out, kicking the offending rat away from him. The rat yelped in pain, and Luis did feel bad about hurting it. Repulsive as it was, the rat was just an animal. Luis was in its world now. As far as the rats were concerned, Luis was just an interesting new food source.

He didn't have to agree, but he could appreciate their point of view.

The other rats withdrew when he kicked the first scout away. At least he'd accomplished that much. Donovan would be proud, if and when Luis made it back to him.

Just as he rid himself of one threat, another one materialized. He smelled the ghost before he saw her. She didn't smell as terrible as Lightfoot, which meant she might not be so much a threat as a companion, but he couldn't count on that under the circumstances.

The ghost took shape before him, her sickly glow muted in the all-encompassing darkness. Her hair was cut short in what looked like a bob, but it was disheveled and seemed to be clotted with blood. One side of her face drooped, like a wax candle that had partially melted, while the other side was perfectly made up into a permanent rictus. Her head seemed permanently tilted, as if her neck had been snapped at some point.

She wore a plain gray dress that came past her knees, with high stockings. She didn't have any shoes.

"Aren't you a handsome thing? Although you've made a mess. They're going to be mad that you made a mess." She *tsk*ed at him, wagging a finger. "They'll put you in the hole, you know."

"In the hole?" Luis blinked. "Who are you?"

"Oh. You're new here. You don't even have your hospital clothes. I'm sorry. My name's Millie. I'm technically not supposed to be out of my ward, but they've stopped yelling at me by now. I don't think they care, as long as I don't make a mess."

Luis ran through what he knew about this place. "I see. Millie, I seem to have . . . ah, lost a few days. Do you know what year it is?"

Millie laughed at him. "Well, you're in the right place, that's for sure. Although . . . I'm not certain myself. Everything happened so fast . . ." Her image blinked for a moment, as if a film projector was malfunctioning. "The last thing I remember was 1924. Yes, that's right. I think I was here for six months by then?"

She smiled sweetly at him. "But it doesn't matter, dear. No one's really supposed to leave. No one gets better."

Luis nodded slowly. "I see." From what he knew about treatment for mental illness back in the 1920s, cures were more incidental than the result of any "treatment." "Millie, how long have you been here?"

"I'm not sure." She tilted her head even farther, the only movement it seemed capable of. "But we can't leave, so what's the point of counting? Have they taken you to your room yet?"

"No." Luis fought back a wave of hysterical laughter. "They seem to have left me here to, um, wait for an escort. Or hospital clothes, or something. I'm not sure. They didn't tell me."

The melted half of her face twisted into a grimace. "That's not good. I'm not sure where the equipment is, but they might want to give you another treatment." She shuddered. "You know. As punishment for making a mess. They don't like messes."

The smell of burning flesh briefly overrode the stink of decay, and Luis understood. Electroshock therapy wasn't used until 1938 at the earliest, but if Millie had been a ghost by then she'd have witnessed its use—and its abuses, especially in an overcrowded hospital. "Well, that's definitely to be avoided." He'd spent enough time in clinical settings to understand what was going on, or what she thought was going on. "Millie, did anyone ever tell you what your diagnosis was?"

She turned away, just a little bit. "Disobedience."

Luis bit the inside of his cheek. Plenty of women had been committed for "disobedience," which covered a range of sins between "declining sex with an abusive or adulterous spouse" to "being in the way when a husband wanted to bring his mistress under his roof."

"I'm sorry." He tried to stand up a little straighter. "You shouldn't have had to go through that."

She blinked at him in incomprehension. "But I *was* disobedient. And I can't see where I would make a different choice. I've earned my place here, I'm afraid, and since I continue to disobey, I don't imagine things would have gone any other way. Why are you here?"

Luis couldn't tell her the truth. She didn't seem to know she was dead. "I'm not sure. I was at work, I passed out, and now I'm here."

"Perhaps you suffered a fit." She raised an eyebrow. "People who suffer fits have to be cared for in hospitals, of course. Everyone knows that. No one could possibly care for them at home."

Luis bit his tongue. Millie was stuck in 1924. She wouldn't know about actual treatment for epilepsy. Most people in Millie's time didn't know about the conditions in public psychiatric facilities either. Part of him suspected they didn't want to know, but he pushed it aside.

"I don't have a history of seizures—fits—but anything is possible. Do you know where we are?"

She smiled blandly, teeth and jaws showing through gaps in her flesh. "We're in the hospital."

Luis counted to five. "Of course. Do you know where this hospital is?"

She laughed. "It doesn't matter where the hospital is, sir. We're never leaving. Even when we die, we stay here."

The disclosure was enough to give Luis pause. "Seriously?"

"Oh, yes. Perhaps some families choose to claim the remains of some of their people, but most of us will be laid to rest in the hospital cemetery." She pointed to the left. "It's a kindness, really, and of course, digging the graves is therapeutic."

The bile rising in Luis' throat had nothing to do with his reaction to the drug his captor had used against him this time. He tried to tell himself his predecessors in mental health had done the best they could with the tools they had, but seeing it firsthand made it hard to believe. "Of course. I just feel like it would help me to orient myself."

The melted half of her face fell. "I'm sorry. I simply don't know. When they brought me here, it was in a kind of truck, like a police wagon, and it was entirely dark. I don't think we went far, but of course, I'm insane. I don't suppose I'd be able to tell reliably."

Luis bit back a scream. This poor woman had finally accepted what she'd been told. He could only see it as a tragedy. "Where did they bring you in from, Millie?"

A slight wind picked up, which should have been impossible in a sealed basement. Luis had gotten used to the effect.

Millie's glow increased, and her clotted hair floated around her head. "I don't like to think about it. I'm not supposed to talk about the time before."

Luis held his hands up. "That's fair enough. The absolute last thing I want to do is upset you, Millie. You've already been so kind to me."

The wind died down. So did Millie's hair. "It's nothing. I hope the doctors help you find your room soon. You don't want to have to sleep in the treatment room, and of course, you've made a mess. They'll be angry about the mess."

A flash of intuition hit Luis. He took off his jacket and mopped up the evidence of his reaction to the drug as best he could. The jacket was already a complete loss, so he wasn't sacrificing anything by the gesture.

Millie beamed at him. "Thank you."

"I didn't want you to get in trouble for something I did."

The air grew colder by at least fifty degrees and fouler by an order of magnitude. Even Millie seemed to notice, although maybe she picked up on the way Luis' teeth chattered just before Captain Lightfoot winked into existence.

"Who on earth is this?" She gaped at Lightfoot. "How did he simply appear here?"

Luis smiled. "This is my friend, Captain Lightfoot. He's a . . . a liaison, I guess, to law enforcement."

"He looks like a ghost!" She pointed at Lightfoot's neck. "Look, you can see the mark from where he was—" She covered her mouth with one hand.

Lightfoot took off his hat and bowed deeply. "I'm Captain Lightfoot, at your service, madam. And yes, I've been deceased these two hundred years, give or take a decade. I suppose this great oaf hasn't bothered to break the news to ye?"

Millie's melted eye widened. "I'm—I'm dead?"

Lightfoot swatted Luis with his hat. "Ye can't sugarcoat it, Luis. We're dead, not stupid."

"I didn't want to upset her. She's already had enough trauma, and she's been so kind." Luis rubbed at his arm where Lightfoot had hit him. "Millie, I hate to be the bearer of bad news, but it does seem as though you might be slightly dead." He glowered at Lightfoot. "There are kinder ways of telling a person, you know."

"Dead." Millie reached for her throat. "It's . . . a lot to take in. It does explain why I'm not confined any longer, I suppose."

"And why the equipment you remember isn't here anymore." Luis managed a smile. "The hospital is abandoned."

She fixed him with a stare. "And yet here you are."

Lightfoot laughed. "Aye, here he is. Luis here is a federal officer. He's been kidnapped, and the woman chose this place as a place to keep him until her demands are met. I suppose it seemed as good as anyplace else."

"And I'm just . . . here." Millie's shoulders slumped. "With the others."

"There are others down here?" Luis caught her eyes, or at least where her eyes should have been.

"Sure. They tend to stay where they were put though. They're obedient." She laughed now, a sound like a bell. "I suppose I never was."

"Millie, I promise once this is over, I will find a way to help you. I'm not an expert at any of this, but I will find some way of freeing you." Luis braced himself for even more cold. "You don't deserve this."

Millie shone for a moment. "I don't suppose I do. I don't know how I can possibly help you though. I didn't even know I was dead."

"It's not about what you can do for me, Millie. You deserve better, and if I possibly can get it for you, I will." He glanced toward the doors. "Everyone does."

Lightfoot gave him a soft smile, which shouldn't have been possible given his ghastly appearance. "First things first, lad. Ye've got to get out of here. I've been to yer man in that house of yours. He's with your friends Kevin and Alex. Talking with them was like bashing me head into a brick wall, especially since they can't see me. I had to write on the bathroom mirror, and it's a good thing Kevin isn't awful to look at because it took far too long."

Luis barked out a laugh. "I never want to think about Kevin naked. I have to work with him."

A pink tinge crept into Millie's pallid glow. "You burst in on a man in the bath?" She smiled at Lightfoot, so Luis suspected her scandalized look was more for show than true disapprobation.

"Aye. We're dead, my friend. Why bother with social niceties? I can show you some amazing things if you'll allow it. There's a whole amazing world out there, a world of laughter and delight, if you want to see it."

Millie seemed to straighten up, just a bit. "I can't leave though."

"Ye can if ye're with me." Lightfoot offered Millie his arm. Then he remembered something. "I couldn't bring yer gun, as it's got too much iron. Yer friend Alex sent a phone."

Millie stared at the cell phone Lightfoot produced from a pocket in his frock coat. "That's a telephone? Without wires?"

"Oh, Miss Millie, wait until you see what I have to show you." He tossed Luis the phone, and the pair disappeared.

Luis was alone.

He checked the phone. He could have predicted the lack of signal before he saw the screen. At least he could use the phone as a flashlight. And Lightfoot had gotten his message through. Donovan knew he was out here, at the very least. He wouldn't give up on Luis.

It took three hours to get the list of people who'd showed up at the courthouse to observe the trial of Santo Gelens. At first, Donovan was impatient. Then he saw just how long that list was, and just how much legwork had already been done on it.

The FBI was more than competent to conduct this investigation. Donovan needed to remember that.

The vast majority of people in the gallery that day turned out to be witnesses, waiting patiently to give testimony. "None of them seem to have been prepared for Luis' testimony to have gone on as long as it was." Kevin scrolled through interviewers' notes. "According to the father of Sarah Bengtsson, one of the victims who is still unaccounted for, he figured Agent Gomes would testify for about an hour. 'His testimony was gripping, and it was good. The jury seemed to be into it—but a day and a half in and we were still on the prosecution's questions. We hadn't even gotten to cross-examination yet.' Yeah, in cases like this the prosecution loves to throw Luis up there to kill them with facts. He could have been up there for days. Cross could have been quick, or it could have been a week. I can't imagine anyone involved with the trial who knew what to expect would have had anything to do with it."

Alex wrinkled his nose and glanced over at

Donovan. "I don't know. Um ... back when we were working together, he told me about a case where a witness was abducted before cross-examination specifically to trigger a mistrial."

Donovan knew exactly why Alex had been so careful with his wording. Donovan could be jealous and boneheaded. There wasn't room for jealousy now. "Did it work?"

"Sort of. They tried the defendant for conspiracy to commit murder. Given that it was in Texas, it got him put on death row. So, all in all, it wasn't a very effective strategy. Desperate people aren't always the most logical, and criminals never think they're going to get caught." He grimaced and reached for his bottle of pain medicine.

"Maybe not the kindest example?" Kevin cringed.

"We know he's alive." Donovan couldn't make himself look up. "At least for now. We need to consider all the facts. What about the parents of the victims? I can see where they might be mad that Luis hadn't found Gelens before he got to their kids. It's the wrong choice, but remember back when Luis and I had that first case together? I thought my mom was going to shoot him when I got hurt."

Kevin's face darkened. Donovan figured he was embarrassed. No one had come out of that serial killer case looking good except maybe Captain Lightfoot, who was a serial killer himself.

"Yeah, I thought so too." Kevin straightened up. "Parents can be irrational. All but one set of parents can be accounted for—"

All three of their phones rang at the same time, echoing off the still-new walls of the town house and waking Tria up from her nap. The three-legged cat jumped and yelled at the noise as the three men groped for their phones.

Agent Holcombe turned out to have called all three in a kind of conference call. Her voice was tense, exhausted. It had been a long day for her too, Donovan remembered, and it was only going to get longer.

"Agents, and Lieutenant Carey. I'm sending a link to your accounts. I want you to watch it and then get back to me right away."

She disconnected the call.

Donovan glanced at the others. Their faces had drained of all color—not difficult in Kevin's case, but impressive in Alex's. Holcombe wasn't usually this terse, so whatever had come through must be pretty negative.

He turned on the TV and flipped through the inputs until he got to the input from his laptop. Kevin raised an eyebrow, and he squirmed a little. "Luis likes to watch soccer. But, like, real soccer, not MLS. So it's just easier this way."

"No judging." Kevin gave half a smile, but it looked a little weak. "It's working for us now. If it helps us get him back, I'll even sit back and watch soccer with him."

It was the work of a minute to get to the link in the sea of Donovan's emails and open it up.

The link went to a video, which Donovan had expected. The woman staring back at him from the other side of the camera had peroxide-blonde hair and feverishly bright-blue eyes. Her face was frozen in a tight, unmoving smile. Her cheeks and her lips both looked artificially plump, which added to the impression of a botched plastic surgery.

Pity rose in Donovan's chest. He wasn't going to sit there and judge women for getting whatever surgery they wanted. The pressure on women, from all kinds of sources, to maintain a certain appearance could only make a botched surgical result worse.

Then the woman spoke. "By this point, you've probably noticed that your golden boy, Super Special Agent Luis Gomes, didn't make it back from his little lunch break. I'm sure you've worked yourselves into a frenzy getting all upset about it. I mean the way that lawyer bitch made it sound, this guy is the second coming of Christ or whatever, but all I can see is some dude who thinks he's hot shit.

"He's not. He's just shit.

"He's shit, but he's shit doing a job. I'm not interested in hurting a dude who's just doing a job, you know?"

Donovan forced himself to breathe and to focus. The speaker hadn't identified herself yet, but she was telling them plenty just by speaking. She had one of the worst Boston accents Donovan had ever heard, coupled with the rasp of someone who'd been smoking at least two packs a day for a decade at a minimum.

Donovan couldn't tell if she was standing or sitting, but her background was a grimy brick wall. He couldn't hear much in the background.

The apparent kidnapper continued. "You fuckers are probably going to want proof that I'm the one who did the deed, right? I slipped him some special K in his water at lunch. Dumbass was too distracted to pay attention. Some hotshot agent. And then when he passed out right in front of the courthouse, I was waiting in my ambulance."

The camera moved, showing a legitimate EMT's uniform.

"You can get away with almost anything in this thing, I'm telling you. So anyway. You're probably wondering what I want, since people don't go kidnapping federal agents for fun." She stared into the distance for a moment. "I mean, I could. He's got a nice body, but as it happens, I'm taken.

"Which brings me to why I'm making this call. These charges against Santo Gelens are bullshit. He didn't do anything to anyone they didn't end up wanting and begging for. If a couple scenes wound up going too far, so what? Can you think of any other industry where you arrest the CEO if a worker happens to bite it in an industrial accident?"

The woman curled her lip as best she could and rolled her eyes. Just like that, Donovan found any sympathy or pity evaporating.

The woman continued. "Be serious. A dude drowned in the water storage tank in Braintree. His kid followed him in and followed him into hell. Did anyone blame the CEO of the company, or even their supervisor? No. So why is it my Santo's fault if some stupid kid croaks during a movie? Make it make sense."

She snapped her fingers. "See? You can't. Now, I'm sure you're going to want proof of life."

The camera changed, showing Luis strapped to a gurney. He was unconscious and covered in vomit. While the camera continued to film, he made a gurgling sound.

"I know you're going to need to make arrangements and stuff. The wheels of justice move slow and all that horseshit, so I'll be in touch tomorrow at noon with a way to make the exchange. I know I don't need to tell you what's going to happen to Barfing Boy here if you decide keeping my Santo locked up is more important than getting him back?" She held a gun up in front of the camera.

"And don't you worry. He won't be escaping in this lifetime. I've got enough ketamine to put down twelve agents, permanently." She wiggled her fingers at the camera. "Ta!"

The camera went dead.

Donovan's blood turned to ice in his veins. "Get Holcombe on the line." His voice sounded harsh even to his own ears.

Kevin rushed to obey. He didn't object to taking orders from Donovan. His face had gone gray, his jaw set into a grim line. Alex sat up straighter, swaying but determined.

Kevin found a way to get Holcombe on the screen. She looked terrible. Dark circles ringed her eyes, emphasizing the washed-out look of her skin. If Donovan didn't know better, he'd think she was one of Luis' ghost friends.

"So you've watched." She closed her eyes for a second. "I need your thoughts."

Alex spoke up. "The kidnapper isn't insane, ma'am. She's completely amoral, but she's sane. She knows what she's doing, and she planned this carefully."

"That'll be very helpful when we put her on trial." Holcombe glared at him. "The charges will depend entirely on whether we find Gomes alive or dead. Did you find anything in that video that will give us clues about her location or identity?" She seemed to notice Alex for the first time. "And go change that bandage before it gets infected."

Donovan cleared his throat. He liked Alex, and Luis had been friends with him even longer. Luis wasn't here to run interference for Alex, so Donovan would have to do it. "The EMT uniform seemed to be legitimate, and she referred to the ambulance as being hers. It's a lead to follow up on. We know the name of the ambulance company. If we can get the names of employees who might be missing, we should be able to compare it against the list of people at the trial."

Kevin nodded quickly. "Luis mentioned, when we spoke on the phone, that he'd noticed someone at the trial who was giving him the creeps. It's not much to work with, but it's something."

It was more than something. It was a good cover for Luis managing to get them information about the kidnapper from wherever he'd been hidden. Kevin was a genius.

"Excellent. What else can you tell us?"

"She's local. I'd say Chelsea if I had to guess." Donovan ran his tongue against his teeth. "Smoker. Age is hard to figure because of the work she's had done, which was botched. There might be a paper trail for the bad surgery, but it would take too long to track that down to be useful in locating Luis. If she's not there when we find him, that's something else."

"She's got him somewhere with brick walls." Alex spoke up. "It looks old and not well kept. Also, she's someone with access to a large quantity of ketamine."

"All right. Good job. Keep hunting. I'll be in touch when I find anything. Donovan, you've got access to RMV records, right?"

Donovan nodded. "Yes, I can get into records from the Registry of Motor Vehicles if I need to."

"Perfect. You can cross-reference gallery visitors against Chelsea residents past and present. Let me know if you find anything." Holcombe ended the video call.

Donovan opened up the Registry's records. "Let's get on it."

Kevin gave him a quizzical look. "I guess I expected more . . . explosive rage."

Donovan ground his teeth together. "Oh, the rage is there. But it's not getting Luis back. We know Luis is alive and awake. We're going to find him. And if I find that . . . person . . . you'll see enough explosive rage to last for thirty years." He stood up. "Come on, Alex. Luis would kill me if I let that wound get infected."

CHAPTER SIX

For half a minute, Luis resented Lightfoot for taking off with Millie and abandoning him to his own devices here in the dark with the rats. He was still in danger, damn it. When he listened to the thoughts going around in his head though, he gave himself a little shake.

Luis was an adult, and Lightfoot couldn't do much besides sit there with him and scare the rats away. Millie was an adult too, but she'd been through a lot of trauma and had been locked away for nearly a century as a result. She deserved the opportunity to see how the world had changed. And Lightfoot, bless him, recognized it.

And hell, if Lightfoot and Millie found something they liked in each other to ease the burden of eternity, Luis would have to be a much worse person than he was to want to block it just because he was afraid of a few rats.

The skittering started up just as soon as Lightfoot left. Luis took a deep breath and pushed the fear to one side. He wasn't going to get anywhere if he sat here and blubbered like an infant. His dress shoes might not offer much protection from razor-sharp rodent teeth, but they were better than nothing.

Hyena Lady had brought him down into this place somehow, and she'd done it on a gurney. Luis was a sizable man. Sure, there were women out there who could haul an unconscious man of his weight around by themselves. He wouldn't pretend it wasn't possible or that Hyena Lady might be one of them. She'd had to ask for help getting him onto the gurney though, and she apparently wanted to keep him alive. She wouldn't want to risk hurting herself or killing him by manhandling him through an abandoned facility like this.

So—gurney. That meant he needed to avoid the door with the stairs. It wasn't hard to figure out which one that was, thanks to the phone Lightfoot had brought him. He had two other doors to consider, neither of which appeared to lead to the outside world. He had to pick one of them.

The one to the right felt better to him. He wasn't sure why at first, but when he looked closer the one on the left had an older lock mechanism that seemed to be rusted shut. The one on the right seemed to be a more modern door, which meant it had been opened more recently.

It was too dark to see tracks, as of a gurney being wheeled through the doors. He could have used the flashlight on his phone, but he didn't want to waste the battery. Fortunately, logic was on his side here. Luis had definitely been brought through these doors.

He closed his eyes for a second and regretted it as soon as he did. The skittering drew closer, brushing against his filthy dress pants again. He fought against a scream and kicked at the push mechanism on the door. After a second, it gave.

He had no choice other than the phone's flashlight to see in here. It was even darker than the main "treatment" room. No windows, however small, lit this corridor. He fought down a wave of panic, and then he closed the flashlight. He had a good sense of the space now, and he needed to conserve his resources.

He slid slowly, like time was a thing he didn't have to worry about anymore, over to the right. A familiar scent tickled the back of his throat. This corridor was blessedly free of the skittering of rats too. Even if he couldn't smell the ghosts, the lack of rats would have been a big clue.

Of course, he *could* smell the ghosts. Lucky Luis.

The walls down here were damp, and they

felt like old drywall as he groped his way along them. His mind's eye saw them as being a kind of dingy yellow, the way they'd been in any of the dozen neglected secure facilities he'd had the pleasure of visiting over the course of his career. He wasn't sure why he assumed this corridor led to secure rooms. There wasn't any logical reason to make that assumption, but the presence of spirits was a big hint.

The first door he came to yielded pay dirt in the form of confirmation and a huge wave of cognitive dissonance. The physical door had fallen across the frame, hanging on by a bent bottom hinge only. A residual image of the door lingered where it had been, looking more like an old-fashioned iron-barred cell door than the comparatively modern door with a large Plexiglas window that had existed when the place was abandoned.

The ghost inside was male, hairy, and nude. He curled his lip and spat at Luis when he noticed him. Maybe it was the suit, destroyed though it was.

"I'm not here to hurt you." Luis looked around the room—or cell, depending on what one wanted to call it. Whoever had decided to "treat" the man in this way hadn't even given him a toilet, just a bucket. His gorge rose, but he fought it down.

He couldn't afford to lose any more fluids. "What's your name?"

"Fuck you."

"What are you in for?"

The patient laughed, a wild, inhuman sound that showed his rotten teeth. Luis couldn't tell if his teeth had been rotten before his death or not, but they made a stark contrast to the white of his jaw.

Then the patient reached into the bucket, pulled out a handful of filth, and grinned. "Boom." The mess in his hand ignited.

Luis jumped back before the flaming shit could hit him. It landed against the wall, providing real light and leaving char marks before it dissipated.

Whatever the man had been sent here for, the "treatment" had only made him worse.

Luis moved on in the dark, the first patient's laughter echoing down the corridor.

A glow from across the hall, roughly kitty-corner to the first patient's cell, brought Luis over. "You had to wake him up, didn't you?"

This speaker was markedly different from the first. He wore a suit and tie, and only his hat marked the outfit as dating to a time before the modern era. Luis had no illusions about the man's status as a ghost—bits of flesh seemed to drop from his bones even as he spoke. Still, he seemed to be fairly cognizant of his surroundings.

"He was awake when I found him, but I do seem to have agitated him." Luis grimaced. "I'm afraid I didn't get a lot of information when I arrived."

"I can't imagine the dame with the frozen face would have given you much dirt to begin with. You were in rough shape." The ghost's rotting lips twisted into a grin. "There's an evil creature for you. You're going to have to put her down, but I think you knew that."

Luis almost flinched at the casual way this patient talked about killing Hyena Lady. "It's a possibility. What's your name?"

The ghost scoffed. "I've subsumed myself in the Archangel Michael. You can call me Mike. These bastards keep telling me it's Walter, but that's not a name anyone's used in decades."

Religious delusions. Luis made the diagnosis almost without thinking about it. "Okay, Mike. Do you know his name?" He jerked his head toward the still-laughing fire starter.

"No one knows. He won't tell. He was dead before I showed up, so it's not as if I heard staff call him anything. I'm guessing he's a fire bug though. Unlike me, he actually belongs here. Hey—can you put him down? I know you're a medium, but I don't know just what you all can do."

Luis blinked at him. "You know I'm a . . ."

"You must be new at this." Mike scoffed again, sending a spray of blood over the space in front of him. "Figures. You're a medium. Someone who can see and interact with and talk with ghosts. Michael tells me you're favored by Gabriel because Gabriel's the messenger. I'm just here to do the smiting." He rubbed his hands together, and then he hung his head. "But I can't smite ghosts, not in my state."

"Is that why you're here? And, er, where exactly is here?"

Mike grinned again. "Oh, yeah. I smote a bunch of demons and a massive creature from the Abyss before Lucifer's minions caught up to me. They locked me into that infernal place up in Danvers. I almost made my escape there. I took out two of 'em, but the bastards managed to break my leg so they caught me again and shipped me down here."

Luis could read between the lines. Mike had religious delusions causing him to act out against people he believed were demons, or otherwise not favored by his angel. "And where exactly is *here*?"

"You know, I'm not entirely sure." Mike took off his hat, revealing a neat, surgical hole in his skull. "They botched the lobotomy. Accidentally, or so they say." He snickered. "I still managed to take out the 'surgeon' after the fact, before he could do it to someone else."

Luis shuddered, but he shook Mike's hand. "Good work." He wasn't sure he believed it, not fully. Lobotomies weren't considered appropriate treatment anymore, and they were cruel even when they were considered standard. Still, if the surgeon had truly killed Mike by accident, it didn't necessarily merit death.

On the other hand, if he'd resorted to murder to alleviate overcrowding, Luis could hardly fault Mike, even with his delusions.

"Have you found a way to get out of your room yet?" Luis tilted his head. Mike was definitely a danger to himself and others during life. Captain Lightfoot was a murderer, both in life and in death. Luis couldn't afford to be picky right now.

"Are you kidding? Do you honestly think if I could get out of here I'd still be moldering away in this box? They even buried me in this dump!" A wind picked up as Mike's rage grew. "Outside, in the yard, without even my name. Just a C and a number."

Luis nodded slowly. Mike still had hold of his hand, and he was going to have to recover it eventually, but he wasn't going to interrupt his companion's righteous anger. He'd certainly encountered this kind of thing before. Most families didn't claim the remains of their institutionalized dead, not back in those days. They were hastily buried on the grounds of the hospital. Where the patients received a marker at all, they'd be marked with a P or C to indicate Protestant or Catholic and their number. Nothing else.

"And that's terrible." He gave Mike's hand a little squeeze. "I might come to regret this, but I want to try something."

"What, you think you can get me out?" Mike sneered at him. "You really are new at this, aren't you?"

"My friend Captain Lightfoot has his freedom. Millie, who was locked up here, seems to have the run of the place at least. I can try to offer you that much. Keep hold of my hand and focus on me, not the bars." Luis focused on Mike, tightened his mental grip, and pulled.

It ached, somewhere deep in Luis' head, but it worked. Mike was on the other side of the bars, right here with him.

Mike laughed out loud, tossing his head back in sheer delight. "Hang on," he said, and disappeared. "I'll be right back."

Luis moved on to the next room. The ghost in this one was a woman, dressed in the same uniform as Millie. She looked relatively sound and even smiled sweetly at Luis.

Then she opened her mouth to speak. Her teeth were jagged, sharp things, as though they'd been filed to points. She had no tongue to speak but managed to get words out anyway. Luis chose not to question the physics of the undead.

"You want to know where you are? You don't need Archangel Boy. I'll tell you where you are, for a price."

Everything in Luis cringed away from this woman, but he approached her room anyway. "Who might you be?"

"My name is Cora. I'm a good girl. I promise." She fluttered her eyelashes at him.

One of her eyeballs fell out and onto the floor. It bounced.

"Okay, Cora." Luis struggled to keep his composure. "What's your price?"

"I just want a little bit of your blood. Just a tiny bit. You won't mind. You've got so much of it, and you'll share plenty before it's all over. Won't you, handsome?"

Mike reappeared in front of him. "Shut it, Cora. The medium's protected by the Archangel Gabriel and has no time for devil spawn like you."

He turned to Luis. "We're in Medfield, Gabe. We're at the Medfield State Hospital, or what's left of it."

Donovan's phone reminded him it was midnight. The phone Alex had sent to Luis wasn't pinging anywhere, which meant wherever he was being held didn't have a signal. Or Miss Chelsea was jamming it, somehow. Either way, they couldn't use it to get in touch with him.

Donovan tried not to panic about that. He knew Luis was awake and cognizant enough to send messages through Captain Lightfoot. That had to be a good sign, right? Of course, he hadn't heard anything new from Lightfoot since that first conversation. Who knew what had happened since then?

This was Luis though. Luis had taken down a serial killer even after he'd been shot in the chest. Luis had electrocuted a ghost with nothing but the power of his own mind—*while that ghost was trying to drown him*. Luis could do incredible things, amazing things, and Donovan should have more faith in him.

Faith was all well and good, but Donovan couldn't expect him to do everything by himself.

His phone rang, and he jumped. Surely, this was Luis. He must have found a way out by now.

The name on the phone wasn't Luis'. It belonged instead to Steve Wong.

"Donovan—Steve Wong here. I just came on shift and heard the news. You've got to be a wreck, buddy."

Donovan slumped and hoped he could keep the disappointment from his voice. "Something like that. How are things downtown?"

"Oh, you know. Had the joy of busting a real brain trust yesterday. If you're going to bring a box truck full of weed into Boston, don't dip into your own supply and don't drive it down a one-way street. I'm just saying." Wong chuckled for a second.

Wong was the brother of State Medical Examiner Dr. Wong and as unlike Donovan's eternal nemesis as two brothers could be. He was closer with Luis, but he'd provided Donovan with a safe place to stay when Donovan had been laboring under false accusations.

"Christ." Donovan managed a little laugh at that because sometimes it did seem like criminals were lining up to be arrested.

"I know, right?" Then Wong sobered. "You know we've got your back. All of us. We're ready to pitch in the second you hear something you can act on."

"Thanks, Steve. I appreciate it."

"You'd do the same for any of us. You *have* done the same for any of us. And so has Luis."

Wong cleared his throat. "And while we're on the subject, I wanted to give you a quick heads-up. My captain called your mom when he heard."

Donovan froze. "Shit."

"Yeah. I'd expect a phone call anytime now. Or she might just show up, who knows? Captain Carey is a force of nature. She'll be good to have on your side."

"Sure. Once they peel her off the ceiling." Donovan closed his eyes. "Thanks for the warning."

"No problem." Wong's radio crackled in the background. "Got to go. Domestic."

"Good luck." He'd need it. Domestic disputes were the most dangerous type of call any cop had to respond to.

"Thanks." Wong cut out.

Donovan reported the call to Kevin and Alex, who'd been dozing but woke up during the conversation. "It's good to know Boston PD has our backs, all things considered."

Kevin pressed his lips together. "I wouldn't count on all of them. I'm not convinced some of them might not be involved, that damned video aside. But we can worry about that once we get him back."

Donovan shuddered to think about the implications of Kevin's statement. "Do we have any news about the location or the suspect?"

Alex ran through his messages quickly. "Nothing about the location yet. She's good at what she does, you know? She definitely seems to know how to pick a nondescript location. *We* know Luis is in an abandoned mental hospital because the ghost told us so. Otherwise, a bunch of red bricks could be anywhere."

"It was still light when she filmed the video, so that leaves former institutions within a few hours of Newton." Kevin pulled up a map on his laptop. "That's . . . still a lot, I guess."

"We do have an ID on Miss Chelsea. Her actual name is Tammie Hatch, born in Chelsea, Massachusetts, in 1980. Graduated from Chelsea High School in 1998 and is an employee of Brainerd EMS Services. Has been since 1999." Alex turned his screen around to show them. An image of Miss Chelsea's senior picture.

Donovan paused. She'd been a pretty girl, fairly normal looking. "How did she get from that, a regular EMT, to looking kind of like an ad for plastic surgery gone wrong?"

Alex scanned through whatever file he'd opened. "In 2006, she responded to the scene of what was reported as a regular barroom brawl in Medford. She wasn't the only EMT to respond, of course, but the situation was out of control and several of the combatants were high on some bastardized version of meth. Bath salts, maybe? Was it during the 'embalming fluid' craze?"

Donovan shuddered. "That was no joke."

"No, it wasn't." Alex made a face. "She got glassed, and some charming soul tried to actually eat her face right off. Naturally, she required massive reconstructive surgery. An EMT can't afford that, and while Brainerd was sympathetic, they weren't about to shell out to pay for the surgery when they weren't willing to give employees health insurance.

"Instead, they worked out a deal with student plastic surgeons. They would repair her face for free, in return for getting to work on her."

"Oh my God." Donovan stared at Alex. "That's . . . that's vile."

"I mean, she did need the surgery. I'm looking at the damage from the before pictures, and I'm not sure the very best reconstructive surgeon in Beverly Hills could have done better." Alex scrolled away. "But yeah—it's pretty awful."

Donovan didn't want to feel sympathy for this terrible woman. "If Luis were here, he'd say something about how she'd probably be feeling vulnerable after an incident like that. The company treated her as disposable—first by refusing to pay and then by treating her as something to be experimented on. He'd make some noise about the pressure women are under, especially at a young age, to prioritize their looks. And he'd make some noise about how she'd be easy prey for someone like Gelens.

"Here's the thing though. Luis ain't here. He's not here because Tammie Fucking Hatch kidnapped him and dumped him into an abandoned mental asylum to try to hold him hostage for the freedom of a pedophile, a rapist, and a child porn distributor."

Kevin shrugged. "I've met a ton of people who've been maimed. Some of them have been maimed terribly, and because of choices someone else made. Yeah, I can kind of follow the logic there. Gelens is a master manipulator, and it can be easy to fall for his BS when you're already feeling low. But most people who survive something awful don't go on to do something terrible like this."

Donovan sat up straighter. "You don't think she's working alone?"

"I'm not sure. She could be. We'll find out. But we did know Gelens certainly wasn't working alone. We didn't suspect a girlfriend, but it's possible Gelens doesn't think of her that way."

"Gelens isn't capable of love." Alex snorted. "Luis said exactly that. Love requires empathy, and Gelens doesn't have an ounce of empathy in his body. He's just not able. He's capable of using someone who loves *him* though."

"We need to talk to him." Donovan jumped to his feet and ran for his coat.

Kevin, who was probably more fatigued than any of them since he hadn't done more than doze, still moved faster than Donovan and blocked the exit. "Donovan, it's past midnight. They're not going to wake him up, rousing the entire row of cells at Nashua Street, just so we can interview a man who's already on trial."

"Try me."

Kevin stared into Donovan's eyes, and then he shrugged. He called Holcombe from another room. Donovan paced while the call happened, but energy surged through him when a shocked-looking Kevin returned to the room.

"Suit up. Holcombe will be here in twenty."

Holcombe was there in fifteen minutes, not twenty, which Donovan felt showed her interest in bringing Luis home alive. She drove as they raced down to Nashua Street, where correctional officers gave them dirty looks but admitted them to an interview room anyway.

Gelens was exactly what Donovan had expected to see. Despite the late hour, his eyes were bright and alert. He was of average height, with a bald head and a weird little reddish-brown goatee that Donovan wanted to punch right off of his face.

The orange jumpsuit marked him as a guest of the state, but the little smirk on his face and the way he seemed to sprawl in his chair proclaimed Gelens to hold the power in the room. Indeed, his presence was such that he seemed to be one of the tallest people Donovan knew. Only by firmly reminding himself of the facts could Donovan remember who was really in charge here.

"You know, not allowing a prisoner to sleep is a violation of the Bill of Human Rights." Gelens smirked.

"Tell us about Tammie Hatch." Holcombe sat down across from Gelens.

"Suck my dick and I'll think about it." Gelens' expression didn't change. "Doesn't mean I'll say anything one way or another, but I'll at least consider it. Good talk."

"So you do have something to say about her." Donovan put his hands on the stainless steel table and leaned forward. "How long have you known her?"

"Has my dick gotten sucked? I don't think so."

"We already know she abducted someone to hold hostage for your release." Holcombe sat back in her seat, completely unruffled by Gelens' crude suggestions. "When was this coordinated by you?"

Gelens laughed. His laugh was deep, coming from his belly, but it didn't seem particularly humorous. "How exactly do you think I'm supposed to coordinate anything from in here, sweet cheeks? I'm not allowed to communicate with anyone other than my attorneys, and if you think they'd have advised me to do something like abducting Luis Fucking Gomes, you're nuts."

"It does seem like an ill-advised plan." Holcombe smiled calmly. "Of course, conspiracy is such an exciting charge. The people conspiring to work with her are just as guilty as she is. If it's just kidnapping, then that's one sentence. If it's kidnapping and assault—say, through drugging someone with horse tranquilizers—then that's a whole exciting other sentence. And if said victim happens to pass away in the course of this crime . . ."

Donovan held his vomit in, just barely.

"Well, *sweet cheeks*, that's murder of a federal officer during the course of his performance of his duties. And that, Mr. Gelens, is a capital crime. What you and Miss Hatch need to understand is that while Agent Gomes isn't a big fan of capital punishment *personally*, the Bureau will cheerfully pursue the death penalty against *anyone* we even suspect of being involved."

Gelens paled, just a bit. Enough for Donovan

to notice. Still, his smirk never left his face. "I already told you, I have nothing to say. Get to sucking or get out of my sight, you psychotic bitch."

"Sweet dreams." Holcombe rose and put a hand on Donovan's arm. She led him to the door, where guards let them out.

One of the correctional officers snorted. "So that was a complete waste of time."

Holcombe's expression didn't change. "On the contrary. We hadn't released the name of the kidnapped individual. Gelens just confirmed his involvement, and since he did it in an interrogation room where everything is filmed, he did it on tape. We'll be needing that to go, please."

The correctional officer gave Holcombe a tired grin. "Lady, you're a genius."

"It's the only way I can keep up with my agents, Officer." She softened a little bit. "Let's try to bring this one home."

CHAPTER SEVEN

Luis kept up his slow crawl through the long corridor of isolation rooms. He didn't have any place else to be, and he knew he'd find his way out if he kept moving. The presence of so many ghosts kept him safe from the rats, so from that perspective he had nothing to worry about.

The ghosts themselves, on the other hand, were something else.

Mike made a decent companion, and he took his self-appointed role as guardian seriously. Luis didn't exactly relish being addressed as Gabe, but he'd get over it. Mike had a decent sense of humor and a good grasp of what was going on in the old hospital, so Luis could accept his new name assignment for the time being.

"The place was a real nightmare for a while," Mike explained, guiding Luis down the center of the aisle. "When I was here and alive, it was crowded. You had all kinds of people all jumbled together, because it wasn't like there was enough room to keep the crazies separate, you know? But it calmed down eventually."

"When you were here, they didn't have any effective treatments for most mental health issues. When they developed medications and other therapies that turned out to be useful, people could live in society again." Luis found himself at a crossroads—or rather, a four-way intersection in the corridors. The wheels from the gurney left tracks going straight, and going to the right. He'd been brought in from one direction, and Hyena Lady had taken her equipment out in another.

"Fabulous." He ground his teeth together. "Any idea which way we should go?"

Mike shrugged, a devil-may-care grin splitting his face and his skin. "I haven't been outside that cell in eighty years, mac. Take your pick."

Luis sighed, which set him to coughing. There was a lot of dust down here. Then he went straight.

"So they really have pills now? I mean pills that'll help folks like that guy with the flaming crap?" Mike stuck his hands in his pockets.

"Depending on what his diagnosis is. I haven't seen him outside of that brief moment, so I couldn't say. But there are definitely solutions that have helped a lot of people, and without having to drill into their heads or resort to electric shocks."

The air temperature, already icy, dropped by twenty degrees.

"You're one of them shrinks?"

Luis shook his head. "I'm a federal agent and a criminal behaviorist. I analyze the psychology of criminals so we can figure out how to stop them before they hurt people—more people, I should say."

A little growl escaped from Mike's throat. "I thought you were a medium."

Luis knew he should be afraid. Mike was, apparently, a killer. At the same time, he didn't strike Luis as someone to get violent simply out of anger. Luis had been wrong before, but he didn't have a choice about trusting Mike. "Apparently, I am. I had a near-death experience and boom! All of a sudden, I could see and interact with dead people." He paused. "Thinking back, there were signs. I just didn't pay attention to them until I was bleeding out onto a forest floor and wound up getting first aid from a deceased serial killer."

Mike scratched his head. "But you're a cop."

"I am. And my best friend is a long-dead highwayman and serial killer." He shrugged. "I've stopped questioning it at this point. It's not like Captain Lightfoot would go away if I told him to, which I wouldn't." He chuckled. "I'm not here to mess with you, Mike. If you want help, I'll help you as best I can. But first, I have to survive."

"That you do." Mike sighed. "So I guess you know a lot about the crazies. You know, chasing them down and stuff."

"Most of the people I deal with aren't mentally ill. Or at least, their crimes aren't driven by their illness." Luis noticed a set of double doors on the left side of the hallway. "What do you think that room up there might be?"

"Could be anything. It's worth looking into." Mike headed in that direction. "What do you mean, their crimes aren't driven by their illness? I thought only crazy people did the really bad stuff."

Luis held his breath as he got ready to push on the doors. Was this his ticket out? Would he find Hyena Lady, or the people helping her, on the other side of this door?

"Most violent crimes are committed by people who know exactly what they're doing, who they're doing it to, and exactly why they shouldn't be doing it." Luis met Mike's eyes. "Lots of people try the insanity defense. They'll say, 'Oh, it's not my fault, I had a moment of insanity because I caught my wife cheating. I didn't know what I was doing.' But it's always a lie. They know.

"Or they say, 'It's not my fault, my crappy upbringing made me not know right from wrong.'

130

But most people who have violent or traumatic childhoods don't go on to hurt people, you know?" He swallowed. "My childhood was pretty bad, but I don't go around hurting people. Most violent crimes are committed by people who choose to commit violent crimes." Luis shrugged. "That's all. People with mental illnesses are more likely to be the victim of violent crime than the perpetrator."

"You feel pretty strongly about that, Gabe." Mike took off his hat and toyed with it, exposing the hole in his skull. "But I got sent here for a reason, you know?"

Luis pushed on the doors. "I know. If you want to talk about it, I'm here. Frankly, I haven't met any ghosts who didn't get that way without a lot of trauma."

Luis braced for the worst, but no hail of gunfire met the creaking of ancient hinges. Instead, he found himself looking into a cold room, with a stainless steel table in the center. Metal cabinets, roughly sized for a human body, lined the walls.

Luis couldn't see much, even with the light provided by Mike's preternatural glow. He could see that the drawer fronts sagged in a few places. He saw the drain cover, rusted.

"I don't think this is what you were looking for." Mike put a hand on Luis' shoulder. "Come on, Gabe. Let's get out of here."

Luis let himself be guided away from the old morgue.

Mike cleared his throat. "So why did they bring you here, if you're a cop?"

Luis ran his tongue along his teeth, giving himself time to consider. "I'm not positive, but I was testifying in a trial when I was grabbed. It was—well, the guy on trial did a lot of bad stuff, specifically to children."

A foul wind blew up from out of nowhere. "I'll kill him myself. That's demonic, it is."

Luis didn't need access to old records to have a sense of what Mike's crimes had been. "It is. Fortunately, we've got him on camera committing said crimes, so he's not getting out of prison in my lifetime."

"Too risky. Demons can be tricky. You have to kill the host to send them back to hell." Mike put his hat back on. "It's a shame, but I frankly wouldn't want to live after I'd been possessed and used for that kind of perversion anyway. So it's a kindness, really."

Luis nodded because he didn't have a strong argument to present. Not one that didn't involve trying to dismantle Mike's delusions about demonic possession, anyway. "I can see your point of view, certainly. I suspect I was kidnapped in an effort to try to derail the trial."

"Hellspawn." Mike glowered upward. "We'll kill the Hyena Woman and send her back to hell."

Luis' blood ran cold. He put a hand on Mike's arm, even though it made his hand ache with cold. "We need to bring her in alive. If nothing else, it's proof I was actually kidnapped and didn't just get sick of testifying so I could wander off to Medfield and go on a bender." He gestured to his filthy shirt and trousers.

"Is that something you're known for?" Mike tilted his head to the side.

"No. I don't drink at all. But defense counsel would be stupid not to make the accusation if it has the slightest chance of improving things for their client." He sighed.

"All this law stuff is complicated. I'm better at smiting." Mike pouted for a moment, actually pouted. "Just let me know when I can do it and I'll make sure their eyes bleed, Gabe. You and me, we make a great team."

Luis smiled, although inside he shrank from the very thought. He wasn't about to go unleashing a ghostly killer with religious delusions onto the people of Massachusetts, however much he hated the place. Even if the thought of letting Mike have at all the pedophiles he couldn't put in jail did have a nice ring to it.

Captain Lightfoot returned just then, Millie by his side. Millie had exchanged her hospital uniform for modern jeans and a tee shirt. Both of them held margarita glasses, and Millie held a blanket out to Luis.

It was a real blanket, gray wool and scratchy. He wrapped it around himself. "Thank you so much! I didn't think you'd be able to bring back something so big."

"I couldn't have done it by myself." Lightfoot smirked and jerked a thumb at Millie. "Two of us together, now, we can do a lot more than just one." He looked Mike up and down. "Who's yer friend?"

"Mike, meet Captain Lightfoot. I think you already knew Millie? Captain Lightfoot, meet Mike. He's been here since the 1930s?" Luis hadn't been so attached to a blanket since he'd been a toddler. He just wanted to wrap himself in it and stay there.

Lightfoot doffed his cap. "Delighted to meet ye. Luis, Ye should know the whole of the FBI, the state police, and the Boston Police are out looking for ye."

Hope sprang up in Luis, but he still frowned. "Wait. What about the people who shot poor Alex? And Donovan's men?"

"They'll get theirs. Right now, they have a

living agent being held hostage by some bird claiming to be in love with the kind of filth you were staring down in court. Their priority is to bring ye back alive. Also, ye're the partner of the head of Major Crimes, ye daft bunny rabbit. Even if ye ran a coffee shop in yer underwear, they'd be calling out the cavalry for ye." Lightfoot swatted at Luis with his hat.

"If you decide to run a coffee shop after all this, I'd take it as a personal favor if you kept your pants on." Mike turned to Luis. "I'm sure plenty of dames won't mind if you left them at home, and maybe a few guys too, but it just don't seem sanitary."

Luis laughed. "No, it doesn't. Fortunately, it's all moot. My customer service skills are best suited to chasing down bad guys and punching them really hard, I'm afraid. Pants are usually a requirement for that too."

Mike shuddered. "Thank God."

"Bah. Both of ye need to loosen up." Lightfoot waved his margarita at them. It sloshed but didn't seem to decrease in volume.

"Where are you going?" Millie blinked at Luis. "Are you trying to get to the elevator?"

"Does the elevator still work?" Luis couldn't imagine how it would. Medfield State Hospital had been abandoned for over two decades. There was no way it still had power.

"No, but I didn't know if you knew that. There are stairs at the end of this corridor." Millie gestured. "Shall we keep going?"

Luis hefted his blanket. "No reason to hold off."

Soon, he'd be out and on his way back to Donovan. He had no idea what he'd do when he could see the stars, but he'd figure it out then.

A key turned in the lock at one thirty in the morning, making Donovan and both of the federal agents in his living room jump up with their guns at the ready. A small part of Donovan hoped it was Luis, but he knew better. Luis would have called.

The intruder stepped over to the security system keypad and punched in a code. "Relax, Donovan. It's only me." Patricia Carey stormed into the kitchen with a stack of plastic containers.

Two of Donovan's brothers followed her. One of them, John, carried boxes of Dunkin coffee. The other, Scott, carried more food.

"Mom?" Donovan blinked at her. Only when Donovan said the word did Kevin and Alex put their guns down. "Since when did you get a key?"

"Luis gave me a key and a code back when you got the place. Said it made sense for someone local to have it. He gave one to Alicia too. She'd be here now, but she's got no childcare for Nicky. Ordinarily, when she gets called out at night she calls you two, but that's not an option right now."

Donovan shuddered. "Yeah, I wouldn't even want to tell the poor kid. It'll devastate him."

Patricia swatted him on the arm. "It will scare him, but he'd only be devastated if poor Luis didn't come home. Which he will because everyone with an ounce of Kennedy blood is going to crawl over every inch of this state and turn up every blade of grass until we find him. Even Tony got his head out of his ass when I called to tell him."

John smirked. "Mom threatened to cut off his balls."

Alex gaped at everyone. "Can someone please explain what's going on here?"

Patricia sized Alex up and turned to Donovan's brothers. "Scotty, heat up some of that stew for this young man. He's too skinny. He's never going to get over that gunshot wound if he doesn't put a little bit of meat on his bones." She looked back at Alex. "You're that fed who got shot yesterday out in Southwick, aren't you?"

Alex bowed his head. "Yes, ma'am?" He glanced at Donovan. "How does she—"

"It was in the news." Donovan sat back down. "Mom, this is Agent Alex Morales. He's an old friend of Luis', and Luis has been kind of a mentor to him. Alex, this is my mom, Captain Patricia Carey of the Boston Police Department. These are my brothers, John Carey of the Boston Police and Scott Carey of the state police."

"Hi." Scott waved from the kitchen, where he was doing Patricia's bidding. No one crossed Patricia and lived to tell the tale. Not for long, anyway. "So. What do we have?"

"Ma'am—Captain." Kevin smacked his own cheek as Patricia seated herself beside Donovan on the couch. "Sorry. It's been a long couple of days. The FBI has this investigation under control—"

"Horseshit." Patricia didn't put any heat behind her words, but she didn't have to. "If you had the investigation under control, you'd have my son back where he belongs He's not, so you need all the help you can get. Plus, you're working another important case out in Western Mass. You people have a willing, trained, and enthusiastic army of volunteers with badges and a lot of vacation time saved up. Get the stick out of your ass and use it."

Alex swayed on his feet. Donovan gently guided him to his seat and patted his good shoulder. "It's okay. You can see how Mom managed to run a department full of macho male cops, can't you?"

Alex closed his eyes. "Yeah. Yeah, I can. Did you just refer to Luis as your son?"

Two spots of color appeared in Patricia's cheeks, but she shrugged. "I didn't always feel that way, obviously, but when he came back into our lives and I found out about him and Donovan, I had a choice to make. I could choose the hate and fear I'd learned from my parents and my church, or I could choose the love I had for my son. In the end, it wasn't much of a choice at all. Now I'm mad I wasted so much time when I could have gotten to know him." She deflated, just a little bit.

Then she straightened up again. "But I'm not wasting any more time. He's part of my family now, whether or not Donovan ever gets around to putting a ring on his finger, and I wouldn't leave any stone unturned for any of my other sons. Even Tony."

"I probably wouldn't show up for Tony." Scott appeared with a bowl of stew for Alex. "Here, eat this. It's the only thing Mom can cook, but she makes it well."

"You damn well would show up for Tony." Patricia fixed Scott with a glower that should have peeled the freckles right off of his skin. "We can't fix whatever's wrong with his head if he's missing or dead. Not the point. What do we know about Luis' kidnappers?"

Donovan knew he should keep outside people away from the investigation. He also knew his mother wasn't going to stay out of anything. If he chased her away, she'd marshal her army and they'd go investigate on their own, possibly creating a disaster.

"We got a videotaped message from the kidnapper this evening. She'd recorded it earlier in the day." He got up and helped himself to some of the stew because he needed to do something with his hands. "She—"

"She?" Patricia did a double take. "She must have drugged him. He's not a small guy."

Kevin grinned and ruefully shook his head. "Trying to keep you out of it was always going to be a losing proposition, wasn't it? Yes, she did. She drugged his lunch and posed as an EMT when he showed the effects. We've got reason to believe he's being held in an abandoned institution somewhere, but that doesn't exactly narrow it down."

"There's only a few dozen of those around the state." Patricia snorted. "And she's not limited to staying in Massachusetts either. That's the problem with New England. Unless you want to go up into the northern boonies, which is certainly an option, everything is only a couple of hours away from everything else. What else did you manage to glean from the video?"

"Not a whole heck of a lot." Donovan put his bowl of stew on the table and rubbed at his face. God, he was tired. "We do have an identity on the suspect."

John swatted the back of his head. "You could have led with that."

Donovan flipped him off. "She's an interesting individual. Her name is Tammie Hatch. She's a legit EMT who's somehow attached to the defendant in the trial in which Luis was testifying. She has one demand. She wants the charges dropped against this guy."

"So not happening." Scott snorted and brought out stew for Kevin, their mom, and John. "I mean even if the guy wasn't a rapist, pedophile, and a murderer, they don't drop charges because someone kidnaps a cop. It's just not a thing. It would be beyond stupid."

"Yes, it would." Kevin nodded. "Holy crap, this stew really is good. Releasing suspects in exchange for hostages sets a terrible precedent. And from what Donovan told me, it sounds like this Gelens dude is in on it."

"Santo Gelens?" Patricia curled her lip. "I busted him fifteen years ago. What the hell is he doing on trial again? He shouldn't even be out on the street from the last time. Never mind. It's not important right now. So we know who she is."

"She's from Chelsea." Alex sat up a little bit. His color looked a little better now that he had some food in his stomach. "I don't know if that's helpful. I'm not from here. I've heard the name, but I don't have any experience with that part of town other than showing up at the field office there sometimes."

"It actually is helpful. I worked in Chelsea for years." John pulled out his phone. "I still know a bunch of people there. And a lot of the beat cops there will answer questions for me. I remember the Hatch family. Her brother was a little shit." He typed with his thumbs as he spoke, already sending messages.

"I'll get on things with the EMS company." Scott pulled out his phone. "They might have some insights."

Kevin stared. Then he turned to Donovan. "Is it always this easy to get help?"

Donovan snorted. "Are you kidding? My little finger still sticks out funny from when Scotty broke it when we were nine and ten. And then he had the audacity to tell Mom I slammed it in the oven door."

"It builds character, dear." Patricia patted his hand. "Now. Let's see the map. Donovan, why don't you put Agent Morales to bed? He looks like he's going to pass out right there."

"I'm fine." Alex sat up straighter. "Really. I can't sleep until Luis is back with us."

Donovan shook his head. "Alex, look. You've got a serious injury. You checked yourself out AMA. You need to take care of yourself if you want to be there for Luis when we do find him, okay? Come on. I'll bring you upstairs."

Donovan escorted Alex back up to the guest room, brought him his pain pills, and made sure he was as comfortable as he could be. Then he headed back downstairs.

Both of his brothers were on the phone with contacts who could help with the search. His mother and Kevin were bent over Kevin's laptop, looking over a map of Massachusetts. Donovan smiled.

The situation was still pretty bleak. Luis was still out there in the wind, and Tammie Hatch could kill him at any moment. Now that Donovan's family had gotten in on the search, Donovan couldn't help but feel like they'd have him home at any minute.

CHAPTER EIGHT

Luis made a mental note never to walk around an abandoned mental hospital in the dark again. At least, he would never do so if he could possibly avoid it. Walking around this place hadn't exactly been a choice. He'd found the elevator just fine. The elevator door, as with many elevators from the time when this place had been constructed, didn't stand out from the rest.

Luis didn't know where the actual elevator car was, but it wasn't in its spot. And while Luis was definitely in the basement, apparently there was a subbasement. At least one. Maybe two. It was too dark for Luis to tell.

Lightfoot and Mike both caught him in time, before he could tumble down the shaft.

He stood there breathing deep for a few moments. Even though the basement was cold enough to store food, sweat dripped down his back.

Then he pulled himself together. Panicking

wasn't going to get him out of this place. He had to find his way out and get back to Donovan.

"Donovan must be worried sick." He only spoke when he could do so without his voice shaking.

"That's one way of putting it." Lightfoot snorted. "It's well yer friend Kevin was with him, otherwise him and poor wee Alex would be spinning themselves into oblivion fretting." He reached out and took Millie's hand. "I'd mock ye worse, lawman, but I suppose I can understand a mite better now. A mite, look ye."

Millie let out a little laugh. "We'll find a way of getting you out of here, Agent. Just you wait." She pointed to another closed door. "There are stairs here."

Luis took a breath and pushed the doors open. These were big solid doors—fire doors. Opening them could only make noise. "If we go back the other way, will we find a ramp leading to the outside?"

"Sure." Millie giggled a bit. "You would, but she's gone and nailed boards over the doors. Hyena Lady is a lot of things, but none of them are stupid."

Luis bit back a curse. "Is it too much to ask for her to assume I'd drink the drugged water and be down for the count?" He shook his head and carefully pushed on the ancient fire doors.

They creaked. Of course they creaked. They didn't creak as loudly as he'd expected though. He glanced quizzically at the hinges, and Lightfoot gave him a smirk and a wink. He chuckled to himself. He should have guessed his friends would have found some way to help.

The stairs were in bad shape, but Luis had expected that. He hadn't expected to see the forms of developmentally disabled children running up and down the stairs, laughing or crying until they tripped and fell.

The ghosts didn't seem to notice him, but they provided a thin pale kind of light that showed him where the risers were.

"They're not really here. Just echoes, thank God." Millie's voice was subdued. She put a chilly hand on Luis' arm. "Their families thought they were doing the best thing for them, leaving them here. They believed they'd get better care than could be provided at home. But there were so many." She turned her head and looked away. "I tried to help."

Lightfoot put a hand on her back. "I know you did, Millie."

Luis couldn't tear his eyes away. He knew the spirits he was seeing were residual, not sentient beings able to interact with him at all. And he knew the history of institutions like this. He couldn't go back in time and change things. At the same time, these were children. They'd deserved better from everyone.

Sure, treatment options had been limited. Sure, people had listened to the experts. It didn't take a higher degree to see that children were harmed.

He closed his eyes and made himself concentrate on the here and now. He had to focus if he wanted to survive this. He'd never forget seeing these children making what looked like a break for freedom or at least a break for fun, but he couldn't help them. All he could do was put one foot in front of the other and get back to Donovan.

One benefit of the ghostly lighting was that Luis could see every hazard on the stairs. The linoleum covering the concrete risers had worn away in several places, which was fine as far as he was concerned. The occasional dead rat was more of a concern. Some had decayed to bone, but some were fresh enough to be a slip-and-fall hazard.

He'd never live it down if he wound up getting carried out of here on a stretcher because he slipped on a dead rat and hit his head. Assuming, of course, anyone could find *here*.

He made it up to the ground floor. There was no light, other than what his companions provided.

There had once been doors separating the stairwell from the main corridor. One of them lay on the ground, glass from the window smashed beyond all repair. At least Luis wouldn't have to try to ease the doors open quietly. He stepped over the mess and into the hallway, making no more sound than any of the spirits with him.

Luis was at one end of the building. He knew freedom lay at the other end. "How many exits are there?" he whispered. "The sooner we can get out, the better."

"Five, not counting windows." Millie didn't have to keep her voice down. Even if Hyena Lady were around the corner, she wouldn't be able to hear Millie. "But this whole building has been boarded up for twenty years and more. The doors have been nailed shut, except for where Hyena Lady peeled them off."

"Not concerned about fire safety, I guess." Luis shrugged. "Awesome. Do we know which entrances she opened?"

"It looks like she's been using the front." Lightfoot pointed. Footprints stretched out in the light from his outstretched arm.

Hyena Lady was definitely prepared for her work. She seemed to be wearing good, solid work boots, or at least the treads visible in the grime and dust suggested. He flexed his hands. He could, maybe, find her, take her down, and bring her in with him when he got out.

It was a nice mental image to hold. He wouldn't be the loser who'd gotten kidnapped because he was too stupid to keep himself safe. Then he'd be the one who turned it around, made the arrest, came out smelling like roses.

Okay, it would have to be a metaphorical smell because everything connected with this place stank. But still.

He let himself bathe in the fantasy for a minute. Then, with no joy at all, he wadded it up and put it away. He had to prioritize getting back to Donovan. He had no way of knowing whether or not Hyena Lady was working with other people or what kind of training she had. He might want to wash away the shame of being helpless, but he couldn't risk everything on his own ego. He could work on *that* wound later.

After a long bath.

He had to move slowly, both because he couldn't afford to alert his captor to his mobility and because he didn't want to outpace his light source. He stuck close to the wall, just in case, but when he put his hand on the wall itself he found slime and mold.

He didn't try to use it to guide him again after that.

The voice of his father, dormant for several months now, put in an appearance. *You always knew it would end like this, didn't you? I mean, you're locked up in an asylum, only the dead for company, and no one is coming to save you. You seriously think Donovan's coming for you? He's glad to be rid of you! God knows the Bureau's long since done with you. They're probably all drinking champagne together right now.*

Luis visualized a cell door slamming shut on his father.

When he got out of here, he was going back to the office, getting that ring out of his drawer, and getting down on one knee. He might not even bother changing or showering first. He had a long list of things he hadn't done yet, but he wasn't going to let a minute go by without letting Donovan know how he felt. Donovan could say no. He very well might say no, and he'd probably be right to do so.

He still needed to know that Luis loved him that much.

Luis found another doorframe. Based on the size, it wasn't the main entrance. The door was gone, like the one to the stairwell, so Luis could look inside.

It was another residual haunting. The dim light provided by the ghosts showed the remains of an office, strewn with papers and office supply containers. Luis hadn't seen so many boxes of staples since he'd had a summer job at an office supply warehouse as a teenager.

His other eyes, the ones that saw the dead, saw a completely different scene. Superimposed over the chaos of a move was an orderly, almost elegant office. A doctor with a handlebar mustache that would have been comical under other circumstances sat at a desk across from a disheveled man with stubble and track marks all up his arm.

"This is your third attempt to rid yourself of narcotics, Mr. Richards. The court has commanded that you be confined to this institution until such time as you are free from your enslavement to heroin. I would dearly love to tell you this will be a matter of several months, but Mr. Richards, we both know you will never be free."

The doctor gave Mr. Richards a thin-lipped smile, and an orderly appeared to guide the addicted man away.

Luis grimaced. Heroin addiction was difficult to beat even in the modern era, with modern therapy and medication-assisted treatment. A century ago, when this building had been built, that hadn't been an option.

And based on Dr. Mustache's commentary, they hadn't wanted to do much but lock people up and throw away the key either.

"That's how it was." Mike spoke softly in his ear. "They had all kinds in here, back then. They didn't separate us out either. You had guys like me—the criminal insane. You had guys like him. You had ladies like Millie. You had folks who had fits, and you had kids like the ones you saw, and you had them after they grew up. And we were all jumbled together. No one was going to get better. Not like that."

"No." Luis looked down. "No, they wouldn't. It's different now."

"I'd hope so." Mike chuckled. "But that's why these places are all haunted. So much pain, and so many people who needed something they couldn't get here. The staff couldn't keep up."

Boots slammed against linoleum. A bright flashlight pierced the darkness. Luis looked up.

"What the fuck?" A female voice, thick with sleep, cracked out from somewhere far too close to Luis. "How the hell are you even awake?"

Luis threw a punch in the general direction of the voice. He connected with something, but not hard enough to do much damage.

A heavy metal bar slammed into his face, sending him staggering into the slimy, moldy wall. Then the light shined directly into his eyes, blinding him.

"Son of a bitch." The woman had one of the worst Boston accents Luis had ever heard.

He grabbed at the area he thought her wrists would be and hit pay dirt. He managed to force her to turn the flashlight away, but she broke out of his hold before he could take it from her.

"That's it."

The gunshot was deafening in the silence of the abandoned hospital.

Donovan jumped up when his phone rang. He didn't recognize the number, although the Miami area code was familiar enough even after all these years. He picked up after signaling to Kevin that he was taking a call from an unknown number.

It wasn't as though phone numbers weren't easy enough to fake.

"Lieutenant Carey." He watched as Kevin started the device that would record any incoming calls. "Who's calling, please."

"Is this Donovan? This is Jose Perez, Luis' foster dad." The caller sounded like a wreck. Donovan heard a computerized female voice in the background, but he couldn't quite understand what it was saying. "We haven't met face-to-face, but I know we've spoken on the phone. It's been a while though."

Donovan swallowed. "Yeah. Yeah, I remember. How are you, sir?"

"I've had better days, to be honest. But I'm sure you have too. Look, I'm on the first flight to Boston. It doesn't leave until eight, but I'll be there as soon as I can, okay?"

A jolt of sheer terror shot up Donovan's spine. "Sir, that's not necessary. We've got the FBI field office, the state troopers, Boston PD, and pretty much every local agency in southern New England working on this." He gulped.

"I'm sure you do, Lieutenant." Jose's voice cooled by several orders of magnitude. "What you don't have is the only father Luis ever really had. I am already booked on that flight, you cannot keep me from that flight, and I will be at your front door whether or not you think it is *necessary*. Is that clear?"

Patricia appeared, as if by magic, and took the phone from Donovan. "This is Captain Patricia Carey, Boston PD. With whom am I speaking?" She paused, obviously letting Jose speak. "Captain Perez, it's delightful to make your acquaintance. This is Donovan's mother. I could wish we were meeting under better circumstances. I'll apologize for my son. He was already dealing with the death of one of his detectives before all this hit, he's badly sleep-deprived, and he's not expressing himself the way he normally would. No, it's not the way he'd normally want to meet his partner's father. What can you do though?

"I'll be honest with you, Jose. I'm hopeful that we'll have Luis back safely before your plane lands. That said, I know he'll be happy to have you here when we get him back, and I know we'll all be thrilled to have you here one way or another." She hung up and shook her head at Donovan.

"What?" Donovan didn't need to ask, but he did anyway. Then he hung his head in shame.

John perked up from the kitchen, where he had his laptop open on the breakfast counter. "Looks like I've got a hit on the type of vehicle she might have used after she transferred your boy out of the ambulance."

Kevin jumped up and jogged over to the kitchen, peering over John's shoulder. "I took a look through RMV records earlier, and all I found was a beaten-up 1980 Honda Civic. No way she'd get a gurney into that. No way she'd get *Luis* into that, willing or no. My first car was one of those, and it was a tight fit for a sixteen-year-old."

"That's why I dug a little deeper, big guy." John winked at Kevin. "Tammie Hatch might even be driving your discarded '80 hatchback, but she's got an uncle in Waltham who's got one of those sweet shag vans. Ford Econoline, 1978. I asked a buddy to swing by the house and take a look-see, and it's not on the premises."

Kevin winced. "He didn't have a warrant. He could have gotten us into a huge mess."

John smirked and held up a finger. "One, you don't need a warrant to look from the street. Two, said uncle has an open warrant for a probation violation. So when he popped out of the house, high as two skyscrapers stacked on top of one another and mad about even seeing a cop car *on his street . . .*"

Even Patricia cringed. "How bad was it?"

"Well, he got Janie to do the drive by. She doesn't play, but she's not going to mess around either. She got him in cuffs and on the ground in something like fifteen seconds."

Donovan grinned and shook his head. Janie McInnes was a cousin. Her mother was Patricia's sister. She was just barely tall enough to meet physical requirements to be a police officer, and she could take down a suspect in seconds without leaving any damage behind whatsoever.

"So he's in custody? We can interview him?" Kevin was all but bouncing in place.

"Your boss, Agent Holcombe, put out an alert for information related to Luis' disappearance. The sergeant in charge of this shift notified her. But it just so happens that he might have also asked a question. You know, during booking. Off the record, since Waltham's favorite creepy uncle was so eager to know why a cop had been in the area in the first place.

"He said he didn't know what 'poor Tammie' was up to or why we pigs would be pestering her, but she'd borrowed the van with his full permission." John scanned through the message on his screen.

Scott was busy typing away, keyboard clacking so loud Donovan worried he'd break something. "Okay. Awesome. So we've got sightings of the van heading south on Washington Street from that country club in Newton. We can call off the search from any of the abandoned facilities on the North Shore."

"Not if she doubled back, we can't." Patricia nudged Scott. "It's what I would do."

Donovan frowned. "How did you get access to the traffic cams in Newton and Wellesley? I thought only locals and State were supposed to have those."

"Oh, that's easy. I went snooping in John's phone while he was in the can one night when we were at a bar and stole his password." Scott didn't even have the good grace to look ashamed. "You'd be amazed at how conscientious the dude is, always logged in, always looking. Good on you, John."

Patricia pinched the bridge of her nose. "Good God, I've raised a monster. Whatever. If it gets the work done, I'm okay with it. How far can we trace this—is that really her van?"

Scott zoomed in on the van in question. It was electric blue. It featured a wizard, with a hat, a long beard, and a loincloth, shooting lightning out from his fingertips while scantily clad redheaded women of questionable age admired his prowess at his feet.

Donovan tugged at his collar. "Um. Well, it's certainly a van."

Kevin shuddered. "If I were abducting a drugged federal agent, I'd want to be as inconspicuous as possible. I'd definitely want to avoid driving something that screamed, *Pull me over, I'm carrying so many psychedelics I've created a wormhole to a different reality.* But then again, that's just me."

"Well, we know Tammie lives her life on the edge." Patricia shrugged. "And she may not have had many other options. She doesn't have prior convictions. She may not be adept at stealing cars. For all we know, she couldn't get another van on short notice."

"Even with plenty of warning, she wouldn't

want to create a paper trail." Donovan nodded, his head spinning as he took in the new information. "Renting a van definitely leaves a trail, and people remember if they have to take out seats and stuff. Scott, how far were you able to track her?"

"There's a camera near the Lookout Farm Brewing Company. That's as far as I was able to track her." Scott made a face and turned the laptop around, so everyone could see his screen. "Don't get me wrong, I'm still running a check to see if any other cameras picked her up. So far though, nothing."

"Okay, it's still a direction." Donovan clapped his hands together. "Who do we have in the Wellesley, Foxboro, Norwood area?"

"Nothing to have kept her from going right into Rhode Island." Kevin sighed. "Or into Attleboro or down to the Cape."

"True. But I think the cameras would have picked her up around there. They're better maintained in that area because Homeland Security gave us a grant." Donovan knew all of the possibilities. He could see them as easily as Kevin could, and they affected him more.

He wouldn't let himself resent Kevin because of them though. He needed to keep a reasonably positive focus, for Luis' sake.

"She's got a drugged-up federal agent

strapped to a gurney in the back of a shag van, and she's not stupid. She's not going to want to take that risk for long. She's going to want to get to a place where she can hide him as soon as possible. All we have to do is figure out where that is."

Patricia pulled up a map on her laptop. "You've said you believe he's being held in an abandoned facility. We've got the Foxboro State Hospital, the Medfield State Hospital, and the Metropolitan State Hospital if she doubled back. The Gaebler Children's Center was right next door to the Metropolitan State Hospital. Both Foxboro and Metropolitan have been at least partially demolished and repurposed, and like hell would I ever buy a condo on those sites."

Kevin did a double take. "You believe in ghosts?"

"I'm not such a skeptic I'm going to choose to live in a place like that." She sniffed at him. "Now. We can have some people go check them out. I can get people to go walk the grounds without a problem, but the issue is . . ."

"It's dark." Scott ground his teeth. "It's dark, the buildings are largely boarded up, and for the places where demolition has happened it's going to be easy to miss something that could be important."

Donovan's heart fell. "Yeah. Yeah, you're

right."

"It'll be easier to pull off at sunrise. Plus, then we can make sure your boss has buy in." John nodded at Kevin. "Don't get me wrong, if she doesn't approve we'll do it anyway. Luis is family, But it's better if we're not stepping on each other's toes."

Donovan stood up. "Yeah. Good point. I'm going to . . . um. I need air." He stumbled through the kitchen until he could get to the patio door.

He fumbled with the handle until he could get through. Then he raced to the far edge of the back deck and leaned over. He inhaled the frosty October air, breathing as deep as he dared. He could only hope the cold would wake him up and help him find Luis faster.

What was Luis doing right now? Lightfoot had told him Luis was awake, so the drugs weren't a problem. He must be scared. Was he trying to escape, or was he waiting patiently to be rescued? The phone hadn't worked, so he must not have a signal wherever he was.

Or his captor had caught him with it.

A sound behind him alerted him to company. He turned around to see Patricia standing there. "We'll find him, love." She walked over slowly, carefully. "We will."

"Will we find him in time though?"

Donovan threw himself into one of the deck chairs. He and Luis had planned to put them away over the coming weekend. He only hoped they'd still get to do that. "I don't . . . I'm worried."

"I know you are, love. I know. And it's easy for me to sit here and say things like 'We'll find him' when I'm not the one in danger of losing my partner, right?" She stroked Donovan's hair, just the way she had when he was small. "Miss Hatch needs him alive. Not that the federal government is going to dismiss charges because she took a man hostage. Nothing works like that. But in her twisted and warped little world, she needs him alive. And that means she cannot kill him. She has to make sure he's alive to trade for this boyfriend of hers."

"In my head, I think I know that. In my heart though . . ." Donovan trailed off. "In my heart, it doesn't make enough sense. She's going to get mad when we won't make the trade, and then she'll kill Luis to derail the trial. No, it won't change anything. But she thought taking him hostage would, and it makes about as much sense."

"Fair enough." Patricia kept stroking his hair. Even though Donovan's heart rate hadn't slowed, he found himself relaxing against her. Even though he was in his thirties, his mother could still make him feel like a little boy. He should be embarrassed, but he couldn't bring himself to be. "But finding all of that out will take time. We're already collecting our resources to put search parties together. We *will* find him, Donovan. And when we do, we'll bring him home."

Now Donovan could hear the smile in her voice. "And you'll meet his foster dad, at long last."

Donovan groaned. "Yes, just how I wanted to meet Jose. 'Sorry I misplaced your son, sir. Mind if I marry him?' "

Patricia hugged him. "You know that won't be how he sees it. And thanks for letting me know you're at least thinking about making this arrangement permanent."

"He'd never say yes. Permanence gives him hives." Donovan slumped, staring at the woods.

"I think he'd put up with a few hives to be with you, but you'll never know until you ask." Patricia kissed the top of his head. "Get a nap in, Donnie. You want to be alert when we finally get out into the field."

CHAPTER NINE

Luis fell to the ground as pain burned through his left leg. He couldn't hold himself up anymore. The agony radiated all the way down to his foot and all the way up into his spine. He reached down to grab at the wound. Blood gushed over his fingers.

Hyena Lady kicked him right where she'd shot him. The pain was so intense he thought he might pass out.

"You stupid moron." She kicked him again. "It didn't have to be like this. You were supposed to stay in the basement, nice and asleep, until your buddies set my Santo free." She switched her target to his ribs. "There was no reason you had to move. No reason you had to get out of place. Now you've gone and made me shoot you."

Luis used his good leg to hook Hyena Lady and knock her down. He couldn't get up and run, but he could definitely drag himself over and punch her. "They will never release Santo Gelens." He had to grit his teeth against the pain. "You can kill me, you can keep me here until time ends, but Santo Gelens is never getting out of jail."

His leg burned. He wondered if the first ghost he'd met downstairs had somehow gotten out of his room and actually set his leg on fire. He couldn't let himself acknowledge it though. He couldn't let himself feel it. He had to focus on the present, on survival.

"Shows what you know." Hyena Lady's face didn't move, even when he punched her. She headbutted him between the eyes and reached for her gun.

Luis recognized that gun. He'd received it when he started at the FBI academy. He hadn't been parted from it since. He barely had time to make the connection as she brought the butt of the gun crashing into his temple, as hard as she could. The first blow dazed him. The second knocked him out.

Oblivion was kind of nice. It didn't hurt, for one thing. Luis could forget that he'd been shot with his own gun, that he might have lost his leg. Oblivion wasn't cold. He wasn't aware that he missed Donovan, so he didn't have that hanging over his head either. Neither did he fear he'd never see Donovan again, or have the chance to give him the ring he'd hidden away.

All in all, oblivion was a pretty sweet place

to be.

Of course, his father could find him even in this nonplace, in the void of unconsciousness. And here, where nothing was real, he was more than a voice. He had form and substance, while Luis was the one reduced to a mere thought.

Carlos wrapped his arm around Hyena Lady and laughed over Luis' mother's body. "You're such a waste of space, Luis." Carlos looked like he had the last time Luis had seen him, locked up in Nashua Street before his transfer out to Shirley. "Some hot-shit FBI agent you turned out to be. Look, your own father managed to torch your house, and you couldn't stop him. You couldn't help your own mother, who died in your place. And look at you now. Bleeding out in filth all alone.

"Your mother died to save you, but we both know she should have saved herself. She should have let you die. She could always have had another kid. Maybe that one wouldn't have been such a fuckup."

Hyena Lady laughed, proving Luis' name for her hadn't just come from her looks. She sounded exactly like her namesake.

"Oh my God, Carlos, I can't believe how easy it was to take him down. He's supposed to be smart? I mean, look at him. I was able to just slip the drug into his water. It wasn't even hard. Can't even escape by himself, and it's not like I tied him up or anything."

Then, to Luis' horror, his mother pushed herself to her feet. She looked just as she had the last time Luis had seen her. Her beautiful face had been mashed to a pulp, and bruises from his father's hands circled her throat. "I gave him the most precious gift I had to give. I sacrificed my life for his. And for what? This stupid worm can't even muster up enough people to care about him to help him get out of this situation. They're leaving him here to rot."

I told them where I was, at least as much as I knew. Luis knew he wasn't really speaking to any of these people, at least on some level. For one thing, Hyena Lady didn't seem to speak Portuguese in the real world. Here, in Luis' head, she spoke it in the same accent as his father. His mother also spoke Portuguese, although when she'd been alive his mother had preferred to speak to him in Nheengatu.

He still couldn't help but plead with this caricature of his mother for understanding.

"Oh, sure." His mother would have curled her lip, if she still had lips. "You got your little hallucination to pass a message along for you. A dead serial killer is helping out an FBI agent." She tossed what was left of her hair over her shoulder.

"If you ask me, you belong where you are."

Luis fought to remember something, anything, from the real world. Maybe oblivion wasn't in his best interests after all. Not if he had to share it with every single one of his insecurities.

He called to mind a recent memory, one from only last week. Alicia and Nicky were at the town house, along with Patricia. They'd had a cookout, a legit cookout with a shiny gas grill. They hadn't had anything fancy, just burgers and salad, but they'd sat out on the patio and enjoyed their dinner like a family.

Nicky asked for help with a school project, so Luis dived right in. Meanwhile, Alicia and Donovan brought up old stories from their childhoods to see who could embarrass the other more, and Patricia brought out a delicious apple pie she'd made only that day.

He gripped the memory tight amid the jeers of his father, his mother, and Hyena Lady. He could still remember every detail, from the way Nicky's eyes still shone with hero worship to the smell of Patricia's apple pie. He could taste the burgers, feel the warmth of Donovan's body beside him. He could even hear Tria yelling at him every time he went back inside to grab drinks or more napkins.

He expanded that memory so it filled every

space in the unreal chamber of his mind. *I am loved.* He kept his voice firm and clear, as though Donovan were right there with him. *I have a family. None of you are real. You're figments of my imagination. It's time for you to leave.*

One by one, the images his insecurities used to taunt him winked out of existence. Then, like a punishment for his sins, consciousness returned.

Luis had no idea where he was, thanks to the complete absence of light. Rats skittered nearby, but considering the condition of the building, he could be anywhere. He lay on linoleum over concrete. His head throbbed in time with his pulse, and his leg alternated between burning and freezing.

He knew what that meant. The bullet had damaged nerves when he'd been shot.

He was on his back, not in the coma position. He could wriggle, which made his head and leg ache worse, but he could not move his hands or feet. They'd been tied together with what he recognized as zip ties.

Whiskers brushed against his ear.

Luis bit down on his lip. He couldn't do anything about the rats, but he wasn't about to give Hyena Lady the satisfaction of hearing him scream.

The stink of the grave assailed his nostrils, a sickly light brought some visibility to the space, and the rat squeaked as it went flying. "Gabe!"

Strong, icy hands hefted Luis into a sitting position. The room spun, but Luis didn't have anything left in his stomach to get sick from so he couldn't throw up. Mike held him up for a second, then produced a shard of broken glass and cut the zip ties on his wrists.

Luis could support himself now. "Thanks, Mike."

"Sorry we couldn't stop her." Mike faded for a second.

"Hey. It's not your job." Luis managed to find a smile. "It's mine."

Mike cut the zip ties on his leg next. "I'm the one who's supposed to smite. That's my whole game. I smite demons. The dame is a demon, a through and through hellspawn. It's my job to take her down, and I failed. I couldn't even make so much as a breeze she noticed. At least your buddy Lightfoot was able to trip her up a little. Me and Miss Millie, we couldn't even do that."

"You'll get there eventually, Mike." Luis focused on his breathing. It was the only way he could think of to manage the pain. "Lightfoot's had a long time and a lot of freedom to practice. I don't get the sense that you've had much fodder."

Mike's light strengthened. "You're probably right, Gabe. You're a good egg."

"Where are Lightfoot and Millie right now?" Luis looked around. He'd been dragged into another room—he could see the streak of blood from where his bleeding leg had trailed along the floor. This space held plenty of debris in the form of boxes and strewn paper files, but nothing immediately useful.

The cardboard boxes and files would make great nesting material for rodents. The thought sent Luis' stomach twisting again.

"They're looking for something to use as a splint." Mike gestured toward Luis' leg. "The demon stole your blanket. We could have used it as a bandage otherwise. You're still bleeding, I'm afraid."

Luis didn't need to be told that. He took off his shirt. It wouldn't make the best bandage. It was covered in filth and vomit. He could worry about infection if and when he got to safety. Controlling the bleeding needed to be his top priority.

He wrapped the shirt around his wound. Even touching it hurt. It wasn't the first time he'd been shot, so he knew what to expect. This time, he suspected bone involvement though. He'd worry about that later.

"How long was I out for?"

"Twenty minutes? Thirty? It's kind of hard to tell. I found the phone, so we've still got that."

Lightfoot and Millie chose that moment to return to Luis' side. "So ye've decided to stay on yer side of the Veil after all." Lightfoot snorted at Luis. "I wasn't sure you'd be wanting that after seeing you go down."

Luis held back a scream as Mike and Millie worked to splint his leg. They'd found—or created—some broken old broomsticks somewhere and were using them to immobilize Luis' leg. Strips of what looked like Hyena Lady's blouse and skirt from court held it in place.

"It's not perfect." Millie shrugged. "It'll have to do."

Lightfoot disappeared and returned with a pair of old wooden crutches. They weren't the right size for Luis, being more appropriate for someone maybe five foot seven or so, but they'd do.

"How are you feeling, lawman?"

Luis almost snapped at him, the absurdity of the question bordering on insulting. Then he got over himself. Lightfoot wasn't being insulting, he was trying to make a realistic assessment of Luis' capabilities. Luis needed to cooperate.

"Terrible. I'm pretty sure I'm going into shock sometime soon, I'm in a lot of pain, and every once in a while, I'm seeing double. But none of that matters. We need to get out of here."

"Can we?" Mike took off his hat and

scratched his head, once again revealing the terrible hole in his skull.

"Absolutely." Lightfoot winked at him. "Leave that to me."

✦————————✦

Donovan jumped when the phone rang again, this time at two thirty. God, this night just seemed to be going on forever. This time, it wasn't his phone ringing, but Kevin's.

Kevin's rich voice was thick with fatigue when he answered it. "Agent Holcombe." He paused. "Yeah. Send it over." He paused again. "No, Donovan's family showed up. His mom chased Morales to bed when he started to turn gray." Another pause. "He got shot *yesterday*, Agent. Of course he shouldn't be part of this investigation. But you couldn't keep him out of it with a crowbar. Yeah. *Oh.* I'm not even going to try, but Captain Carey and her sons are—"

Donovan closed his eyes as Agent Holcombe went into a longer speech. He could only guess what it was about.

"Ma'am, I understand what you're saying, but this is a special case. They have the motive, means, and opportunity to help us, and they've already provided information we hadn't gotten

174

any other way. It gives us boots on the ground all over southern New England, which is something we couldn't afford otherwise considering the situation in Western Mass. And the entire weight of the Federal Bureau of Investigation couldn't stop Patricia Carey from doing what she thinks needs to be done, as we've seen before, so we're going to work with her in the best interests of Agent Gomes."

Donovan sat up straighter, pride surging through his body. All of these things were true. He'd spent a lot of time in his youth, especially during that last year of college facing the end of his relationship with Luis, bemoaning his family ties. Right now, he couldn't be more proud.

"Thank you, ma'am." Kevin's shoulders lost some of their tightness. "I'll pass that along. If you want to send that video over, we'll give it a look. I know it'll be hard, ma'am."

All activity in the room stopped as Kevin hung up. Donovan, his brothers, and his mother stared at Kevin.

Then Patricia crossed over to Kevin and hugged him. "Thank you for sticking up for us. I appreciate it."

Kevin blushed but submitted to the embrace. "Thank you. You've already helped more than I can say. I didn't have to exaggerate anything at all, and Agent Holcombe was just a little uptight about protocol. She's the one who has to think about covering our asses if things go south." He swallowed. "Which they might. Our kidnapper sent a video."

Donovan's heart seemed to stop beating for a moment. "That's unexpected."

"It is. Tammie was pretty mad too. We need to watch it, but I just want to warn you it's going to be hard to see."

Donovan had to force himself to breathe. "Right. Thanks for the warning." He went to the kitchen and fixed coffee for everyone. No one needed the extra caffeine. They were all jittery enough, especially Donovan, but he needed to do something with his hands or everyone would see them shaking.

Not that he needed to be afraid of showing weakness. Not in front of these people, and not weakness about Luis. He was allowed to be scared for his partner. Still, allowing his hands to visibly tremble meant admitting Luis was in trouble, and Donovan wasn't going to be ready to do that for a long time.

He distributed the coffee and took his place in front of the laptop, between Kevin and Patricia. Kevin opened up the message and clicked on the video.

Tammie didn't waste time on niceties. She seemed to be in a completely dark room, lit only by the flash from her camera and a Maglite. Her reconstructed face, marred now by a hell of a shiner, was still stuck in its permanent grin, but her voice told the story of her rage on its own.

"All right, listen up. Your boy here has the reputation of being some kind of super genius or whatever. Well, I'm here to tell you that reputation is seriously overblown. He thought he could run on me. On me!" The image shook, as if she were thumping her chest. "Like I wasn't going to find his sorry ass. I had to take steps.

"I wasn't planning on hurting him. All he had to do was stay downstairs like a good little piggy. He'd have been just fine. He wouldn't have had to do much. The water would have kept him asleep, so he wouldn't have even gotten bored. I'm not a bad person. I'm an EMT for fuck's sake. I save lives. I don't go around hurting people.

"But he made me do it. He made me fix it so he couldn't get away. Because he was stupid. He couldn't just sit there like a good boy, he had to go off and play hero."

The camera and the light moved. Donovan saw Luis' face, with a huge bruise over the temple. Luis was unconscious and covered in grime and filth. He'd lost his jacket somewhere along the way, and as the camera panned down Luis' body, Donovan could see his wrists were bound with zip ties. His skin bulged a little over the restraint, showing it was too tight.

Tammie didn't stop. She trailed down Luis' still form until she got to his legs. His right leg bled profusely. Donovan could see bits of bone through the injury, or at least he imagined he could.

He dropped his coffee.

Luis' legs were bound at the ankles. Tammie had taken his shoes too and left him on the floor. Donovan could just see dirty linoleum under his partner's still form. It had probably been black-and-white at some point. Now, it was just gray.

She brought the camera back up to her face. "You can see your boy's in a bad way here. I'd almost feel bad for him, if it wasn't for the fact that he forced me to do this. I would have been perfectly happy to leave him in peace downstairs in the cellar. He had water. If he drank it, he'd have been perfectly good until my demands were met. Hell, he'd probably never know he'd had a problem. Instead, now he made me put a bullet in his leg. Stupid fucker.

"So my conditions have changed. You bring Santo Gelens to the Whole Foods parking lot in Dedham at exactly seven in the morning, or the next bullet goes into this fucker's brain."

178

The video ended.

Donovan stared at the laptop screen. The colors were too bright. Even the room itself was too bright. His family was breathing too loud. The hum of the electric lights was a buzz saw in the back of his head.

This was Luis. Luis, who had saved Donovan's life several times over. Luis had been shot in the chest and still taken down the serial killer who'd shot him. Luis had survived a near drowning and destroyed the ghosts behind it. He wasn't supposed to be bound and still. He was supposed to be fighting, running, and showing everyone else up.

"We've got till six to find him." Patricia stood up. "My guess is that this psychotic little troll is close to Dedham. That's why she picked it. That eliminates most of the defunct facilities south of Boston as well and everything out of state. There's construction on I-95, and she's not going to want to get caught in traffic."

"Good point." Kevin's voice was subdued. "You've got a BOLO out on the shag van, right?"

John gave him a thumbs-up. "No hits so far. Staties in Danvers, Attleboro, and Haverhill did pull over similarly customized vans leading to significant narcotics arrests, but that's not here or there."

"It's a win for the good guys." Patricia shrugged. "Luis got his start in Vice, if I recall. All right. Foxboro, Westborough, Waltham, and Medfield all have abandoned mental health facilities that fall within our criteria. We're cutting it too close to wait for sunrise to search the premises so we'll have to go in now. I'll get Cecelia and her people in Waltham on the sites there. Davy and the other boys can help out in Foxboro. Westborough and Medfield will be more problematic."

Donovan saw Kevin's quizzical glance and answered the question he hadn't asked. "The decision makers there are family on my dad's side. They might be open to helping, but they'd have to be approached carefully." His own voice echoed in his ears. "I'll call Lieutenant Power. Captain Power, I mean. He's probably asleep, but he did say to reach out if we needed anything. And, frankly, we need it."

Patricia's eyes gleamed with quiet pride, but she just nodded. "I'll leave you to it."

Donovan grabbed his phone and fled to the bedroom, where Tria was nesting in Luis' laundry. She'd done that ever since they brought her home. What would she do if they couldn't save Luis? Eventually, the scent would fade from his clothes. Tria would be devastated, and Donovan wouldn't be able to console her because he'd be a useless and blubbering sack of grief in the corner.

He pushed the thought away. They'd save Luis, because no other options existed. He owed it to Luis, and he needed to do it for himself. Luis was the love of his life, and he wasn't giving up.

He sat down on the edge of the bed and called Captain Power.

Power picked up right away. "Carey. Any news?"

"We've narrowed his possible location down to four abandoned psychiatric facilities, sir. We do know he's badly injured and unable to assist in his own rescue."

"Well, shit." Power breathed deep. "What do you need from me? Give me something to do, Carey."

Donovan's stomach settled just a little bit. Captain Power was a godsend. "We've got family able to check out two of the locations. The Westborough and Medfield police have folks from my dad's side of the family. If Mom, my brothers, or I ask for help, it could blow up in our faces."

"Yes, it will. I know the captain out in Medfield. We've had words. Let me handle it. What's your deadline?"

Power never wasted time or minced words. Donovan wouldn't either. "The kidnapper will execute Luis if we don't have him at an exchange site in Dedham by seven. She changed the time after he tried to escape."

"Crap. Okay. It's going to take me a minute to pull together enough people, but I'm hoping we can get it done. I'll keep you posted. We might have some angry local LEOs by the time we're done, but right now, I don't give a good goddamn."

Donovan almost sobbed with relief. "Thank you, sir."

"You're welcome, son. Get back to work and find your man."

Donovan hung up.

The bed was a mess. Donovan hadn't bothered making it after he napped. He'd had other things on his mind. It wasn't as if the state of the bed was important when Luis was out there suffering God knew what.

Donovan knew "what" now.

Luis wasn't the most domestic guy. He liked their house, but he liked it because Donovan was in it. He hadn't even unpacked in his old apartment. When they got him home though, he was going to be in a lot of pain. Donovan wanted to do something to lessen that pain as much as he could.

From a practical perspective, he knew he couldn't do much. The bullet had shattered bone. Maybe things looked worse in the dark than they were, but the wound had looked catastrophic. Donovan couldn't exactly numb the injury. He could give Luis a clean and comfortable home to return to, and it started with the bed.

He stripped the bed and put new clean sheets on it. He made sure each pillow was perfectly placed, and he even found a clean comforter to top the bed with. The old sheets made it into Tria's heap because they had Luis' scent too.

It wasn't much, but it was a start. Donovan nodded once, looked around, and went downstairs to report back to the others.

He cleaned up the coffee he'd spilled too. It was only right.

CHAPTER TEN

Luis checked his phone. He still didn't have a signal, and the screen was cracked thanks to its unceremonious tumble to the ground. Still, he could see by the face that it was 2:45 in the morning. He had no idea what time he'd been brought in, and no clue what schedule Hyena Lady was operating under.

The pain in his leg was agony in layers, like an onion or a gift-wrapped present padded by tissue paper. The crutches helped, but they were ancient, wooden, and not adjustable. Hyena Lady hadn't shot him with the intention of killing him. She'd shot him with the intention of immobilizing him, and so far, it was working.

Sticking those crutches into the ribs she'd bruised wasn't a picnic either, but he could ignore that.

"We need a plan." He looked around at his ghostly companions, who stared back at him.

"Yer friends are working to find ye. Ye know

that." Lightfoot glanced at the door.

"It's true." A part of Luis, the part that still spoke with his father's voice, had its doubts about all of that. He knew Donovan would be beside himself with worry though. Donovan wouldn't just let him rot down here.

He ground his teeth and edged toward the door. The first step made the whole room swim, like when the controls on a television went haywire. He couldn't afford to pass out. He had one more shot at getting away.

"They're looking for me, but Hyena Lady is *here*. She's here, she's got my gun, and she's likely to take me out when she sees them coming. She knows where I am. Even if you go back to Donovan right now and tell him exactly where I am, it will take him time to get here. He'll have to marshal reinforcements, and they'll be pretty obvious even if they come up with sirens off. They'd need lights to see.

"Knowing she's caught, trapped, she'd shoot me on general principle. She's not getting her guy back, and if she's involved with Santo Gelens, she's not exactly concerned with the sanctity of human life, you know what I mean?"

"Bah." Lightfoot waved a hand. "That doesn't make her daft enough to slay a lawman in cold blood. That's something that would get her hanged for sure."

Luis managed a grimace. He'd been trying for a grin, but a grimace was all he could get. "We go for lethal injection these days. And, yeah, kidnapping and murdering a federal agent usually does get a person a date with a needle, not that I approve of stuff like that. But here's the thing. She knows all the ways in and out of here. I doubt Donovan, his state police buddies, or even Kevin know those.

"Right now, I'm the only living person who can get my ass out of this."

Mike's face had grown pinched, at least as pinched as a mostly skeletal face could get. He reached out and put a hand on Luis' arm. "I'm glad you made that little rider, Gabe. You're not alone."

"He's never alone." Lightfoot leered at Mike. "You can bet your hat on that."

Millie sniffed as though she disapproved, but she managed to grin. "That's enough of that, men. We do need a plan. What is it you think we should do?"

Luis took as deep a breath as he could. A SEAL he'd been with briefly had taught him one of the breathing techniques they used to keep themselves cool in the face of panic. In for four, hold for four, out for four, hold for four. Box breathing, they called it. Luis could barely remember the SEAL's name, but he remembered that. It was helping him now. "Does anyone know where we are in relation to where her vehicle is?"

Lightfoot disappeared. He reappeared a few seconds later. "There's a ground-level door at the end of this hallway. It takes us to that great cart of hers. An ugly beast it is too."

"It could be a custom 1970s shag van with a goddamn wizard on the side, and I wouldn't care, as long as we could get it out of here." Luis stood up. "Our plan is to get down this hallway, go through the door, and get out of here."

Mike crossed his arms and shook his head. "I can see a flaw with your plan already, Gabe. The demon is keeping an eye on you. You've already tried to escape once. Believe me—I know from experience. Once you've tried to make a run for it, no one ever just figures you've learned your lesson." He laughed darkly.

"The lad's right." Lightfoot scowled. "I hate to admit it. We need a plan for dealing with Hyena Woman. Right now, I'm the only one who can do anything to her, and I can't do much."

"And she's got my gun, unfortunately. Which puts a damper on things I can do about her." The crutches dug into Luis' chest, making his chest ache.

Millie brightened a little. "Oh, but we're not

188

completely helpless."

"It feels like it."

Millie held her head up high. "We're forgetting someone. The cursing man. The one who throws . . . stuff."

Luis remembered back—was it only a few hours? Time had no meaning down here. "The hairy one. He's a little volatile, isn't he?"

Mike grinned. "We're all a little volatile, I suppose. Maybe he was able to hold it together a little better before he got locked in a cell for a century. It's worth letting him out. I mean look at me. You let me out, Gabe, and here I am being a productive member of society already."

Lightfoot rubbed his hands together. "It doesn't matter if he gives us his name or not. He's going to make the perfect distraction." He disappeared.

Luis looked at his companions. "I have a bad feeling about this."

"Has the captain ever steered you wrong before?" Millie tilted her head to the side. Bones crunched, echoing off the walls.

"Well, no. But he did kill a few dozen people, to include a businessman only about a year and a half ago."

"I'm sure he had his reasons." Millie shrugged.

Luis chuckled softly. Lightfoot *had* reasons, and most of them wouldn't stand up to much in the way of moral scrutiny. Then again, Millie had been confined for being a disobedient wife. That didn't stand up to much scrutiny either.

Lightfoot reappeared with the hairy man Luis had encountered in the first solitary confinement room.

The ghost had one of the most ghastly appearances Luis had ever seen, hair growing from solid bone alternating with patches of burned and blasted skin. He grinned at Luis with his rotting teeth, held up a hand, and laughed. "Boom," he said, and cackled.

"I canna get a word out of him, besides 'Boom.'" Lightfoot pursed his lips and wrinkled his nose. "Nor can I convince him to cover himself. Even in the presence of a lady."

"He's been in solitary confinement for a century, and who knows how long before that." Luis shook his head. "That kind of torture can do terrible things to the brain. For now, let's just call him Boom-Boom." He tried to meet Boom-Boom's eyes, which were the same voids as all ghosts. "You okay with that, Boom-Boom?"

Boom-Boom tilted his head to the side the same way Millie did, so far he almost fell over. "Boom!"

"Right. Sounds like consent. For these purposes, at least." Luis turned to the others.

He still couldn't quite understand how Boom-Boom's presence was supposed to help them escape. Mike and Millie hadn't been able to do anything to affect the living world. Boom-Boom had managed to scorch a wall, but that wouldn't help when it came down to dealing with Hyena Lady.

He wasn't about to leave Boom-Boom down there in the dark. He had obviously been a danger to himself and others when he was alive, but back then, there hadn't been any way to treat someone with Boom-Boom's obvious problems. Now, Boom-Boom was as harmless as a fly. He'd suffered enough in life. He didn't deserve to be tortured in the afterlife as well.

"All right. Let's get out of here." Luis headed toward the door.

"Boom."

Luis almost didn't notice the smell of damp, smoldering paper in their wake. The stink of decay produced by so many ghosts in one place overpowered it. And, of course, he couldn't see the smoke. He could see the faint glow of paper getting ready to ignite.

His companions didn't need to breathe. No wonder they'd thought a fire would be a fine distraction.

He sped up his pathetic attempts to get out of the room. He wasn't in a position to complain. Hyena Lady could come and investigate. It was in Luis' best interests to be elsewhere when she did.

"Boom."

Donovan called Holcombe to update her with the details about Captain Power's assistance. She still sounded twitchy about it, but Donovan understood. "Look, it's a risk. I understand that. The way he was bleeding, I feel like the bigger risk is waiting." He kept his voice calm and neutral, as if Luis was just another hostage.

His brain replayed images of Luis' still form over and over again, in his mind's eye so he couldn't stop seeing it. But he stayed outwardly calm, at least. It was something he could pride himself on later.

Holcombe sighed. "I know. And I agree with you. I'm just worried she's going to shoot him when she sees so many people coming at her, you know?"

"Me too." Donovan swallowed hard. "But it isn't like we're going to trade for what's his face anyway. It's something we'd have to consider

192

eventually."

"Valid." Donovan could hear the sad smile in her voice. "I feel like I'm running out of time here, and I don't like that. There's not much I can do about it, I suppose. Oh—Bianca's still here. She never went back to Virginia."

"That's fantastic." Donovan waited a beat. "Who's Bianca?"

"She's an image analyst from Quantico. Ordinarily, we'd have to wait for them to get to the office to do anything about the image—sure, we can wake someone up in an emergency and this is definitely an emergency, but they still have to physically get to the office. Bianca came to the Chelsea office as soon as we found out about Luis and hasn't left. She's got a soft spot for him. So we woke her up as soon as we got an image and she's been working on it ever since."

Donovan found new energy rising up from the ground. "That's awesome. Seriously, that's fantastic news. Thank you so much, Agent."

"I'll reach out to you or Agent Rourke as soon as she finds something to tell us. Be ready to run at a second's notice, all right?"

"Absolutely."

When they hung up, he turned to the others and explained the call.

Kevin chuckled a little when Donovan told

them about Bianca. "Yeah, she does have a soft spot for him. Any requests he sends get moved to the top of the pile, no questions asked. I'd say I'm jealous except I'm his partner and it works out for me." He shook his head. "I wonder how he got such an in."

"It's probably the abs." Scott made a face.

Patricia swatted him. "Don't be an ass, Scott. I'm sure he solved a case that disturbed her." She paused. "The abs probably don't hurt. All right. So we've got the image person working on the video. We've got state troopers going to two of the abandoned asylums. What else can we do?"

"Agent Holcombe said specifically to be ready to go at the drop of a hat." Donovan put his shoes back on. "We should have been ready to go anyway, but it's good to be reminded. We should maybe wake Alex."

Patricia shook her head. "Absolutely not. That young man is in terrible shape. What's he going to do, bleed on your suspect? Would Luis want you to kill his colleague to support his ego? I don't think so. He'd tell you to leave the boy alone and make sure he's comfortable."

Donovan bit down on his lip. "You're not wrong. Alex just wouldn't be able to forgive himself if something happened and he wasn't there to try to stop it. You are a cop, you've raised cops, you *were* raised by a cop. You know how this works."

Patricia nodded. "I'll stay here with him. We can coordinate information and details from here. That way he'll know exactly what's going on, and he'll be able to help without making himself into a liability. Because we both know Luis would never forgive *himself* if anything happened to Alex while looking for him."

"True enough." Donovan bowed his head.

Alex wouldn't like it, but Patricia was right. Alex wouldn't be allowed into the field in his condition anyway, not under normal circumstances.

In an ideal world, Lightfoot would come back with some kind of report. Surely, they had to know where they were by now, right? There were limits to the whole ghost thing, but it had been hours. Hours in which Luis was conscious and had tried to escape. That meant he must have done some exploration.

Donovan pushed the thought out of his head. He didn't need to be building resentment toward a dead man. He needed to focus.

The first report came in from the crew in Waltham, in the form of Donovan's cousin Cecelia. Cecelia was more of a second or third cousin, Donovan was never quite sure which. He just knew she and Patricia were tighter than the warp and weft on most fabric, and Cecelia would do just about anything Patricia asked.

"I sent a handful of guys from the night shift up to where the Metropolitan State Hospital used to be and to the Gaebler Center. The buildings are pretty much demolished. There's nothing left for the abductor to use to hold someone, not the way you described, Patti." Cecelia was on speakerphone. "I went up there myself, because the demolition was relatively recent. The boys might have missed something, because the grounds on that place were huge. I mean the facility crossed into Belmont and Lexington, remember?"

Patricia sniffed. "I remember. What a sad place to be."

"Well, yeah. They didn't really treat people back in the day, you know? Didn't know how. But that's not here or there. We broke up three teenage parties, which is going to get some angry parents calling in the morning, but that's about it. There's no place for this sick person to be hiding our sweet Luis."

"Thanks for checking it out, Cici." Patricia sighed heavily. Waltham was relatively close by. It wouldn't take long to get there. "I appreciate it."

"Thanks, Aunt Cecelia." Donovan made sure he spoke up before Patricia ended the call.

"We'll find him, Donnie." He could hear the smile in Cecelia's voice. "You can count on that."

The call ended.

Kevin stood up, hands in his pockets. "Well, that's one place eliminated. Down to the other three." He headed up the stairs. "I'm going to wake Alex."

Ten minutes later, as Kevin helped Alex down the stairs, Donovan's phone rang. He didn't recognize the number, but it had a Virginia area code.

"Lieutenant Carey."

The voice on the other end of the line belonged to a woman, one who had a thick Queens accent and spoke almost too fast to be understood. "Lieutenant Carey? Donovan? My name's Bianca Laterza. I'm a friend of Luis', I work with him at the FBI. I do the image analysis. I'm looking at the video the kidnapper sent right now."

Donovan blinked as he tried to make his exhausted brain catch up with someone clearly in a permanent state of fast-forward. "Hang on, let me put you on speaker. I think I've heard the name, Doctor—" He switched from the handset to speaker.

"Oh, just call me Bianca. I don't stand on ceremony with Luis, and you're his boyfriend, so whatever. Look, I've started my analysis of the video, and there's a lot there, but it occurred to me to start with the basics. And I do mean really basic. We're talking you-don't-need-a-PhD-to-do-this-shit basic, which is kind of insulting because I have two. Anyway, not that it's a big deal. So I did take a look at the most basic information and it turns out your lunatic is using her own personal, very own cell phone, under her very own personal name."

"She shot the video with her phone." Donovan translated more for himself. "I know that's important, but I'm not exactly tech savvy. Why is that an issue for her?"

"Well, it's important because it was easy to figure out where she was at the time. See, we'd normally have to get a warrant for that, and as it happens, we did get an emergency warrant once we knew who we were dealing with. But once I had everything, like the phone number, it was easy enough to trace the phone signal. I mean, I couldn't pinpoint the exact location without being back in Quantico, but that would be kind of weird and I'm pretty sure you don't want the satellite coordinates for air strikes—"

"Bianca, this is Kevin Rourke. I love you, you're amazing at your job, no one else does it like you do. I've got four of us ready to head out the door right now, so maybe you could give us a general area without the air strike coordinates?"

198

Kevin sounded fine, but Donovan recognized the look of a man who was barely holding it together.

"Right. Sorry. She's in Medfield. I don't know where Medfield is. Is it made up? It sounds made up. I bet there are cows."

"Oh my God, you're a miracle worker. I'm sending you fifty fruit baskets. Thank you so much."

"Go get 'em, tiger." Bianca hung up.

Donovan grabbed his coat, hugged his mother, and ran out the door. He headed toward his car, already dialing Captain Power, when Kevin turned him around and directed him toward his giant "inconspicuous" FBI-issued SUV.

Scott and John were already in the back.

Donovan decided not to argue. He updated Power on their destination as Kevin peeled out of the driveway, lights on, and headed toward the highway.

It only took a few seconds to realize exactly why Luis had such a low opinion of Boston drivers. Driving with Kevin was a challenge to Donovan's own agnosticism. Before they'd gone even one exit, Donovan remembered every prayer he'd learned in Sunday school. By the time they'd gone two, he remembered some of the Portuguese curses Luis muttered. He might not be able to give a literal translation, but he knew they were appropriate for the situation.

Even John and Scott were holding on for dear life in the back seat. John had a set of rosary beads in one hand. He clutched them so tight his knuckles were white.

Scott swatted him. "Don't stiffen up your trigger fingers, dumbass. We might need them."

"Who knows anything about Medfield?" Donovan asked, hoping no one noticed how tight he was gripping the passenger-assist bar.

"Medfield was built later than most of the other abandoned hospitals." Kevin barely noticed as he passed a slow-moving gold-toned Buick on the right. "The biggest problem we're going to have is that most of the buildings haven't been demolished, just boarded up. And there are a lot of them."

"Awesome." Donovan covered his mouth for a moment, fighting down a wave of nausea. He didn't know if it came from the prospect of searching through dozens of buildings in a race against the clock or if it came from Kevin's oblivious approach to driving. "What are we looking at here?"

"Well, they decided when they built the place that 'cottages' were more conducive to healing than a big Kirkbride-type building. They do have a big creepy main building, but they also have a lot of buildings that would look like large single-family homes to an outside observer. And Luis could be in any one of them."

Donovan shook his head. "They'll be in the main building."

"Why do you say that?" Scott leaned forward.

"She's going to want to keep him secure. The smaller buildings might be easier to break into, but they'll be easier to break out of too. She caught him trying to escape, so it's not like he was able to just get out quick. That means it has to be the bigger space—the main building."

"Plus, she had to get him in there on the gurney." John scratched his chin, where his five o'clock shadow was threatening to eclipse his face. "I'd be surprised if the buildings designed to be 'cottages' had the facilities to accommodate that— especially for a woman working alone."

"Good points." Kevin sped up. Donovan hadn't thought it possible.

Medfield, with its abandoned hospital, awaited.

CHAPTER ELEVEN

Luis could be patient, especially when he was on a case. He wasn't used to being patient with himself, and right now he needed more patience than anyone. Every inch he moved took five times longer than he was used to, and hurt so much he had to bite his lip to keep from crying. The building could have been used for cold storage, but he'd sacrificed his shirt and jacket already. His pants were in shreds.

The shivers wracking his body weren't entirely due to temperature either. If he didn't get help soon, shock would set in. Or get worse. Luis wasn't sure at this point, which he figured was a good argument in favor of shock already being a factor.

"You're doing great." Mike patted him on the back. "Just a few more feet and we'll be at the next door. You can take a little rest there."

"Is that a great idea?" Millie scratched the back of her neck. "Don't you think he should maybe keep moving?"

"Aye. That hyena could be along at any minute, look you. We'd best keep moving."

Luis forced a small smile. "If I stop, I won't be able to start again. Let's keep moving."

"Boom!" Boom-Boom jogged back a few feet and tossed a fireball into a room marked as a women's bathroom. "Boom!"

The resulting explosion rattled glass.

Luis hobbled as fast as his crutches would carry him. Maybe bringing Boom-Boom hadn't been the best idea after all. There was no way Hyena Lady could possibly fail to notice that little gem. His arms trembled with the effort, even though Luis was a strong man. What was the point of staying fit and in shape if he couldn't escape a burning abandoned asylum?

His mind drifted back to the last time he'd seen Donovan, the morning before he'd been taken. Was it only this morning? It felt like a thousand years ago. Donovan was sleep-deprived already, thanks to some jackass who'd decided to shoot up a bunch of cops. He probably wasn't any better off now.

But he'd been there, and he'd been so Donovan about everything. He'd tried to take everything onto his own shoulders alone, answering questions from the families and trying to take care of Alex too.

Poor Alex—that injury had been awful. Luis had taken shots like that. They hurt like hell. Rehabbing could be its own special misery, and then there was the guilt that came with surviving when others hadn't.

How bad was Donovan's guilt now, with one detective dead, another likely never working again, and now Luis gone?

He almost fell over as a wave of guilt hit him. How could Donovan even stand to be around him when all he did was cause him pain? Sure, Luis hadn't meant to get kidnapped, but a basic awareness of his surroundings would have prevented all of this. He hadn't asked for water. He shouldn't have drunk the water. It was that simple.

Captain Lightfoot flicked his ear, but gently. "I recognize the look on yer face, lawman. Whatever's going through that head of yours, squish it like a bug and get back in the game. We're not near the exit yet."

"Sorry." Luis took a ragged breath and tried to focus on the space in front of him. He had to rely on the ghosts to provide light, which didn't give him much to work with. It was better than nothing though. He didn't want to see much more, not when the ghostly light reflected off tiny living beady orbs at ground level.

"It's okay, lad. Your body's having a rough go of it. There's only so much ye can do. It's good we're here to snap ye out of it, that's all." He cackled, like a brisk wind through ancient trees. "It's what we're here for."

Boom-Boom ignited a heap of what might have been bedsheets once. "Boom!"

"Well, and that." Millie averted her eyes.

Luis hadn't thought about paint as flammable. He supposed anything was possible, but he'd never given much thought to interior design or decor before. Whatever was in the paint used on these walls was enough to ignite, given their proximity to Boom-Boom's flaming bedsheets. The fire spread right up the wall in a beautiful little line.

Skitters and squeaks filled the air as every rat in the institution sought a way out.

"Boom?" Boom-Boom stared, wide-eyed and smiling, at his handiwork.

"You got it, Boom-Boom." Luis pushed himself to move faster, even as smoke filled the air. "Boom."

Luis coughed as smoke created a haze in the air. Sure, the fire created a little bit of light, but the smoke undid almost all of the good it had done.

Where was Hyena Lady? He couldn't assume she was just off somewhere sulking. He knew she'd show up to try to block his exit at some point. She couldn't ignore the fire.

The sound of gunfire was his answer. Thankfully, Hyena Lady couldn't shoot at this distance. Maybe the darkness and smoke affected her aim. The bullet ricocheted from a light fixture and bounced into the darkness.

"How the hell did you get up so fast? You should still be out cold!" Her bad accent and the rasp of a thousand cigarettes echoed through the corridor, spreading along with the flames and the smoke.

Luis didn't make time to answer her. Adrenaline lit his nerves and flooded his muscles. He had always been disciplined. He had always been able to ignore outside issues in pursuit of a goal. Right now, that goal was escape. Pain, shock, and fear were all pushed to the side in pursuit of the ramp out of here.

His lungs burned. They burned with the effort of exertion, and they burned with the smoke and fire. The part of his brain that was wandering—*that's shock, Luis*—thought the place should have been more fireproof than this, but evidently, it had just been waiting for the right time to do its Roman candle impersonation. The sooner he could get out of here, the better.

A living hand caught him by the wrist. He

didn't even think about it. He balanced on his good leg, turned, and slammed one of his crutches into Hyena Lady's head as hard as he could.

She collapsed into a heap without a word.

"Shit." He barely regained his balance before joining her in the heap. Maybe that was the point of staying in fighting form after all. "What do I do with her now?"

"Leave her here?" Mike blinked at him. "Demon, remember?"

Luis bit his tongue while his mind raced. He didn't have time to try to argue Mike out of his religious delusions, and he didn't have the strength to rescue her himself. "You're not wrong," he said slowly. "She's evil, and she's participated in a greater evil than I can articulate right now. But it's not up to me to visit judgment upon her. If she's possessed by a demon, she should have the opportunity to be healed and repent her actions, right?"

Luis wasn't a theologian. Sometimes, when his dad had been hungover, he'd sent Luis to church, but that was about it. Jose hadn't been at all religious, and Luis hadn't found a welcoming home in the Church himself.

He *had* been forced to learn enough about certain forms of religious mania, since they tended to show up under professional circumstances.

"You're right." Mike hung his head. Then he picked it up. "But not at your expense, brother."

"No." Luis chuckled. "But I'm okay with leaving her behind the fire doors while we make our escape. I just can't do it myself."

"Boom?" Boom-Boom looked at Luis much as a child would, plaintive and hopeful.

Luis couldn't quite guess what Boom-Boom might be hopeful about, but when the dead pyromaniac moved over to Hyena Lady's head and picked it up, Luis figured it out.

Mike picked up her legs. Luis retrieved his gun, painfully, and let the ghosts get to work. Lightfoot and Millie helped, although Lightfoot did it with his lip curled and his nose wrinkled.

"Look at what I'm driven to. I was the terror of the road to Worcester, and now I'm saving an actual evil wretch from a fire who by all rights should hang just because a lawman doesn't want to have her death on his conscience. Ugh. I feel almost clean." He gave a full-body shudder as they carried her over to the fire doors at the end of the corridor.

Luis followed along behind, after making sure his gun wasn't going to go off in his pocket. That would just be embarrassing.

They secured the fire doors behind them, so Hyena Lady would have some protection from the fire, and inched their way down the ramp into the cold October air.

And Luis saw it—their ticket to freedom.

The van looked like something from a bad late 1970s rock and roll fantasy flick. It had to have been a custom job. Electric blue, the airbrushed art featured a white-bearded wizard wearing nothing but his hat and a loincloth, shooting lightning bolts from his fingertips. Two young women with red hair and breasts that defied the laws of physics sat by his feet, gazing up at him and his beard adoringly.

"This is it. I'm dying, and my brain is throwing up this hallucination because even I hate me."

"If it's your dying hallucination, at least ride it out to the end." Lightfoot gave him a nudge. "Come on, before you bleed out."

Luis couldn't find any fault with Lightfoot's argument. He propelled himself forward and found the shag van locked. It was easy enough to solve, considering that he had two crutches he could use to open the thing. He smashed the window, unlocked the van, and opened the door.

The world spun, but he wasn't out of the woods yet. Sure, he could dial 9-1-1 and wait for rescue. It would take too long to get here.

He let the ghosts blow the broken glass away and climbed into the driver's seat. This took a lot more strength and athleticism than he'd expected, considering that he couldn't put any weight on his left leg.

At least he could let himself scream out here.

He finally made it, though the old thing was full of cigarettes, beer cans, and joints. He shook his head. Fine. Whatever. He wasn't working Vice anymore, and he didn't care enough to try to preserve evidence. He just needed a spare key.

He didn't find one, even though he risked certain infection and death groping around under the floor mats looking for one. He found a screwdriver instead.

He'd worked undercover in Vice long enough to pick up a trick here and there. He stuck the screwdriver into the ignition. This didn't work on most cars, not even on older cars. It was always worth a try though, especially in a pinch.

Thankfully, it worked on this monstrosity from ancient times. The engine turned over right away. He let it idle while booting up the phone Alex had sent.

He fumbled until he found the GPS app. He knew he was in Medfield, but that didn't mean anything to a guy from Miami. There had to be a real hospital near here, not just an abandoned psychiatric facility that was currently on fire.

The GPS told him the fastest route would be

twenty-one minutes. He aimed for the hospital and cast his gaze at the ghosts. "Mike? You're probably my best bet. Tell me you remember how to drive a car."

"Of course I remember how to drive a car." Mike scoffed. "Used to drive a cab, you know."

"Awesome. Because there's a good chance I'm going to pass out between here and there, and I'm going to need you to make sure I don't accidentally kill anyone on the way. Can you do that?"

"Sure thing, Gabe. You can count on me."

"Swell." Luis showed him the phone. "This will tell you how to get to where we're going."

Darkness closed in around him. Luis didn't even fight it.

Medfield State Hospital looked strangely familiar to Donovan, but he didn't have time to ponder why. When the giant SUV pulled up Stonegate Drive, his heart almost stopped in his throat.

He could see all the little "cottages," which dwarfed the town house he shared with Luis and Tria. Of course, the town house had the advantage of having many big beautiful windows that weren't boarded up. Every last cottage was sealed, very thoroughly, with messages in bold letters on hunter-orange paper stating that the building was unsafe.

The main building, a huge red brick thing that looked like every evil asylum in every movie Hollywood had ever made, was also boarded up. Donovan could see the remnants of additional warnings, but he couldn't make them out between the scant light from the SUV's headlights and his panic.

The main building was on fire.

Smoke billowed from small fissures in the boards covering the windows, openings no one would have noticed in daylight. It poured from the main doors, which looked sealed but weren't.

Kevin grabbed his phone. "Dispatch, this is Special Agent Kevin Rourke, FBI. We need fire and rescue at Medfield State Hospital. The main building is on fire, it's believed one suspect is inside with one hostage. The hostage is a federal agent. The suspect is armed and highly dangerous."

Kevin paused, while Donovan stared at the building with his jaw slack. Were they too late? Had Hatch killed Luis and torched the building to hide the remains?

"Dispatch, it's fantastic that we have state troopers en route. I'm looking forward to their assistance. Please advise them to report to

Lieutenant Carey on-site, he's with me. What we need, in addition to those troopers, is fire trucks. And ambulances." Kevin's voice had the clipped tone of someone who might well shoot someone on general principle.

"Awesome. Thank you." Kevin hung up. "I know they're trained to be calm in the face of whatever. I never understood just how annoying that was until this moment."

The words snapped Donovan into action. "I've got to get in there." He passed his phone to Kevin so it wouldn't melt in the heat, and raced toward the main doors of the building.

Scott and John tackled him, just in time. It took both of them to hold him back.

"Christ you're dumb." John gritted the words out from between clenched teeth. It took all of his strength to hold him back. "Would you put some of that bull strength into your brain for once?"

"That building is massive and has no electricity. It's full of smoke, dumbass." Scott swept Donovan's legs out from under him, although he and John kept hold of Donovan's arms. They had to fight to hold Donovan up, but at least he couldn't get purchase on the wet leaves carpeting the ground anymore. "You think you'll be able to find Luis in there?"

214

"I have to try." Donovan stopped fighting, despite his words. He knew his brothers were right. They had to wait, even longer, to find Luis.

And every second was precious.

The state troopers showed up first, led by a night shift guy by the name of Phil Hamilton.

Phil was a short wiry guy with a reputation for brains and a short fuse. He glanced up at the burning building and shuddered. "Captain Power said we were supposed to be searching the site?"

"Yeah." Donovan ran his hand through his hair. "We, uh, found the hostage, sort of. But the situation has deteriorated. The suspect used her own phone to make some threats, and it was traced to this location."

"This location covers a lot of ground." Hamilton grimaced and glanced around wryly. "And it's got a couple of ways in and out."

"Fabulous," Kevin snarled.

"Allow me to introduce Special Agent Rourke. His partner got drugged and taken hostage." Donovan took a deep breath. He could handle this if he didn't mention Luis' name. "We can't get into the building until the fire department douses it, so we need to search the grounds for any clues they might have gotten out." He raised his voice. "Suspect is Tammie Hatch. She's five foot eight, blonde, and her face does not move due to a surgical accident. Hostage is six foot two, Latino, with a bad injury to his leg. We're looking for blood, drag marks, anything. Also looking for a 1970s Ford Econoline with unique artwork."

The troopers, about twenty in all, dispersed. Donovan stayed upright until they were out of visual range. Then, and only then, did his legs buckle.

Kevin caught him. "We'll find him, Donovan. You know we will."

Donovan bit the inside of his cheek. "He's a strong guy. We both know he'd fight as long as he could, but she has plenty of ways of taking him out. She's drugged him before, what's to stop her from doing it again? He could be dying from smoke inhalation right now and can't even fight."

Kevin looked away. "It's possible." Then he settled his shoulders. "But I can't let myself think it's likely." He glanced at Scott and John and left it at that.

Donovan wished he had as much faith in Captain Lightfoot as Kevin. Sure, Lightfoot had come through for Luis in the past. He was also a serial killer. Donovan wasn't in the habit of trusting the people they hunted.

He straightened up, pulled out his Maglite, and circled the building. He wasn't about to just stand around and hope that someone else found the clue that led to Luis' rescue. He needed to do something about it himself.

The worst years of the state hospital system were behind it by the time Donovan was old enough to know what was going on in the world. He'd experienced the hospitals as places for people who truly needed help—safe places, really. That didn't mean the stigma attached to them didn't exist.

He could see how a place like this would make people think of the absolute worst history had to offer.

He crept around the exterior. All of the buildings associated with the hospital were abandoned and disused, but the site itself was open to the public as a park. It was apparently a popular dog-walking spot, although Donovan didn't see many colorful baggies near the main building. Apparently, it disturbed even people who wanted to leave their dog's mess on-site.

Luis had been in this building.

It didn't take a rocket scientist to figure that out. He'd have been able to sneak out of any of the other buildings long before Tammie Hatch found out. And if this old building wasn't just as haunted as that old jail they'd holed up in, Donovan would hang up his detective badge and go back to catching speeders.

How awful had it been for him, being trapped in here with some severely disturbed dead souls? What had they done to him, to take out their anger and aggression?

He sneaked around the corner. The main building was *massive*. According to the website, it had been abandoned in stages. It had to have been creepy as hell, to receive modern treatment in a building only partially in use, perhaps tuning in to the whispers of the damned.

He spotted what looked like pay dirt—a pair of ramps at a side entrance. One went to the main floor. The other went to the basement. Both doors were boarded up, but the main floor door hung ajar.

Donovan bolted towards it. For one thing, less smoke came from this exit—even though the door was ajar—than from the other options. For another, an open door meant someone had been in a hurry. They might have been sloppy.

He didn't find Luis in the vestibule. He found stairs, wretched and slimy with mold. He also found Tammie Hatch.

Hatch groaned when he rolled her over. She had a bump on the side of her head, just above her temple, and bruising around her eye and jaw. Luis had put up a fight, then. Pride surged through Donovan, its only outlet a grim twist of his lips as he pulled his gun.

He grabbed his radio. "I have the suspect. Side entrance. Requesting backup."

Hatch blinked up at him. "I'm a damsel in distress! I'm not a suspect in anything! How could I be?" She reached for her hip. "Goddamn it, the son of a bitch even stole my gun."

"It's his gun, you psychopathic little shit. Hands where I can see them."

Hatch stuck her tongue out at him. "Finders keepers, handsome." She kept her hands still. "Look, I'll cut you a deal. Give me what I want, and I'll tell you where to find Agent Lightweight there."

Donovan ground his teeth. "You left him in a burning building?"

She scoffed. "Who do you think roughed me up like this? Don't get me wrong, I don't mind a little horseplay, but don't go for the face. That just gets awkward for everyone involved, don't you think?"

Donovan tightened his grip on his gun. Where was his backup? He wanted nothing so badly as to put a bullet in this woman's brain, but he couldn't afford it. He needed to find Luis, and she was the only one who knew where he was.

"Agent Gomes didn't do that during rough sex, lady. He wouldn't touch you with a ten-foot pole."

"Shows what you know." She tossed her hair over her shoulder, holding her eyes with his own.

"I've known Luis Gomes for fourteen years—almost fifteen, I guess. He's got as much interest in sex with women as he does in sex with jellyfish. The thought would literally never occur to him. Not even to get out of being locked up in some abandoned asylum with the kind of woman who defends a child molester, rapist, and murderer." Donovan forced a tight smile as his brothers ran up behind him.

John saw what was going on, caught on, and grabbed his handcuffs. He hauled Hatch to her feet, none too gently, and bound her wrists behind her. "What did I tell you about going into the building, bro?" He shook his head.

Donovan shrugged, not taking his eyes away from Hatch. "Saw an opportunity. And now this lady is going to tell me where Luis is." He stepped closer.

Scott got between Donovan and Hatch. It wasn't egregious, but it was enough to bring Donovan to his senses. He wasn't *that cop*, even if he wanted to be right now.

"First things first, bro. Even someone like her's got rights. And she gets reminded of them. Besides, there's a good chance that Luis isn't here."

Scott put a hand on Donovan's shoulder.

"Oh, he's here all right. Your darling Luis is right where I left him. He's in the dayroom, all tied up, roasting away like the pork roast he is." Hatch lunged for Donovan but wasn't able to balance herself with her arms restrained. She fell into the floor face-first.

Scott picked her head up—by the hair—and read her rights to her.

"Bro, this is a parking lot," he continued, gesturing to the clearing around them. "What do you not see?"

"It's an abandoned hospital, Scott." Donovan glowered as his brother let Hatch's head fall back into the tiny stones. They probably didn't feel great, especially on an already battered face. "I'm not expecting to see visitors lined up."

"No, but I would expect to see her shag van. I don't. I did find a little puddle of antifreeze and some broken glass." Scott waggled his eyebrows.

Hatch picked her head up. "The little fucker stole my car too?"

CHAPTER TWELVE

The ride to Norwood Hospital was one of the most surreal experiences of Luis' life. He had four dead companions in a shag van from the seventies fighting to make sure he stayed conscious. It even worked, some of the time. Thankfully, there weren't many people on the road at three thirty in the morning or whatever it was. He might be conscious for half the trip, but there was no way he could keep the car going in a straight line.

And now that the need to escape was past, Luis couldn't focus on that instead of on the pain. He had to actually feel everything, and that wasn't fun at all. The pain came with Luis' familiar friend—fear. He'd survived Hyena Lady, but what about the injury? Would he be able to keep the leg?

There was no way he'd be able to stay in the field.

He yanked the wheel to the right as an oncoming motorist flashed their lights at him. He'd drifted into the wrong lane again.

"Close call, Gabe." Mike eyed him from the front passenger seat. "Why don't I just take over behind the wheel?"

"Yeah. Okay." Luis nodded and moved over, which was agony, but he knew he wasn't in shape to drive.

It would look odd, if anyone looked. They'd see a battered man in the passenger seat and no one at all behind the wheel, unless they were able to see ghosts. Then they'd get a real sight to behold. Luis laughed at the thought and turned the heat on.

The heater wasn't working. Of course it wasn't.

"I'm pressing charges against Hyena Lady for the van alone." He shuddered, and then he realized he couldn't stop shuddering. It was more of a shiver, and that wasn't good.

He tried to focus on his breath. He could do this, if he kept his cool. He'd been in worse situations, right? He'd been shot in the chest and survived, and taken down a serial killer to boot. He wasn't going to die out here on some backcountry road, in some filthy van with his leg held together by a makeshift splint.

He was going to get back to Donovan. He was getting back to his desk, getting that damn ring, and giving it to the man he loved. Donovan could decline, but at least Luis wasn't going to —

Mike sideswiped someone's mailbox. The sound of metal against metal hurt his teeth. He hoped it at least took out the improbable breasts in the artwork.

He passed out for a few minutes again.

Captain Lightfoot revived him with a slight jolt. "Can't have ye sleeping on the job. Not for long, at any rate. Some of us need ye if we're going to be able to touch things in the living world." He jerked his head toward Mike.

Mike grinned, manically, and honked the horn. "I won't pretend this doesn't feel good. I miss driving. Think anyone would mind if I did a few doughnuts on their lawn?"

"I think this old wreck would fall over if you did doughnuts on someone's lawn, and we'd be screwed. Well, I'd be screwed." Luis chuckled, even though his stomach lurched at the thought. If they wrecked the van, his trip to the hospital would be delayed, and he'd never make it. "Once I'm at the emergency department, you're welcome to do all the doughnuts you like. Do them on the hospital's lawn. It'll be fun."

"Do you think I could?" Mike's features got a little more solid as the idea took hold.

"Sure, why not?" Luis' leg felt like it was on fire, even though he was so cold he had to have hypothermia by now. Or frostbite. One of the two.

"Everyone's grumpy at the hospital. They won't be able to see you, so think about it. They'll just see a beat-up old van, driving in circles on its own. Think about their reaction. Think about them going home and telling the grandkids or the grandparents."

Millie laughed and clapped her hands. "I'm going to see how fast I can make the wheelchairs go in the hallways!"

"Boom!" Boom-Boom shouted in glee. A pile of leaves on someone's lawn ignited as they drove past.

Lightfoot patted Luis' bare shoulder. "Ye're a good man, lawman."

Mike brought the shag van skidding to a halt in front of the emergency department. A security guard gaped as Luis let himself out of the passenger-side door and braced himself against the van. The guard could see that Luis hadn't been driving.

Luis didn't care. He couldn't waste time on that kind of thing right now. "I need help." He gestured at his leg. "I've been shot."

The guard nodded and stepped into the hospital. Luis lost track of him as he let himself fall to the ground. He'd done what he came here for. He could pass out now.

He came back to himself a few minutes later, on his back, moving through a hallway. A white woman in maroon scrubs looked down at him. "Sir, do you know where you are?"

Luis' teeth clattered. "Norwood Hospital. My name is Special Agent Luis Gomes. I need to tell—"

She looked at someone on Luis' other side. "He's delusional."

The person on Luis' other side mumbled something unintelligible. Luis could barely make out the word *courthouse*.

"Yes!" Luis seized on the word and hoped he was doing the right thing. "I was grabbed outside the courthouse. She drugged me. I just escaped. Let me call my—"

The first woman just patted his hand. "It's okay, buddy. You can tell us all about it when you're feeling a little more coherent."

Luis let out a little shout of frustration as the unknown people wheeled him into a treatment bay. It looked like any other room in any other emergency department. He'd been in a few, as a patient and an investigator.

Another woman, Black with short hair, strode into the room and looked Luis over. "Good morning. I'm Dr. Anderson. I'm going to order imaging on your leg, but I can tell you right now we're not the facility to treat it. You've lost a lot of blood, your temperature is dangerously low, your heart rate is erratic, and you're having trouble staying conscious."

"Shock." Luis closed his eyes for a second. Then he grabbed the rails on the gurney and hauled himself into a sitting position. "Listen, please. I need to get in touch with my supervisor and tell her where I am and where the suspect is."

Dr. Anderson glanced at the two nurses. "You were found with a gun in your pocket and a cell phone, but no identification."

"Yes. That's my service weapon. The bullet in my leg will be a match to it." Luis fought for breath. "Just let me call SSA Holcombe. Or my partner."

"Sir, you're in bad shape. We need to stabilize you for transfer to a level-one trauma center—Tufts, most likely." She pressed her lips together, and then she sighed. "But yes, bring him his phone."

"What about the gun?" The nurse in maroon glanced back at her friend, who grimaced.

"If he is who he says he is, he needs to know where it is at all times. I don't feel comfortable having it in my ER, but we'll make that call when we get to it."

Maroon ducked out and returned quickly. She carried a plastic tub and brought it to Luis' side. He checked the gun without taking it out of

228

the tub, since it seemed to make the staff nervous, and took out the phone.

Before he could call anyone, it rang. Luis blinked and answered it.

"Agent Gomes." He closed his eyes as the room lurched to the right.

"Luis?" Patricia sounded close to tears. "Oh my God, you have no idea how glad I am to hear your voice. Donovan said the building was on fire."

"Patricia." Luis let himself fall back onto the gurney. Who would have thought he would be so relieved to hear Donovan's mother's voice ten years ago? "Thank God. Yeah, the building's on fire. It's part of how I got away. I'm at Norwood Hospital, but they're going to transfer me. Would you maybe explain to the doctor who I am and tell Donovan I love him? I think I'm going to pass out again."

Dr. Anderson took the phone from Luis' hands. He didn't pass out, but he did surrender to the lassitude of shock and exhaustion. Nurses asked him questions about his blood type, gave him fluids, washed his filthy body as best they could, and covered him with warmed blankets.

He liked the warmed blankets.

Through it all, Dr. Anderson spoke with Patricia. "Hello, this is Dr. Anderson at Norwood Hospital. Who am I speaking with?" She straightened up a little. "Captain Carey. I see. Well, he's only just arrived. He appears to have driven himself? He's in terrible shape, honestly, and we don't have the facilities to treat him here. We can stabilize him and pass him on to Tufts. Yes, ma'am. They're a level-one trauma center, and they'll be best equipped to deal with his leg. The technical term is a hot mess, ma'am. I can't give a more accurate diagnosis until I get some imaging, but first we need to get him stable. Yes, ma'am. That will absolutely take long enough for family or colleagues to get here." She caught Luis' eye and winked. "They might want to bring him some pants. The ones he came in with are trashed."

Luis cringed as the nurse cut away the offending garments, but he couldn't argue about it. They were shot.

Kind of like his leg.

"Thank you, Captain. I'm glad to help." Dr. Anderson hung up the phone and handed it back to Luis. "Captain Carey sounds like the kind of mother-in-law everyone wants—as long as they can stay on her good side."

Luis hummed in contentment as he burrowed into his warm blanket. "I'm a lucky man."

"You certainly are. She's going to make the necessary phone calls for you. Someone from your office should be here soon to help you out. In the meantime, let's get down to business. She grimaced down at Luis' leg. "That probably doesn't feel great."

"The kidnapper shot me with my own gun, ma'am." He closed his eyes. "Close range."

"You did a pretty good job of splinting it up, considering the circumstances. We're going to have to undo the splint to get the images we need though. And I'm going to redo the splint with better materials, because we have them. That's going to suck."

Luis winced. "The good part is I might well pass out in the middle." He managed a grin.

He didn't know if he could trust this. Maybe he'd wrapped the van around a tree on the way off the hospital grounds, and this was another deathbed hallucination.

He'd ride it out, if that was the case.

Donovan got in touch with Phil Hamilton, who he'd decided was in charge of the uniformed officers right now. They sent some units out to look for the van, which must have left an impression on at least someone. Donovan didn't want to think about the state Luis would have been in if he was driving.

He'd lost a lot of blood. Donovan could see that in the video. He'd been drugged and beaten, shot, and he'd be in a ton of pain. If he made it more than a few blocks, Donovan would start going to church again. It would be the clearest proof of the existence of a kind and benevolent deity anyone had seen yet.

He almost ignored his phone when it rang. Luis didn't have his phone, and Luis was the only one he wanted to hear from right now. Then he remembered the phone Lightfoot had sneaked to Luis. It must be giving off a signal. Maybe Alex or Patricia had picked it up and had a clue about which direction Luis had chosen.

"Carey." He didn't waste words as the fire department came screaming up the long dark driveway.

"Don't you *Carey* me. I just spoke with Luis." Patricia's grin was evident in her voice.

Donovan lost his breath for a moment. Scott had to come over and pound him on the back. "He's okay?" he sputtered, when he remembered how to speak.

"Pretty far from it, actually. Get your butt over to Norwood Hospital. They're stabilizing him as best they can before they send him on to Tufts, where they'll have the facilities to treat him. He needs the level-one center, I'm afraid. But he's alive and more or less coherent."

"How come he called you?" Donovan turned away from the burning building.

"He didn't. I saw that the signal was active, and I called the number, just in case it went dark again. I'm glad I did. Apparently when half-naked men show up with gunshot wounds and no ID, the doctors don't believe it when they claim they're with the FBI. Go figure. I'll come down with Alex when you get settled in at Tufts, and then I'll go pick up Jose at the airport. Are you in the car yet?"

Donovan chuckled, even as his heart raced. "I've got to go tell Kevin. He's got the keys. Thanks, Mom. I love you."

"I love you too. And you tell sweet Luis I love him when you see him." Patricia disconnected.

Donovan hugged John and Scott and told them the good news. Then he ran to go find Kevin.

Kevin was arguing with the fire chief. "Look, I know it's an old derelict building, but there might be a living federal agent trapped inside. We can't just stand back and watch it burn—"

Donovan put a hand on Kevin's arm. "Agent. He's alive."

Kevin turned around. "Excuse me? Do we have an ambulance? Did you not see how much blood he lost?"

"Escaped. By himself. Stole the suspect's vehicle and drove himself to the hospital." He couldn't hold back the hysterical laughter. "I kind of need a ride."

"Isn't someone going to stay here to supervise the scene?" asked one of the firefighters.

"Yeah, aren't you worried about there being more hostages or something?" The chief curled his lip a little.

Donovan's fist clenched, but Kevin stepped on his foot just in time to restrain him. "We're not, actually, but thank you for your concern. Officer Phil Hamilton is on the scene. So is Sergeant Scott Carey." He handed the chief his card, as well as one for Captain Power just to be safe. "Thank you for your assistance."

He jogged toward Kevin's giant gas-guzzling SUV. If he keyed the fire truck on his way past, Kevin didn't say anything about it.

Kevin needed the GPS to take them to Norwood Hospital. It wasn't one of the larger hospitals in the area. It was a small community hospital. The ER could probably handle basic childhood accidents like broken bones or sports injuries, but gunshot wounds would be pretty far outside their typical practice. Kevin didn't know Medfield well at all, it not being a hotbed of federal-level crime, and Donovan wasn't all that familiar with it either.

The GPS said it would be a twenty-one minute ride. They made it in twelve.

Donovan didn't notice much along the way. His thoughts were all on Luis. How close had it been? Had they passed in the darkness or had Luis already been gone by the time Donovan arrived on-site? Did Luis just not have faith in Donovan or the FBI to save him, or had he felt he was in too much danger to wait?

He did notice a few smaller fires on the way—a dumpster here, a pile of leaves there. He couldn't make himself believe there wasn't a connection, but he couldn't tease it out of the ether either. "The hospital caught fire, which allowed Luis to make his escape. Right?"

"That's what it looks like." Kevin gripped the wheel and took a corner on two wheels.

"So why are there so many fires along the way? I don't see him stopping to lob Molotov cocktails while he was driving."

"Maybe it was Lightfoot. He's volatile enough." Kevin shrugged. "Could be his way of trying to attract attention, if he didn't think Luis could get himself to the hospital in one piece."

"Hm." Donovan couldn't think of an argument against it, not one strong enough to distract Kevin from his awful driving. Lightfoot was certainly volatile, but he wasn't a firebug either.

They screeched into the parking lot at Norwood Hospital's emergency department. Donovan barely let the car stop moving before he jumped out of the vehicle and ran toward the entrance. The receptionist looked him up and down. "Have a seat and tell me your symptoms, sir."

Donovan glared and pulled out his badge. "Lieutenant Donovan Carey, Massachusetts State Police. I'm here about a gunshot wound victim who showed up a short time ago."

She widened her eyes and picked up the phone. "Hi, can you tell Dr. Anderson someone's here about that patient? Thanks." She turned back to Donovan. "Sorry. Are you sure you aren't here for yourself?"

Kevin popped in behind him. "It's been a rough couple of days. There's nothing wrong with Lieutenant Carey that a good night's sleep won't fix." He patted Donovan's back and showed the receptionist his credentials. "Agent Kevin Rourke, FBI."

Some of the hacking, miserable patients

236

waiting their turn for treatment took an interest. This was definitely more excitement than a typical community hospital saw on a weeknight. Donovan couldn't help but feel uncomfortable.

Fortunately, a nurse in maroon scrubs appeared. Her cheeks were bright pink. "Are you here about the gentleman who came in earlier? Please, follow me."

Donovan forced himself to breathe as he followed the short curly-haired woman down the corridor. He could hear an elderly man moaning in a treatment bay and someone vomiting in another. The smells in an emergency department could be overwhelming, and today was no exception.

Luis had been put into a room with walls, if not a door. It gave him a little bit of privacy and dulled the shouting from the other rooms. He looked downright gray. He was covered in blankets, more than Donovan had ever seen on a hospital patient. He was receiving fluids and blood through an IV, and a nasal cannula provided extra oxygen. His eyes were closed, but they fluttered open when Donovan and Kevin walked into the room.

"I'm dead." His voice was soft and a little loopy. "I'm dead, and somehow made it into heaven. I guess Mike was right after all." He smiled blissfully.

Donovan glanced at Kevin, who shrugged.

"Who's Mike?" Donovan took Luis' hand, the one that didn't have the IV in it. "Luis, was there another hostage?"

"Not living."

Donovan groaned quietly. They were going to have to keep Luis quiet while he got the painkillers out of his system. They couldn't afford to have him talking about ghosts while he was high as a kite.

"That's fortunate." Kevin stood behind Donovan. "How in the hell did you get out?"

"Almost made it the first time, so she shot me. Hyena. Didn't think there was time to wait. Bleeding too much. Lightfoot found crutches. Whacked her in the head."

"She told us she left you in the dayroom." Donovan shuddered with his whole body at the thought.

Luis nodded. "She did. But had help. Got them to put her on the other side of the fire door." He yawned. "Did you find her?" Then his heart rate—monitored carefully by what looked like a hundred little sensors coming out from under his thin polka-dotted johnnie—spiked, and he struggled to sit up. "Did you find her? The building is on fire."

Luis' eyes burned with fear. Sweat poured

down his face. An alarm rang somewhere outside the room, and a tall Black woman in a white coat rushed into the room. "Who exactly is agitating my seriously fragile patient?"

"She's going to burn." Luis reached for Donovan. "Fire doors are only so good."

Donovan kissed Luis' sweaty forehead. "We found her. She's safe and on her way to Nashua Street. It's okay. I promise. I found her myself, okay? I'm not just yanking your chain."

Luis' panic subsided immediately. "Don't want that on my conscience." His heart rate began to ebb back toward normal, and he relaxed against Donovan. "Sorry I smell bad."

"You smell alive, and that's what I care about."

"Sorry I distracted you from the Southwick thing."

"Luis, this isn't your fault."

But Luis had already fallen asleep.

The stranger shook her head, a gentle smile on her lips. "Let me guess, you'd be Captain Carey's son."

Donovan blinked in confusion. "I'm sorry, have we met?"

"Your mother called when Agent Gomes was first brought in. He was about to call you, I believe, when the phone rang. He passed the phone to me, as I didn't believe him when he identified himself. You wouldn't believe how many people try to claim they're secret agents when they come in here, usually after doing something embarrassing." She rolled her eyes. "I'm Dr. Anderson. I'm working to stabilize your partner until we can transfer him to Tufts."

"I'm Donovan Carey. This is Agent Kevin Rourke. He's Luis' work partner." Donovan stroked Luis' hair. "How bad off is he?"

Anderson glanced toward the door. "I'm going to operate on the assumption you're his next of kin. He's in bad shape, honestly. He was already fairly dehydrated when he came in, and the blood loss isn't helping. We're doing what we can for both of those things, and he seems to be responding well. With any luck, he'll come away without permanent damage to internal organs such as his kidneys.

"I'm not sure what the conditions were like where he was being held, but it's almost like he's been held in cold storage. We're talking refrigeration. I'm seeing some signs of early hypothermia, and maybe tortured with frozen items?" Anderson indicated marks on Luis' arm and shoulders. They looked almost like finger marks, except for where they were more like bone impressions. Donovan knew what they were, but

240

of course Anderson wouldn't. "He told me he was drugged. We did a blood test and he did test positive for ketamine, and a large dose of it too. That could explain why he was able to escape—the pain from his leg should have been unbearable, but the drug is routinely used as an anesthetic."

Kevin made a face. "It's possible. Luis is also the kind of guy who thinks pain is a problem for future-him."

"We see a lot of those guys around here." Anderson smirked. Then she sobered a bit. "Unfortunately, while he may have saved his own life, he might have caused more damage to the leg. We're going to have to see what the experts think. His heart rate is still erratic, I'm afraid, and I don't like that at all. The leg is secondary to the brain and heart."

"You're not suggesting he's going to lose it?" Donovan held Luis a little closer, even though he didn't seem to notice. He'd love Luis no matter what, but even the perceived loss of independence wouldn't sit well with Luis.

"I'm not ruling anything out. Like I said, we'll get him to Tufts and go from there."

CHAPTER THIRTEEN

Tufts was a blur. Luis was content to let it be a blur. Now that he wasn't in danger, or at least not in immediate danger, he could surrender to the oblivion that had been calling him ever since Hyena Lady shot him. He had a few moments of lucidity, such as when the new doctor started poking around at his leg. The pain from even the slightest touch yanked him out of his state and sent him howling nearly to the ceiling.

The new doctor was a white guy, with gray hair and cold gray eyes. He informed Luis that the pain was "good news, son. It means some of the nerves are still attached."

Luis wasn't so far gone that he missed the *some* in his sentence.

He couldn't remember a time when he'd had more images taken, and that included during the FBI application and intake process. Fortunately, they didn't need him to be awake or coherent during the imaging process, so he let himself drift in and out. Donovan was around, willing to stand there and hold his hand even though Luis stank and was more or less useless during the whole thing.

Then they wheeled him into a bay, like a presurgical area. It was like a room, but with curtains for walls. He could hear murmurs and, occasionally, shouts from other patients he couldn't see. His nurse, thankfully, turned out to be Brazilian. She spoke to him in Portuguese. "I'd love to give you something for the pain because I know you're really feeling it right now, but you'll be going into surgery just as soon as a room opens up. We can't give you anything that might interfere with the anesthesia."

Donovan set his jaw, but didn't say anything. He didn't like being excluded from conversations, but he didn't seem to want to deny Luis this little comfort right now. "Did I introduce my boyfriend Donovan?" Luis squeezed Donovan's hand. "He's the best."

The nurse smiled kindly at both of them. "I'm so happy you've got someone who can be with you right now. I don't suppose he has brothers?"

"Three, but one's an asshole." Luis grimaced as a wave of pain overtook him. "You'll like the other two though."

The nurse laughed and switched to English to speak to Donovan. "The anesthesiologist is on her way in. Once she's here, I have to chase you away. I hate to do it, but we have to keep the OR as clean and as distraction-free as possible."

"I understand completely." Donovan managed a little smile. He bent down and touched his lips to Luis' forehead. It must have been disgusting, considering how filthy Luis was, but he didn't seem to mind. "I'll be pacing in the waiting room."

"Along with the squad of people in suits and cops, I'm sure." The nurse winked. "There's even a small child waiting."

"Nicky's here?" Luis tried to sit up. Donovan gently pushed him back down. "He shouldn't be in a hospital. It's too scary. Shouldn't he be in school?"

"He's not going to be in school when his favorite uncle has been shot and is in surgery." Donovan stroked Luis' cheek, and Luis tried not to lean into it too hard. "It would be useless to send him. He wouldn't be able to focus anyway. Come on."

A white woman with brown hair, about Luis' own age, popped into the scene. "Hi, I'm Dr. Wilson. I'm your anesthesiologist. I understand you're the agent who got taken hostage and freed himself on a shattered tibia?"

Luis heard one of the monitors beep, saw Donovan's look of consternation. "I shouldn't have let myself get—"

"None of that." Donovan's voice turned gruff. "It could have happened to anyone, you didn't have any reason to think someone was gunning for you, and you didn't just get yourself out, you made sure she was safe before you escaped. Which you did. On a leg that's so shattered it needs—"

He cut himself off at a warning look from the nurse. Luis didn't understand what that warning look meant, but his brain was too foggy from pain, shock, and fatigue to care.

"You're amazing, and don't you forget it." Donovan broke off. "I guess I have to go now?"

Dr. Wilson gave him a gentle smile. "You can stay until he's under, if you want. Agent Gomes, do you have any known allergies to any medications?"

"I don't drink." Luis frowned. "My dad was a drunk."

Donovan huffed out a little laugh. "He doesn't. He also doesn't take any mind-altering substances, so he's probably a little bit of a lightweight." He'd answered the same question for Luis five times already, or at least five times that

Luis could hear. God, it was embarrassing.

"Fair enough." Dr. Wilson approached Luis with a mask.

"Wait." Luis squeezed Donovan's hand. "Tell Kevin I need the thing in my desk. He'll know what I'm talking about." He nodded to Wilson, and let the darkness take the pain away.

The world was fuzzy when he came back to consciousness—fuzzy, and painful.

His nurse, whose name tag he could now process, was still Cila Castro. "How are you feeling?"

Luis took stock. The world was indeed still fuzzy, and he wasn't sure if his stomach was on board with the idea of food or even water. His head felt a lot clearer, so that was something, but his leg was still on fire.

"A little more with it than I was. That's not saying much." He grimaced. "I apologize if I was out of line before. I don't remember much."

"You were fine." She took his hand and smiled. "You told me your boyfriend was the best and said I'd like his two brothers. That's about it." She glanced around what Luis assumed was a recovery room. "He said you wouldn't want morphine for the leg. I argued with him, and I'll still give it to you if you want it, but the people with him backed him up . . ."

Luis smiled and let himself relax as much as he could. "They were right. It hurts—it hurts a lot. My father was—is—an addict, and I'm leery of following in his footsteps. Also, I get incredibly stupid when I'm on painkillers. It's embarrassing."

She laughed a little. "Well, if you change your mind, we'll see what we can do. If you think you're ready, we can bring you up to your room."

He stopped her with a gesture. "Sorry. I don't mean to be rude. But, um, everything kind of hurts, and I can't really tell the difference. My leg . . ."

She gave him a soft smile. "It's still there, Agent. Your doctor will talk to you about the surgery and everything else. I'm not qualified to discuss your prognosis or any of that. But he did save the leg."

Luis let out a long sigh of relief. "Thank you."

He knew he wasn't out of the woods yet. He'd known the bone was a mess when he'd been shot. Still, he'd have a hard time making a case for staying with the Bureau if they'd had to amputate.

An orderly appeared, and between him and Nurse Cila, they wheeled him out of the recovery room and out into a long sterile corridor. They took a ride in an elevator that smelled strongly of disinfectant, only to end up on an unmarked floor.

"This is a floor we use for people who need a little extra privacy." Cila continued to speak Portuguese, as if there wasn't anyone around. "Most of the people on this ward are trauma patients who might need the protection, but occasionally, there are celebrities who don't need fans popping in to gawk while they recover from surgery or whatever."

They wheeled Luis into a room with two uniformed officers—one Boston cop and one state trooper—standing outside the door.

The first thing Luis noticed, strangely enough, was that it was dark outside. The second was that the room was full. Patricia was there, along with Donovan, Kevin, SSA Holcombe, Alicia, Nicky, and Jose Perez, Luis' foster dad.

Luis stared. All these people had come to see him? All these people had to see him like this— covered by a sheet and a hospital smock? Overwhelm made his mind spin, and threatened to make the room do the same. He wrestled himself back under control and pulled the blanket farther up his body, making sure everything below his ribcage was hidden.

Somehow, he'd learned shame over the past couple of years, or at least modesty.

Nicky, being all of eight, had no use for restraint. He didn't even wait for Cila and the orderly to finish wheeling Luis into the room before he flung himself at Luis, wrapping his arms around him and squeezing tight.

The gesture made Luis gasp. He'd almost forgotten about his bruised ribs in the fuss about his leg, but he'd gladly endure the pain in exchange for the warmth and love of this small innocent person.

"I didn't think I'd see you again!" Nicky soaked Luis' johnnie with tears in only a few seconds. "I woke up, and Mom told me you'd been hurt. I got scared!"

Luis stroked Nicky's hair and swallowed hard. He couldn't make himself look into the eyes of anyone else there, not even Donovan. "I'll admit it—I was scared too, buddy. When I woke up in that basement, in the dark, I was pretty sure I was never going to get out of there. But you know what?"

Nicky sniffed. Cila twitched. If Luis had to guess, he'd figure she was running through the laundry list of germs small children carried with them.

"What, Uncle Luis?"

"I wasn't going to let go without a fight. I had too much to get back to. Especially you, Nicky." Now he did look up and meet Donovan's eyes. "So I worked hard to get out. It wasn't easy, and the first time, I failed. But the second time, I managed it."

Holcombe hid her grin with one hand. "And burned down a historic building while you were at it."

Luis let Cila help set Nicky into a more comfortable position for both of them, raising the back of the bed so Luis didn't have to hold himself in a sitting position. "It smelled bad. What can I say?"

Everyone laughed, even Jose. Marriage looked good on Jose. He'd gotten grayer over the years, with maybe a few more crow's-feet, but he still looked every inch as strong and vibrant as he had the day he shook Luis' hand on his way out the door.

Now Jose stepped forward. He took a deep breath and hesitated. "It's been a while, Luis."

"Too long." Luis looked down. "How are you?"

Jose shocked him by throwing his arms around him. "Better now that I can see you're alive and talking." He switched to Spanish. "I heard you'd been taken from a damn crime wire. I thought I was going to have a heart attack right there in the office."

"I'm sorry." Luis buried his face in Jose's shoulder. "You shouldn't have to worry about me."

"Of course I should! I'm your father. Maybe

I didn't show it the way I wanted to, the way you needed me to. There were reasons for that, but, Luis, I'm proud of you. And I'm always going to worry about you because that's *exactly* what I signed up for when I brought you under my roof." He gave Luis a squeeze, including Nicky for good measure, and turned to the rest of the room with a smile.

"I've been getting to know your Boston family while you were lazing around downstairs," he said, switching back to English so everyone else could understand him. "I can probably worry a little bit less. Just a little though." He winked at Nicky, who laughed and hid his face in Luis' chest again. "I mean you did get shot. *Again.*"

"You should see the other guy. Er, person." Scott perked up from his perch on the windowsill. "She definitely didn't expect the fight she got out of him, that's for sure."

Everyone laughed, even Luis. He could laugh now. He distinctly remembered Donovan telling him Hyena Lady was in custody.

Something deep down inside Luis didn't want to trust this. There was too much that could still go wrong. For now though, he couldn't do much to affect anything either way. He forced himself to relax into the moment. He would take whatever came as it came.

Donovan hadn't met Jose when he and Luis lived together back in their college days. Donovan had still been in the closet, and Luis hadn't wanted to burden Jose with his life any more than he absolutely had to. During the long hours of Luis' surgery, he'd had a chance to experience the man who gave Luis the confidence to live as an out gay man for pretty much his entire life.

Jose was, on a lot of levels, exactly what Donovan would expect from a cop parent. Donovan had grown up around a fair number of them, after all. He made his expectations clear—Luis would take his meds, he would rest and not try to sign himself out AMA, he would eat the hospital food when it was offered. He wasn't given to flowery displays of emotion either.

At the same time, he had a subtle, wicked sense of humor that put everyone around them at ease. He was just as welcoming and loving toward Nicky as Luis himself was, and wasn't that something?

And he didn't try to interfere with Donovan at all. Donovan did find Jose staring at him from time to time, but it wasn't with that touch-my-kid-and-I'll-kill-you vibe he half expected.

A pair of doctors stopped in early the next morning, before Alicia and Nicky could return. Ordinarily, Donovan knew, they wouldn't have so many visitors to contend with. Luis' position as a federal agent made the extra law enforcement presence inevitable.

That didn't mean the doctors were enthusiastic about the audience. "Er, Agent Gomes, do you really want a big crowd for this?" The surgeon asking was a tiny Asian woman with a flat New York accent.

The crowd, at this hour, consisted of Donovan, Patricia, Kevin, Jose, Holcombe, and Alex Morales.

"They're all pretty much family at this point." Luis waved a hand. "And, honestly, pain causes memory lapses in a good number of patients. It's important to have other people present."

"Fair enough." The surgeon grimaced and glanced over at Holcombe, specifically. That alone told Donovan she knew who Holcombe was, and her relationship to Luis. "I'm Dr. Wattana, I'm your orthopedic surgeon. I specialize in traumatic reconstruction. This is Dr. Ihejirika, he's a neurosurgeon."

Luis and Jose both winced. The expressions were identical, and it would have made Donovan

254

laugh under other circumstances.

Luis ran a hand through his dark, curly hair. "I suspected there was nerve damage after it happened."

"You're a smart man, Agent." Ihejirika gave him a grim smile. "A gunshot of that caliber, at that range—well, it would almost have to cause nerve damage. The amount of damage still remains to be seen. There's a lot of swelling, and a lot of reaction to the injury itself."

Luis' face went cool and smooth, a professional mask Donovan had seen before. "And the rest of the leg?"

Wattana nodded once. "Right. Well, the bone shattered. We had to do a bone graft. We used synthetic bone because the body is less likely to reject it and we didn't want to put you through that if we didn't have to. The graft is held in place with metal plates."

Jose cleared his throat. "What are the long-term consequences?" He took Luis' hand. Donovan already had the other.

"Well, his recovery period is going to be a long one." Ihejirika gave Luis a sympathetic glance. "The recovery from the simple gunshot wound would have been long. The nerve involvement is a complicating factor. We did surgically repair some nerves during surgery, as we found clear evidence of the need to do so. What remains to be seen is what damage we couldn't see due to inflammation and what damage may have been caused by the graft or the plates."

Luis met the eyes of each surgeon in turn. "Thank you for your hard work. I know it's delicate surgery and you did everything possible to save the leg. I don't mean to sound ungrateful. How long before I'm back out in the field?"

Wattana huffed out a little laugh. Ihejirika nudged her with his elbow. "Agent, right now we can't even guess when you'll be able to leave the hospital. You know infection is still a risk. We're blasting you with broad-spectrum antibiotics because of the conditions in which you were held and in which the injury took place, but that's only so effective. We'll consider the operation a success if you're walking with a cane at the end of six months."

Donovan saw Luis pale, and he saw Holcombe turn away. She already knew. She'd already gotten the skinny from the doctors.

And while half of Donovan wanted to rise up in fury at the violation of Luis' privacy, the other half understood. Holcombe needed to make preparations for dealing with the Bureau. She needed to figure out a plan—how she'd help her department, how she'd deal with the human resources red tape, and how she'd help Luis.

He turned his attention back to the conversation at hand. He'd never be able to come up with an answer to this dilemma, and he'd just get mad and lose his focus on Luis if he thought about it.

Luis raised his eyebrow at the doctors. "Six months, huh?"

"This isn't something you can rush, Agent." Wattana leaned forward, just a little. "I can see you're an athletic guy. It's good to keep up that energy. I'll personally make sure we find you a physical therapist who gets that, who doesn't assume the same exercises that work for a ninety-eight-year-old woman with sciatica are going to be right for you. But, Agent, you have an entirely artificial section of bone in your leg that's essentially held together the same way furniture from Ikea is. It's always going to be more delicate than the rest of your body. You're always going to have a concern about the bone breaking again.

"There may always be pain, from nerve damage. We still don't know. You're going to be here in the hospital for a while. We're going to keep an eye on your leg and see what additional nerve damage we have. This situation could still turn on a dime. I know this isn't the news you wanted to hear, but it's the honest truth."

Luis' smile looked forced. "I'd still rather have the truth than a lie. Thank you, Doctors."

"We'll send someone in to check your vitals and clean your bandages in a little bit." Wattana acknowledged the crowd with a nod and left the room.

Donovan heard Ihejirika speaking under his breath as they left. "You orthopedists have the worst bedside manner."

"You think he's the first cop I've worked on? You can't sugarcoat anything, or they think they're Superman and go out and fuck things up worse." Their voices faded away.

"She's right about that." Patricia sighed and glanced toward the door. "After I got stabbed, they told me I 'should consider' staying in bed for six weeks. I went back to work a few days later, popped all my stitches, and bled everywhere chasing a suspect."

"But did you catch him?" Jose tilted his head to the side.

"Of course I caught him." Patricia snorted and tossed her hair over her shoulder. "I'm not letting a little blood and guts keep a pervert on the streets."

Holcombe laughed out loud. "Okay, so maybe the doctors are right about some things." Then she turned to Luis. "It sounds grim, Luis."

"It is grim. But I'm not going to drag down the whole team." Luis took a deep breath, like he was about to resign then and there.

Holcombe held up a hand. "Do not finish that thought. Please." She softened. "There's a lot going on, for you and for the Bureau right now. I have a plan. You are too valuable to lose. I haven't always been the best, and I know that. But please—give me some time. Like I said, there's a plan in the works. I just have to ask that you trust me. And if I ask you to fill out some paperwork—well, you're basically a captive audience, right?"

Luis sighed. "I am that."

"Good man." She beamed at him. "Same goes for you, Morales."

Alex deflated as Holcombe walked out the door, already on her phone.

Donovan frowned over at Kevin. "What's going on with that?"

Kevin shrugged. "Once you make her level, you get sucked into all sorts of weird head games. The pay raise would be nice, but it's not worth it at all. Although we are concerned about Agent Morales' arm." He gave Alex a harsh look.

"It'll be fine." Alex looked away and blushed. "Luis got shot in the actual lung and recovered."

Jose hid his face in his hands. "Oh my God."

"Took forever." Luis made a face. "And luck runs out." He gestured at his leg, which was still covered by a sheet. He hadn't moved to look at it since he woke up. There was probably a complex psychological reason behind that, but Donovan didn't need to know it. He just knew Luis was hurting, and he couldn't do anything about it.

Luis squirmed a little and reached for the bedside table, the one that could become a tray. It had a little drawer in it. Donovan had always kind of thought these were a work of genius, and wished they made them in more refined models for home use. Of course, he'd never get out of bed if they did.

Luis reached into the drawer and cleared his throat. "Um, listen." His cheeks darkened. "This is a bad time, and I get that. I smell, and I need a wash in the absolute worst way."

"You're fine. You're here and I wasn't sure that was going to happen, so I don't really notice any of the other stuff." Donovan managed to smile a little. "I'm going to have to bring that johnnie home for Tria when they change it though. They wouldn't let me bring her to you to prove you're okay. She's getting super twitchy."

Luis grinned. "I can't wait to see her. Think we can get away with telling them it's an ancient Brazilian custom?"

"Your nurse is literally from Brazil. No, you

can't pull that off." Donovan laughed.

"So I'll tell them it's an ancient Puerto Rican custom." Jose smirked. "Problem solved."

Luis was hiding something in his hand. Donovan shook his head to correct himself. He wasn't so much hiding the object as he was clutching onto it for dear life.

He cleared his throat again. "Look. Um. While I was there, in that place, I couldn't help . . . I was scared, you know? I'd picked this thing up. And I was waiting for the right time to offer it to you. I know we've had our share of troubles. And right now—I mean I'm about to lose my job, maybe my leg, who knows. But I need for you to know, if that makes sense. I couldn't get over the thought that I might die down there and you'd never know how I felt—how I wanted to show my commitment."

He thrust out his trembling hand. When Donovan accepted the unseen offering, he found a wide platinum band, with a small diamond in the center. A groove had been cut around the middle of the band, to draw attention to the single tiny jewel.

Donovan gasped and almost dropped the ring. "Luis, my God. It's gorgeous!"

"I don't mean to put you on the spot." Luis' eyes shone with something—sincerity or maybe unshed tears. Donovan couldn't quite tell. "I don't want you to feel pressured because I said something in front of everyone. I just—I was so scared, that I'd die down there and you'd never know." He glanced over at Kevin. "Thanks for grabbing this for me."

"It's what your partner is for." Kevin winked.

Donovan blinked back his own tears. "I was scared too. Really scared. I mean—I don't even have words to—"

Alex slipped a small velvet box into Donovan's hand.

Donovan stared at him for a second. Then he threw his arms around Alex. "You're the best. How did you know?"

"Have to be pretty smart to get into the FBI." Alex smirked and patted him on the back. "Go on."

Donovan presented the ring he'd been hoarding to Luis. "I'd been waiting for the right time too. And I realize that the right time is now—because we don't know what's going to happen tomorrow. We're here, together, today. And if you'd . . . well, if you hadn't come back, and you didn't know that I wanted to make it official, and legal, and forever, I don't know if I could have taken it."

Luis pulled Donovan in for a hug. It pulled

the oximeter off of his finger, which set off all kinds of alarms, but neither of them cared. They only saw or heard each other.

CHAPTER FOURTEEN

Most of Luis' visitors filtered out during the day, or at least rotated. Donovan and Alex still had work to do on the Southwick case, and Kevin had been assigned to assist. This freed up Donovan to spend more time closer to home (actually at the hospital), but he still had to be out and about with his detectives.

The work didn't stop, not even for family. Donovan's department were his family too, and if anyone understood that, it was Luis.

He didn't exactly have time to be bored. He had Jose to keep him company, and Camila from Mattapan stopped in to visit when she heard what happened. She brought food, since "Hospital food is dreadful and obviously those doctors don't know a thing about healthy food anyway."

A spate of fires broke out around the hospital, but never inside. A clergyman of undetermined denomination died on his way into the hospital, but a little bit of discreet snooping proved to Luis that said cleric had a history that would put him squarely on Mike's "demonic" list. Not that Luis condoned vigilantism, but the guy should have been defrocked or whatever a long time ago.

The ghosts didn't enter the hospital itself, but Luis knew they were around. Maybe he shouldn't have felt comforted, but Luis had made his peace with the inconsistencies of his unique position a long time ago.

The first day and night after his surgery passed in a haze. Luis slept a lot, and he didn't feel too bad about it either. He knew he should be spending time reconnecting with Jose, but he also knew he wasn't going to be capable of much right now. He'd spent too much time interacting with the dead, which had exacerbated his shock symptoms. He'd lost too much blood. And while Jose didn't understand the shock aspect for what it was or where it came from, he definitely didn't expect more from Luis after everything he'd just endured.

Plus, he seemed to like Camila's cooking.

The second day, they let Luis try to shower. It wasn't easy. He had to have a bench in the shower with him, and two nurses waited outside just in case he couldn't get out. Still, the shower was possibly the best feeling in the world. It was better than sex, or at least better than sex with anyone

266

who wasn't Donovan. That alone surprised Luis.

He mentioned it to Jose, when he got out. He didn't miss the fact that his bedding had been changed while he scrubbed every available inch of his body in water as hot as hospital plumbing would allow.

"I never thought of myself as prissy, you know?" They spoke in Spanish, just as they had while Luis was growing up. "I mean sure, I like to dress well, but I never couldn't get a job done because I got a little dirt on me. I've crawled through sewers to catch a suspect. I never thought I'd be *that guy* who needed a shower to feel like a human being."

Jose managed a little grin. "I didn't see you right when you got out of there, and they did a pretty good job with the sponge bath thing. But that wasn't *you*. That was nurses acting for you. You'd been drugged, held against your will, in a place with a lot of negative associations—I'm not surprised. It's going to leave a mark on you. Up here, I mean." He tapped his temple. "It's normal. Donovan's already restocking all of your favorite soaps and shampoos."

Luis froze. "He's repulsed by how I smell now."

"No. But he knows you're thinking about it. You don't think of yourself as prissy, but apparently, you make a habit of getting shot and you're kind of predictable when you're recovering. By the way—I didn't raise you to make a habit of getting shot. Are you kidding me? I taught you to *avoid* getting shot. I bought you your first vest!"

Luis ducked his head, face burning. "I didn't want to scare the homeowners," he muttered, thinking back to the last time he'd been shot while working with Donovan. "This time was a little different."

"Obviously." Jose chuckled. "No more getting shot at for you. Are we clear?"

Someone knocked on the door so Luis didn't have to answer his foster father. When Jose answered it, he admitted SSA Holcombe and a gray-haired white guy with a corduroy sport coat. The sport coat had actual patches on the elbows. He couldn't have been more of an academic stereotype if he showed up in his cap and gown.

Luis pulled the blanket up, even though it was already up to his waist. He wasn't exactly up to meeting strangers right now, not without pants, but he wasn't going to chase his boss out of the room either. Not while she was still his boss.

"Luis, how are you feeling?" Holcombe approached the bed slowly and carefully, as if she were afraid of waking him up. That in and of itself was weird. "I'm sure you're in pain."

"I can get to wherever you need me to be." Luis reached for the walker hospital staff insisted he use. "I know Donovan brought me some pants, they have to be here somewhere."

"I told him to take them home." Jose gave Luis a hard look. "You can't go 'anywhere she needs you to be,' son. Your leg is held together with duct tape and prayers, and you're an atheist. You need to stay right where you are until you're medically cleared."

Holcombe laughed, although she blushed when she did. "I see he's been like this for a while."

"Since he was nine." Jose smirked at Luis. "Did you know he fought his captor *with his crutches*?" He shook his head. "This kid."

Academia Man gulped. "That's . . . inspired."

Luis fought to keep his voice neutral. "She did have my gun at the time." He held out his hand. "Special Agent Luis Gomes."

Academia Man took his hand gingerly. "Dr. Richard Norton, Harvard University Department of Psychology. I was wondering if you might be able to help me out with a problem."

Luis gave Holcombe a long measuring look, and then he shrugged. "I'll admit you don't exactly find me at the top of my game right now, but I'm happy to offer what I can."

Norton nodded. "I had a pastor approach me about a parishioner. The parishioner is in his midforties, white, from a middle-class background. He has served in the military, although he didn't distinguish himself. He has trained as an accountant and worked his way up through the profession, although he's recently been faced with setbacks. It seems he's been unable to keep up with the changing demands of the profession, and his personality isn't conducive to the advancement or recognition he craves.

"Finding himself blocked, he's bounced from job to job in the past three to five years, with each job becoming less stable and less remunerative. He is married, and the marriage is troubled. He is the father of three, as well as a stepfather, and his mother lives with the family. The mother and the subject share a conservative religious fervor not shared by the wife. The stepdaughter has already left the family nest due to religious conflicts.

"The pastor approached me with concerns because the father has become increasingly anxious about his financial state, disproportionately so based on what appears to be appropriate given his situation. And the pastor claims that while he has not witnessed any symptoms of domestic violence, the children have recently become extremely fearful—again, disproportionately to external appearances.

"A recent incident shows us an example of the children's fear. The eldest child is a daughter of sixteen years. Due to recent civil unrest, their city has been under a curfew. Police stopped the daughter and a friend due to their being out after curfew, and they brought them home. They were nowhere near the protests and were brought home instead of arrested.

"The father began berating the daughter in front of officers, calling her a whore, among other things. The rest of the family emerged from their rooms and the father continued, even in front of her brothers. The mother shielded the daughter, although she didn't argue with the husband—it appears as though she's ill. The father expanded his description to encompass the mother as well—both were 'whores.'"

Luis' blood ran cold in his veins. Carlos, his father, had accused his mother of the same thing. Jose put a hand on Luis' shoulder.

Norton didn't seem to be aware of Luis' history, or if he was he didn't care. He kept going. "According to the pastor, the daughter told a teacher at school, 'If my father tells you we're going on an emergency family trip, he's killed me.' Agent, how do you recommend I proceed here?"

Luis reached for his water, which Jose passed to him. "The first step would be to have the pastor encourage the father to check himself in for treatment for his anxiety and depression. He'll decline, but it's a step that needs to be made and documented. In the meantime, the teacher has a legal obligation to report the daughter's claims to authorities. Social Services should already be involved, and if they aren't, the pastor needs to get loud about it. And he needs to do so right away.

"The children need to go stay with a relative until Social Services can intervene. This isn't optional. It can take some time before the legal authorities can get all their ducks in a row, and it definitely sounds to me as if your subject is on the verge of a significant crisis. He's already told the children what he's planning. They're in danger, right now."

Norton smiled and relaxed, beaming over at Holcombe. "Congratulations. You just saved the List family."

Luis shook his head and closed his eyes. His leg throbbed, and he didn't know if it was psychosomatic or not. "No one could have saved the List family, Dr. Norton. Times were different in 1971. For one thing, the teacher in that case reported his concerns to other faculty, which was the standard operating procedure at the time. Not only were his concerns dismissed, but the bodies weren't discovered for a month after the fact because the teacher was told to stand down *even though the father did exactly what the daughter said he would* and claimed they were going on an emergency family trip.

"The pastor in the case was so caught up in his patriarchal ideals, he believed the father and husband still had the right to determine how the bodies should be disposed of after the fact, even though the father was the murderer. He would never have approached law enforcement with his concerns. He wouldn't have *had* concerns. It took a lot for people in 1971 to worry about domestic violence in other people's homes, and a father calmly sitting his children down, telling them he was going to kill them, and telling them to choose burial or cremation was not the red flag it is today."

Norton gaped at Luis, and then he smiled ruefully. "You were right, Alison. He's definitely something else. I'll talk to the higher-ups and call you, probably tonight or tomorrow." He shook Luis' hand and left the room.

Luis stared after him. "Agent Holcombe, I don't mean to be rude. I'm just a little bit confused though. I need to know what that was all about."

Holcombe's smile just made her look tired. "I don't want to say anything yet. Nothing's really in place. Just a little while longer, okay? I promise. I'm not going to leave you hanging."

Luis didn't want to trust her. At the same time, he didn't have anything to lose by sitting back and letting her do her thing. He couldn't get himself fired until the FBI's massive bureaucracy decided if his injury merited workplace compensation or not, so he just nodded.

Just then, Donovan raced into the room. He didn't knock. His eyes were wild. "Luis, I've got some news."

Luis' eyes fell to the ring on Donovan's finger. Whatever the news was, it hadn't made him jettison his ring—their engagement. He didn't need to panic. Not yet.

"What's up?"

Donovan took a deep breath. "Tammie Hatch had her arraignment today."

Luis stared. "Congratulations?"

Holcombe cleared her throat. "That would be the woman who abducted you."

"Hyena Lady." Luis nodded. "Right. Okay." He didn't like feeling stupid, but he wasn't going to fight it right now.

"And she overpowered her guard in the bathroom and escaped."

◆——————◆

Nothing could have prepared Donovan to have to make that notification. He knew Luis wouldn't show much of a reaction, even if they'd been alone. Having to inform Luis in front of his foster dad though—that was something Donovan hadn't bargained for and didn't want to ever have to do again.

"What the hell is going on at the courthouse?" Jose got to his feet, eyes blazing. "How did she manage to pull this off? They know they've got a dangerous offender in their custody. What are they doing, just letting her skip along merrily?"

Donovan winced. He knew Jose wasn't mad *at him*, but he still didn't want to be his future father-in-law's target. "They sent her into the bathroom with a guard. They followed protocol. She used the cuffs to choke her out, traded uniforms, and made her escape that way. There's a manhunt out there now looking for her."

"And you're here why?" Jose's voice was like a whip.

Luis cleared his throat. "Because he's more useful directing people right now than he is with his nose to the ground, Jose. Remember, he's already built the resources to find her once. He can direct fresh eyes, people who haven't been running themselves ragged trying to rescue their damsel in distress fiancé, find a cop killer, and run a department. Because going out there himself would increase the risk of mistakes, and right now, mistakes are getting people killed."

Luis closed his eyes and leaned back in his bed. "I should have killed her back in the asylum. This is my fault."

"I didn't raise you to be that kind of cop, Luis." Jose ruffled Luis' hair. "You did the right thing, although I have no freaking idea how. You saved her, and I'm proud of you." He turned to Donovan. "Luis is right. I lashed out, and I apologize."

Donovan sat gingerly on Luis' other side. "No, no. I know I'm not actually responsible for prisoner transport or courtroom security, and I'm kicking myself for it too. I totally get it." He massaged his temples. "My mom is updating the team looking for her with as much information as we have. Which, I'll admit, is a lot."

"Captain Carey is a force of nature." Holcombe gave a little smile. "If it weren't against recruiting rules, I'd be trying my damnedest to get her into the Bureau. Who's leading the search on our end?"

"Kevin Rourke, of course." Donovan huffed out a little laugh. "He's convinced Morales he needs a lot of assistance, now that Luis is in the hospital. In reality, he's keeping Morales from doing too much."

"Good. Morales' mom would reassign me to Alaska if I let him get hurt worse." She shuddered. "I'll keep Borchard and Wragge out in Southwick to work on that case. You get Fontana for Hatch, along with anyone from Organized Crime who Rourke catches looking at social media when he walks through their space."

"Awesome, ma'am." Donovan pulled out his phone and started texting. "Luis, I know you're tired, but what can you tell me about Hatch?"

Luis winced. "I barely interacted with her at all. Certainly not enough to build a proper profile from." He took a deep breath. "She's local. She doesn't believe she's acting out of malice. She put water in the room where she left me at first. It was drugged, but her plan was to drug me up so I wouldn't cause trouble, then release me when you handed her boyfriend back. I think she sincerely believed you'd give in to her demands. The thing is, when I didn't follow her plan, she showed her sadism directly. She incapacitated me with the shot to the leg but chose to pistol-whip and kick me well past the point where I lost consciousness."

Donovan saw red, but only for a moment. "I had the chance to shoot her when I arrested her. I should've taken it."

"Hindsight is always twenty-twenty." Luis flashed a quick grin at him. "In all seriousness, I wonder if we shouldn't be looking at Hyena Lady—er, Tammie Hatch—for some of the deaths Gelens is currently on the hook for. She has a lot of rage, and she's supremely loyal to Gelens, past the point of reason. And he's an extreme narcissist, so there's no way he feels the same way about her. She's bound to have some jealousy issues, even if Gelens' other partners aren't there of their own free will."

"Good point." Holcombe passed Luis his tablet. "This should keep you out of trouble until you can get home. You can take a look at the other cases and flag the ones you think are suspicious."

An objection rose up like bile in Donovan's throat. Jose's face darkened, so he was probably thinking along the same lines. Luis was injured. They still weren't sure they could save the leg. Why on God's green earth would Holcombe be trying to eke productivity out of a man injured on the job?

Then he saw the way Luis' face lit up.

"I'm on it." Luis accepted the tablet and opened it. "Is there anything else you want me looking into while I'm at it?"

"You can feel free to answer any messages looking for a consultation. Obviously, nothing that would require you to be in the office or traveling, but if they just want your opinion, that's fine. You're good at what you do, and there's no reason you can't keep using your brain while you recuperate." Holcombe straightened up. "I've got to go. Judge Sullivan still wants you to finish testifying, so I've got to go negotiate to figure out how to make that work." Her sensible shoes made almost no sound on the linoleum floor.

Jose glanced between Donovan and Luis. "I'm going to go back to the hotel and clean up a little, okay?" He directed his gaze at Donovan. "I can trust that you've got him?"

"Yes, sir." He didn't need to ask to know exactly what Jose meant. "We're good for a while."

Jose softened a little. "I'll see you tonight." He ruffled Luis' hair again and left.

Donovan and Luis were alone. They sat in silence for a long moment. Donovan had no idea what was going on in Luis' head, but he knew the turmoil in his own. It kept bubbling up until he couldn't hold it back.

"Luis, I'm so sorry I wasn't there to protect you."

Luis stared at him for a long moment. Then he put his hand on Donovan's. "I love you. I respect you. You're an incredible detective, you're an amazing lover, you're a brilliant man, and it's not your job to protect me. Don't get me wrong—I appreciate that you want to. I love that you want to. I spent a long time feeling so exposed and so unprotected that it . . . it kind of confuses me and thrills me at the same time that you'd even want to.

"But it is not your job. We both have dangerous jobs. Things happen, and we can't be attached at the hip." He winked. "For one thing that would make sex kind of weird."

Laughter exploded from Donovan, surprising even him. "Christ, Luis."

"He ain't here. Right now it's just you and me." He squeezed Donovan's hand. Then he brought Donovan closer and kissed him.

Donovan glanced at the door, which Jose had helpfully closed. Then he threw himself into the kiss. He'd missed this. He'd been so focused on finding Luis, and making sure he was going to recover, that he hadn't taken the time to treasure the little details. Luis hadn't shaved, and his stubble tickled where it brushed against Donovan's skin. His toothpaste was still fresh, his hair still a little bit damp from the shower.

And he held on to Donovan like he thought he might disappear at any minute.

"Was it really bad there?" Donovan kept his voice down. They were alone, but anyone could walk in.

Luis kept hold of Donovan, but he looked up at the ceiling as he spoke. "There were times I thought I must be unhinged if I thought I was getting out. Um." He scratched at the soft cast on his leg. "I didn't . . . I just didn't want to be the guy who just sat there and patiently waited. I couldn't have gotten out without help. You get that, right?"

"Lightfoot?"

"Among others." He closed his eyes. "I think they're staying out because hospitals freak them out, but they're still around. The clergy members who keep dropping dead outside? That's Mike. And the fires? That's Boom-Boom."

"Boom-Boom?" Donovan almost didn't believe him. If he'd been dealing with anyone else, he wouldn't have.

"He doesn't really talk much. He curses, he mutters, and he starts fires. No one's quite sure how long he was in there or what he did to get there. He started the fire that torched the place. We needed a distraction. They're the ones who carried her out beyond the fire doors. They didn't want to do it, but I insisted." He swallowed hard and looked up. "I don't . . . I let them help me. I asked them to help me. And I showed them how to get out of the asylum. Mike's a murderer with religious delusions. Boom-Boom is a pyromaniac. Mike's a good guy—"

Donovan snorted. "Except for the killing?"

"I know why he does it." Luis shrugged. "I don't agree that it's the best way to address his issues, but I'm not about to pretend that they aren't valid. And, hey, look at Lightfoot."

The temperature in the room dropped by at least twenty degrees, and a foul stench polluted the air.

Donovan edged closer to Luis. He still couldn't see or hear Lightfoot, but he could feel the temperature drop and anyone could smell the stench in the air. "If that's one of the ghosts that helped Luis, I owe you a massive debt."

Luis didn't tense up at all when the ghost showed up, so Donovan knew he had to be on fairly solid ground in terms of his assumption.

"Captain Lightfoot says you're welcome." Luis took a breath. "And wants us both to know he's keeping Mike away from clergymen who aren't perverts, so there's that."

"Thanks, Captain." Donovan tried to follow Luis' eyes so he could directly address their unseen ally. "I appreciate it." God, this was weird. Had Luis felt this weird when he first started seeing ghosts? At least he'd had something to see.

"Also, Millie approves of you." Luis blushed. "She, er, yeah I'm not going to repeat that. We'll just leave it at she approves."

Luis didn't get embarrassed easily, especially not by anything sexual. Donovan almost wanted to know what this Millie character had said, but he kept quiet.

"The whole place? Really?" Luis glanced up at Donovan. "The whole building—the main building at Medfield—is gone. Burned to the ground. I guess Boom-Boom is pretty thorough."

"I guess he is. I mean there's a reason they boarded the buildings up. It's a shame—I think the town made a good amount of money renting the building out for movie shoots and stuff." Donovan couldn't bring himself to care much, however much money the town had made. Whatever evidence had been lost when the building burned was mostly superfluous. Hatch had filmed herself confessing to the crime.

There was still plenty that could go wrong. She could possibly convince a jury that Luis had gone along with her willingly, that he was an accomplice, but the idea was far-fetched enough that Donovan refused to worry about it.

"Please let them know I'm recovering. I'm in a surgical ward—for bones, not brains. And I've got people with me pretty much all the time, so I'm not in danger." Luis smiled at the air, which probably contained Lightfoot and this Millie person. "Seriously, though. Thank you for all you did to help me."

The room returned to normal temperature. The rotten stink departed. All that was left was Donovan and Luis.

Donovan turned to Luis. "How come you didn't ask the ghosts to help find Tammie?"

Luis sighed. "Because they'll kill her. And we still need to try her."

Donovan grimaced. Managing people who could face no consequences for their actions was more of a challenge than he thought.

CHAPTER FIFTEEN

Luis had dreaded this moment, which was odd for him given that it moved the case against Gelens along. Until now it hung in limbo, the jury sequestered lest media coverage of the missing agent prejudice them in the case. Now Luis could complete his testimony against a serial predator and, hopefully, send him to prison for the rest of time.

Er, for the rest of his life. Luis knew a little too much about the afterlife to make statements about the rest of time.

Now that the time was here though, he dreaded it. He'd showered carefully and dressed in a collared shirt and shorts that could be hidden by a blanket. The outfit was a compromise. Luis hated to appear as anything but a consummate professional before a jury, but they'd see the bruising and the hospital setting. And the doctors didn't want him in anything they couldn't get rid of easily if they had to.

The first person to arrive was the defense attorney, Andrew Morello. He brought a giant gift basket of coffee-related products and looked ready to cry. "I am so sorry. You wouldn't have been in that position if I hadn't helped to get you onto the gurney."

It was true, and Luis knew it. He also knew better than to hold a grudge about it. "What, you mean you didn't think too closely interrogate the EMT who showed up just when a witness collapsed in a heap on the ground? For shame, Mr. Morello. For shame." He made himself laugh. "Honestly, I should have been more careful. I should have brought lunch from home, for one thing. And I definitely should have picked up on the water I didn't order."

Morello looked at him a little funny. "You're not blaming yourself, seriously?"

"I'm supposed to pick up on stuff like that. It's literally my job. Sure, there were extenuating circumstances, but I'm still supposed to know better." He made a face. "You know how it is."

"I do." Morello gave him another look, long and searching. He opened his mouth like he wanted to say more, but the arrival of Fahey and Sullivan chased the words away. He stepped to the side and let the AV tech following them set up a camera and wire them all with microphones.

Sullivan held up a hand. "Before we start, and before we go live to the jury, I need to make one thing clear. Agent Gomes, I'm very sympathetic to your situation. I can see you're in pain, and I know what you've been through must have been terrifying. I spent five months as a POW in Vietnam, so I'm not pulling your leg here. I really do know."

Luis looked up. He hadn't known about Sullivan's background. He'd assumed Sullivan had just kind of sprouted there on the bench. "Thank you, sir."

"Don't thank me yet, Agent. I'm sympathetic, but I do have a job to do. I've got a perfect record going. I haven't had a single case overturned because of technicalities or judicial errors, and I'm goddamn proud of that fact. I'm not willing to risk it.

"I know exactly who did this to you because we have her on camera confessing to it. Mr. Gelens may have instigated it, and may not have. But he's not on trial for the kidnapping. That's still under investigation. I cannot, and will not, allow questions or references to his potential involvement in the abduction into evidence before the jury. Mr. Gelens is entitled to a fair trial, even with the serious charges against him, and I will not jeopardize that right. Do I make myself clear?"

Luis hadn't noticed tight bands around his chest, but he found one of them releasing at Judge Sullivan's words. "I wouldn't have it any other way, sir."

Fahey looked mildly put out, but she nodded. "Crystal clear, sir."

Morello looked away, but his nod was vigorous. "Thank you, sir."

The tech started the broadcast, and the show began.

Sullivan started off. "Members of the jury, I'm sure you'll recall that Agent Gomes' testimony had to be rescheduled due to unforeseen circumstances. As it happens, he was injured in a work-related incident and is still hospitalized. Doctors are only now willing to allow him to testify, but it has to be here, due to medical issues."

Luis would have been perfectly happy to go to the courthouse. Then he remembered he couldn't even make it to the bathroom and back without help. He'd still rather Sullivan didn't make him sound quite so weak.

"Ms. Fahey, I believe that you were questioning the witness when we last heard from him." Sullivan nodded at Fahey.

She cleared her throat and rose. If she had any qualms about being on camera, Luis couldn't see them. "Thank you, your Honor. Agent Gomes, let me refresh your memory. When we last spoke, we were talking about what might lead someone to behave the way Mr. Gelens has."

Luis could see it all—the courtroom, the jury, even the suit he'd been wearing that day. His mouth went dry for a moment. He'd chosen that suit because it was Donovan's favorite, and now, it was scattered in rags across Norfolk County.

Then he grabbed for the water and locked those thoughts away. "Yes. There's no one factor you can point to and say, 'Yes, this will lead to a pattern of sexual sadism and murder for profit twenty years down the road,' because you'll always find that a majority of people who've had those same experiences—or who share those same biological traits—do not share those behaviors. The only intervention that could have helped would have been something to stop him one of the prior times he was convicted, and again here, Gelens doesn't fit the classic mode. He doesn't have a preference for children, but he'll make use of them for profit or if nothing else is available."

Luis took a deep breath. "He is driven entirely by his own interests—greed and lust, in that order."

Morello winced, but he raised his hand. "Objection. Witness is engaging in speculation."

"Agent Gomes, can you clarify your

comment or is that indeed speculation?" Sullivan gave Luis a cool glance.

Luis nodded and pushed himself up a little. "Yes, sir. I don't have my copy of the report I did after the arrest right here, but I did write one up in detail. I spoke with Mr. Gelens for several hours, and he was very explicit about his motivations. While I might have to extrapolate from behavior in some cases, Mr. Gelens didn't feel the need to hide."

Fahey piped in. "Paragraphs twelve and forty-seven, Exhibit Forty-Two."

"Thank you, Ms. Fahey."

Luis could have kicked himself. He should have known the exact location of the quote.

"In your expert opinion, both as a law enforcement professional and as a psychologist, do you believe Mr. Gelens is capable of redemption?" Fahey met Luis' eyes.

Luis had to think for a long moment about how to respond. He saw, or he thought he saw, Mike and Lightfoot standing behind her. "I think anyone is capable of redemption. Whether or not it's *likely* is a different story. At this point, Gelens shows no remorse for his crimes, and he is highly likely to reoffend. In his own words, he has no other skills, and he enjoys the work.

"Ted Bundy was a monster, but in the end,

he helped us catch a monster. I think if Gelens makes a choice to change, he can probably still do something good with his life—but not on the outside."

"No further questions, Your Honor."

Morello cleared his throat and stepped forward as Sullivan glanced at him. "Your witness, Mr. Morello."

Luis closed his eyes for a second. He could get through this. It was funny though—he never got nervous about testifying when he was in a courtroom.

"Agent Gomes, forgive me. I know you coauthored a study on child pornography, but you yourself stated that you are not an expert on the subject. Can you help us to explain that contradiction?"

Luis didn't roll his eyes, even though he'd already answered the question in his prior testimony. It felt like a month ago, even though it had only been days. Morello was here to do a job, and the best he could hope for at this point was to let his client see the light of day someday. "Sure. I study criminal psychology and behavior, but I don't specialize in one specific type of offense. Our child pornography unit will study all aspects of the child pornography business, whereas I'm more of a specialist in the offender themselves—whether it's the producer, the distributor, the consumer, or an outlier such as Mr. Gelens."

It wasn't the answer Morello was looking for, but Luis wasn't under any obligation to help the defense.

"But you're not an expert in child pornography, correct?"

Luis let a little smirk cross his lips. "No. I'm not."

"So what qualifies you to speak as an expert witness about child pornography?"

"Other than the study I coauthored?" Luis shrugged. "My honors thesis from my master's program, three additional academic publications, and forty-seven case closures with convictions in child pornography cases."

Morello blinked. "Moving on." He swallowed. "You said you believe everyone is capable of redemption, but you don't think Mr. Gelens should be released. Can you help us understand *that* contradiction, please?"

Luis nodded slowly. "Of course. Some people can learn the difference between right and wrong, even if they didn't understand it before. Gelens doesn't fall into this category, simply because he already understands that difference. He doesn't care. Gelens' view is different on a fundamental level. He views people as a means to

292

an end, and morality has no place in his decision-making. If he needs money, he'll make that money in the most profitable way possible for him—whether that involves making snuff films, child porn, or murder for hire. Or all three at the same time. And if he can get sexual satisfaction at the same time, so much the better. He's not . . ." Luis tried to find a way to explain this that wouldn't be prejudicial. "It would surprise me on a fundamental level to see him change this aspect of himself. It would take a deep desire to change and a great deal of effort from both Mr. Gelens and from mental health providers within the correctional system.

"And, even then, it's probably about a fifty-fifty chance of working for five years."

Morello blinked again. "I thought you said he had a chance for redemption?"

"He does. He can still find ways to give his life meaning from inside prison. That's why I referenced Ted Bundy in the first place. I don't think Bundy could ever have been released. But I do think he found a way to give something to society while he was there. He probably had his own interests at heart, but he found a way to make his own interests and the interests of the world coincide. Other offenders acknowledge their crimes and go on to help other offenders inside. It's hard, but it's not impossible."

"No further questions, Your Honor."

Sullivan did a double take, but he rose. "In that case, court is adjourned. We'll play this back for the jury. Thanks for your time, Agent. I hope we'll see you on your feet in short order."

"I hope so too, Your Honor." Luis didn't have to fake his grin this time. "They've been good to me here, but I'm eager to get back to my own space."

"I'll bet you are." Sullivan shook Luis' hand. "I hear congratulations are in order too?"

Luis' face got hot. "I—yeah. Yes, sir. It turns out we were both waiting for the right time to ask, and with all this, we realized the perfect time was never going to get here. So we've got a few details to iron out, but at least now we both know."

Sullivan chuckled. "And knowing is half the battle. I'll bet you're not going to wait quite so long this time, right?"

"No, sir. In fact, if you're not busy . . ."

"I'm pretty sure the other groom should probably be here. But if you should happen to bring him by sometime, I'd be honored." Sullivan beamed at him, and he and the two attorneys left.

Luis fumbled for his phone. He needed to tell Donovan.

Donovan yawned and shut down his laptop. One of the new uniformed recruits, some kid fresh out of the academy, had said something in front of Power the other day. By the time Donovan heard about it, the quote had become something like, "Must be a pretty sweet gig to make lieutenant and only have to work five hours a day."

Power ripped into the kid and made sure he got reassigned to the graveyard shift out in the boonies for good measure. Donovan almost felt bad for him.

He knew how it looked, to someone who wasn't involved with the investigation—or investigations, really. Sure, he was showing up at eight and leaving at two or whatever. He was still setting up shop in Luis' room at the hospital until eleven or twelve, whenever the nurses decided Luis needed his beauty sleep. Then he went home to do it all over again.

Yeah, it was a grind. But at least he got to see Luis and be part of his recovery, however one wanted to define recovery.

As soon as Donovan walked into the room, he could see that Luis was a wreck. His face had that grayish tone he got when he'd been overdoing it at work, and sweat dampened his hair. He was half-asleep with his tablet in his hand when Donovan eased himself into the room.

Holcombe was there too, silently waiting in the visitors chair. She looked up when she saw Donovan, put a finger to her lips, and glided out into the hall. Donovan followed, although he couldn't understand what exactly Luis' boss might want with him.

She closed the door behind them. "I spoke to the doctors. Luis is going to need more surgery."

Donovan bit back a curse. "How bad?"

"We'll have to see. But it's going to be a long time before he can come back to work as a full-time field agent, if ever." She bit her lip and glanced at the closed door.

"That's going to kill him. I know we're engaged, and that's a lot. I know things are better for him than they were when he was transferred here, but this job is his everything." Donovan didn't have to think twice about that. He knew it as well as he knew his own name.

"Do you think I don't know that?" She slumped against the wall. "And it will hurt our department too. I've got a solution, but I have to think of how to present it to him."

Donovan sucked in his cheeks. He couldn't think of a single way to present *You're losing your job because you got kidnapped and shot in the leg* in a positive light. "Okay. Well, tell me what you've got, and we'll see if we can come up with something."

"The Bureau is willing to keep him on in a non-field capacity while he pursues his doctorate." She took a deep breath. "And Harvard is willing to take him on."

For a second, all Donovan could do was stare. "Wait. What?"

"I know it's not exactly the career path he had in mind. But he's got the brains, and this recovery is going to be long and drawn out. It's going to be miserable if he doesn't have something to do with himself in the meantime. Why not let him do something productive? And he'd still be part of the Bureau, he'd still be involved."

Donovan ran his hand through his hair. "It's . . . I mean I like the idea. Don't get me wrong." He glanced back at the door. "I'm sure you had to do a ton of work to ram it through."

Two red spots appeared in her cheeks. "It wasn't easy. But we managed."

"Now all we have to do is convince Luis, right?"

"Thank you for seeing it my way." Holcombe stood up a little straighter. "Do you want to talk to him about it, or do you want me to go first?"

"Why don't we try it together?" Donovan shrugged.

Luis woke up when they headed back into the room. Donovan set his laptop up and checked his messages while the trio made small talk. Approaching Luis while he was still groggy wasn't usually the way to go, unless it was about sex.

After a few minutes, Luis glanced between his two visitors. "All right," he said, a little smile on his face. "Out with it. You're dancing around something. What are you trying not to say?"

Donovan glanced at Holcombe and shrugged. They'd known they couldn't put it off for long.

Holcombe bit her lip. "Luis, how much have your doctors told you about your leg?"

Luis glanced away. "I've been trying not to think too much about it. I know I need at least one more surgery, probably this week. There's nerve damage, and they're hoping it's something they can fix. We're not sure though." He sighed and looked down. "Is this the part where you thank me for my service and talk about early retirement options?"

"God I hope not." Holcombe didn't hesitate. "It did come up, but you're too valuable to the Bureau for that to be a first option. It, er, it is going to be a long recovery period, and you're not going to be able to be in the field while you recover."

Luis moistened his lips. "So they're sending me back to Quantico?" He glanced at Donovan. "I'm not sure—I mean I love the Bureau but I just got engaged—"

Donovan took Luis' hand. "I know."

"And he can't up and move down to Virginia. Even if there's a lot less snow down there."

"That's not what the Bureau's asking, Luis. They want you to stay here. Kind of a lot, actually." Donovan squeezed his fiancé's hand.

Luis knit his brows together. "I don't get it."

Holcombe smiled, just a little. "You met with the gentleman from the Psych Department at Harvard, remember? They've agreed to let you pursue your doctorate, based on your publications and your history with the Bureau. You'd continue to work for the Bureau while pursuing your studies, of course."

"Which is fine, because the Bureau's picking up the tab. Along with you keeping your job." Donovan nudged him.

"There's got to be a catch." Luis glanced between them both. "What are you not telling me?"

"You just won't be out in the field chasing people down. If and when you get medical clearance to do so, you can jump right back in."

Holcombe's smile broadened. "But in the meantime, you'll be working from the office or from home. We're still ironing out the day-to-day details. But the Bureau feels strongly that keeping you, and that brain of yours, available to the rest of us is important. We'd like for you to seriously consider it."

Luis scratched the side of his head. "Things that sound too good to be true usually are."

Donovan had to laugh. He couldn't help it. The laughter came bubbling up from his chest like a brook. "This is one of the things I love about you, Luis. Someone comes to you and says, 'Hey, we want to put you out of harm's way, but we're going to double your workload by sending you through a grueling PhD program while still having you work a good part of your regular job,' and you're like, 'Twice the work! There's got to be a catch here somewhere.'" He bent down to kiss Luis. "You're the best."

Luis chuckled. "I like my work." He glanced over at Holcombe. "I'm sorry. I didn't mean for you to feel like I was accusing you of lying or anything."

"It's okay, Luis. I know it's a challenge sometimes. But we're not going to hang you out to dry. Morales is in for a long rehab too. I've got some ideas for assignments to keep you both productive and busy while you recover. And, of course, you'll be able to take advantage of all those student discounts." She winked at him.

Just then, Donovan's phone rang. He glanced at the caller ID and recognized Kate Dunican, one of his second-shift subordinates. "Carey," he greeted, heading out of the room to take the call.

"Hey, boss." Dunican sipped from a drink he assumed was coffee. "I hate to bug you during your time with Agent Gomes, but I knew you'd want to hear about this. We got a hit on your suspect."

"Would this be the one who shot Fitch and Nguyen or the one who escaped custody a few days ago?" He glanced around. Most of the people he could see were familiar—people he might not know, but nurses and visitors he'd seen before. Still, he couldn't be too careful.

"Tammie Hatch, sir. She's got relatives up in Gloucester. Local police up there have stayed alert for anything suspicious around those properties. They spotted a stolen car abandoned in a nature preserve not far from one of those properties today."

Adrenaline surged through Donovan's veins. "Stolen cars get ditched all the time."

"They do, sir. But fresh tire tracks led away from the spot, matching a type used on a car registered to Ms. Hatch's family members." She cleared her throat. "They live in a school zone."

Donovan's stomach dropped. "All right. Send cars into the area but send them in quiet. If she's there, we don't want to alert her. And if she's not, we don't want to panic people. I'll meet up with folks . . ." He wracked his brain to think of some good landmark in Gloucester. "Over by the Fisherman's Memorial, I guess. Alert the local PD, but warn them not to alert the suspect or to engage." He swallowed hard. "I'll inform the feds and have someone come here and keep an eye on Luis."

"Got it, boss." Dunican cut out, but she'd never been one to waste time when there was work to be done.

Donovan stepped back into Luis' room and kissed him again. "I hate to do this, Luis, but I need to take off." He debated explaining exactly why, but then he stopped himself. Luis was a strong guy, but he'd already been through so much. He didn't need the additional anxiety of worrying about Tammie Hatch while he was sitting here vulnerable in the hospital. "Agent Holcombe, could I speak to you for a moment?"

Holcombe narrowed her eyes, but she followed him out into the hallway. A few nurses gave them funny looks, and Donovan supposed they were treating the hallway like their own private conference room, but he couldn't exactly do anything about it right now.

"What's going on, Lieutenant?" She stood straight and spoke crisply. Obviously, she knew something was up.

"We've got a lead on Hatch." He relayed all the information he had. "I'm headed up there now to hopefully make the arrest, if you wanted to send some people along. I was wondering if you could do me a favor though."

She raised an eyebrow. "A favor?"

Donovan plowed ahead. "Yes. In case this lead is false, something to just lead us in the wrong direction, I'm feeling a little uneasy leaving him here alone. If you could maybe just . . . call my mom or something, make sure he's got armed protection twenty-four seven until she's caught?"

Holcombe's face relaxed. "It's not a problem. I'll take care of it personally, Donovan." She put a hand on his arm, just for a moment. "Now go and take this lunatic down, for all of our sakes."

Donovan didn't need to be told twice. He grabbed his laptop and his jacket and headed out into the crisp October air. He wasn't coming back until Tammie Hatch was in custody.

CHAPTER SIXTEEN

Luis knew he was a pretty smart guy. Not to toot his own horn, but he'd just gotten into Harvard. Apparently, that was a big deal. He didn't need to be a genius to know something was happening though, and that it was big. Donovan hadn't even unpacked his things when he got a call, turned around, and left again with a quick kiss for Luis. And then Holcombe got on *her* phone, communicating mostly by text.

His leg burned. That was the nerve damage. It might never be fixed. They "might" be able to fix "some" of it. It was all about waiting and seeing. They'd do a little surgery here, a little surgery there, see how it went. And in the meantime, Donovan was out there putting himself on the line, and Luis wasn't going to be there to protect him.

He wiped his palms on the sheets, hoping Holcombe didn't see.

Useless as two shits. Might as well finish the job. His father's voice echoed from his cell in Luis' brain, cackling as phantom flames licked higher.

Luis gritted his teeth and reached for his tablet. They kept offering him opioids, and even Donovan seemed to think Luis should consider accepting them. He had to admit the idea of at least dulling the pain in his leg had its appeal. Two things stopped him. For one, his father's history of addiction (and the utter asshole his father had become) kept him strictly away from anything habit-forming.

More importantly, in the immediate term anyway, Hyena Lady had taken away Luis' career and his self-image. All he had left was his brain, and apparently, it was quite the asset. There was no way he was going to throw that asset away in the name of a little bit of relief—especially when that relief wasn't real, and was only temporary.

He scrolled through the conversations he could see on his tablet. He still had access to everything—he was, technically, still an agent. So far, he couldn't see a lot of movement on the Southwick case. He didn't expect to see much, not without the right pressure point to apply. After all, this was gang related, and gang members didn't typically snitch.

A message from Holcombe to Kevin Rourke caught his eye. He stared at it for several seconds, biting down on the inside of his cheek. He would not shout or throw things at his supervisor. She'd done a lot for him, and he knew it.

That didn't mean the temptation wasn't there.

She must have noticed something about him. Maybe his face had darkened, or maybe it had gotten gray. Maybe the medical instruments stuck to him like new appendages had gone haywire. Luis had no idea. He could only see the words on the screen.

"Luis, you'll be perfectly safe. Captain Carey is coming down here, along with Captain Perez. You don't have to worry; we're not going to let Tammie Hatch get to you."

The world snapped back into focus. "I'm not worried about that, ma'am. Give me my gun back, and I'll be just fine. It's Donovan I'm worried about. He just up and took off after an armed-and-dangerous fugitive with nothing to lose, in her own territory, who has already shown she has no regard for law enforcement officers? No. Hell no."

He didn't tell her that Kevin had already brought him his gun. He wasn't the kind of agent who used his gun often. Guns were permanent solutions, and Luis tended to prefer to leave his suspects alive. Sometimes that couldn't be done though, and he'd already made that mistake once with this suspect.

Besides—he no longer had the tools to craft a more peaceful solution.

Holcombe sighed. "It's not like he's going in alone, Luis. He's got a whole army of state and local officers with them. I know none of them are you, but they are competent."

Luis straightened himself up. "I certainly didn't imply that they weren't. This is *Donovan* we're talking about."

She grinned, wry and patient. "It is. And you love him, which makes you terrified of losing him. I get that, believe it or not. But he did find the place where you were. He and this team of people he pulled together did the work, and they found where she was holding you, and they missed rescuing you by maybe half an hour. He's going to be fine."

Luis gnawed on a knuckle. He wasn't sure how to phrase the gaping anxiety inside of him. On the one hand, he knew anxiety could lie. It *did* lie, all the time, and he was well aware of the way those lies manifested.

This wasn't like that.

"Hatch is smart," he said finally. "She's incredibly smart. She's also a fanatic."

"I see you've read up on her." Holcombe raised an eyebrow. "Is that healthy?"

Luis squirmed. "Depends on who you ask.

The point is, she's also tough as nails. If she'd decided to go into the military, she'd be their poster child. Her abysmal self-esteem dumped her in Gelens' lap, but once she's got her mind set on something, she's the more dangerous of the two. There's nothing she won't do to get what she wants, and right now, what she wants is to not go to jail."

"You think she's liable to do something." Holcombe leaned forward.

"I'll be shocked if she doesn't. At the very least, she'll have access to a firearm and try to take out officers who try to arrest her. She's more likely to be more efficient." Luis reached out for his water and took a giant gulp.

"You don't think this is maybe a little bit of panic?" Holcombe came to sit on the end of his bed. "I know it's kind of terrifying."

"It is. But no." Luis closed his eyes for a moment. "Look. She doesn't like to waste time or energy, right? She didn't tie me up, because she had enough ketamine to knock out all of those beer Clydesdales. She assumed I'd take the bait—water left out for me if I woke up—and just left me to it. But she didn't care if I overdosed or had a bad reaction—I had already had a bad reaction, and she still left me alone with it."

"I'm listening." The only emotional

indicator on Holcombe's part was a little line on her forehead, that hadn't been there before.

"When I turned out not to take the bait, she took more drastic action. She shot me."

"In the leg. She wasn't trying to kill you." Holcombe glanced at Luis' leg, still covered by a blanket. Luis didn't want to have to look at it any more than anyone else did.

"She left me unconscious and bleeding, ma'am. If I weren't in the shape I was, I'd have bled out and died down there." Luis wished he could admit he'd only survived with help. He didn't like taking credit for other people's work. "My death wasn't her goal, but she wasn't going to waste time worrying about it either.

"Here, the goal is avoiding prison. If Donovan gets her cornered, she's not going to just say, 'Oh, good collar, I'll go quietly now.' She's going to have something up her sleeve." Luis scrambled to type in the search terms on his Bluetooth keyboard.

"I'll admit she might be a little reluctant to go quietly, but there's no reason to think she's going to do something stupid." Holcombe craned her neck to try to see Luis' screen.

Luis bit his lip. For a second, just half a second, he considered knocking her out and just sending Lightfoot after Donovan. Lightfoot wouldn't solve the problem though. "I'm still relatively new to New England. Forgive me. Gloucester is more of a seaside community, right? Fishing. Boats. Tourism. Fish."

"Correct. Why?"

Luis turned his screen around. "So why would a guy by the name of Hatch be suddenly buying small farm-sized quantities of fertilizer and sending it to a residential address in a town that just does fish?"

Holcombe paled and pulled out her phone. "Rourke? I want you to get on the phone with everyone involved with this case—now—and tell them the house is likely bombed. Get the bomb squad up from Framingham. And don't let anyone the fuck near that site."

She paused, apparently for Kevin to respond.

"Just do it. I'll explain when everyone's safe. And for the love of God, call Carey first. He's already heading up there full steam ahead." She hung up and looked back at Luis. "I know you're a genius. I know you have a better grasp on the criminal brain than anyone else I know. But you have got to tell me how you figured that one out. You barely spoke with her."

Luis blushed and gripped his phone. He couldn't relax until he heard from Donovan, not yet. "Well, I mean like I laid out for you, most of it is just logic, you know? I read her file. It gets pretty dull in here. It's not like I can work out."

She snorted. "You're supposed to be doing physical therapy."

"There's only so much of that I can do right now. I'm doing what I can." Luis looked away. Intellectually, he knew he had to take the time to heal the right way. He still felt helpless, and hated it. "But anyway, I've never done well while being idle. So—not idle."

"It's true." Jose's voice rang out against the sterile walls of the hospital room. "He always got into trouble if he didn't have some kind of task. We wound up making him an intern in the evidence room just to give him work to do." He grinned at the memory. "Fun times. Hey, Agent Holcombe, I got your message while I was on my way here already. What's going on?"

"We've got a situation." Holcombe explained why Donovan wasn't here anymore. "I need to take off and coordinate from the office— more communication is better. But I'm also not willing to leave Luis alone, just in case."

"Well, no." Jose glanced back at Luis. "You finished your testimony today, right?"

Luis nodded. Fatigue overwhelmed him suddenly, the way it did these days. It was like his body recognized Jose's presence as making the room safer and sucked out the adrenaline keeping him upright. "Yeah. I hope it was enough."

"Well, I hope so too. That Morello guy doesn't have a lot of witnesses—like, two, I think. Psychiatrists who want to talk about his mental disorder, if I remember correctly." He curled his lip. "I think he's grasping at straws, personally."

"He's definitely grasping at straws." Luis shrugged. "But it's his job. Everyone gets a fair trial. Even sacks of crap like Gelens."

"That just lends more weight to you, Luis. She's more likely to act out today because on some level she knows Gelens is never going to see the light of day again." Holcombe shuddered. "Okay. I'm on my way out. I'll keep you posted. Keep an eye on your tablet. We might need your expertise later."

"I was planning to run a marathon around midnight, so you know, keep an eye on the time." Luis smirked.

Jose playfully smacked the back of his head. "Don't sass the boss."

Holcombe laughed as she headed out the door, moving so fast it could almost be called a jog.

Jose stopped grinning and closed the door behind her. "How bad is it?"

"I think she's going to blow up half of

Gloucester to avoid going to jail." Luis looked away. "And if I'd just figured it out earlier—"

"Stop it. You are not the only agent in the FBI. Someone else should have noticed that large fertilizer purchase long before you thought to look. There's a whole program in Homeland Security for that shit. You did catch it, people are being warned, you've done more than anyone could have expected.

"But that's not what I'm here to ask." Jose smiled and sat on the edge of his bed. "How bad is the pain?"

Luis didn't meet his eyes. "I can handle it."

"Of course you can. From what I'm told, you got all cut up, slapped a Band-Aid on it, and decided you could *handle it* until you passed out from the infection. How bad is it?"

"It's . . . it hurts." Luis took a breath. "I kind of want to cut it off myself, just to make it stop. But I know that won't help. And I'm scared for Donovan. So I'm trying to distract myself as best I can." He waved the tablet. "So I work."

Jose covered Luis' hand with his own. "I'll wake you if there's any news. Go ahead and close your eyes."

Luis did.

<hr>

Luis' warning about the potential bomb had seemed overwrought at first. The whole reason Donovan hadn't wanted to tell him where he was going was so Luis wouldn't worry, wouldn't get all worked up. He knew Luis wasn't dealing well with being confined to a hospital room or with the possibility of being restrained to a desk in the future. It was only natural for him to try to find some way to stay involved.

At the same time, Luis was probably the smartest guy Donovan knew. And when Donovan got the message about the fertilizer, he had to admit Luis' instincts hadn't been dulled at all. Maybe he was anxious, and maybe he was struggling with his own identity now. That didn't mean he wasn't right.

The bomb squad discreetly sent a robot into Hatch's relative's garage, a converted old barn that predated the house by at least a century, and found it was rigged to flatten everything in a two-block radius. *Everything* included an elementary school and a day care center. They had to act carefully and quickly to contain the area and make sure civilians were safe.

The robot showed no sign that Tammie was in the barn—not Tammie, and not anyone else either. That was one good thing. Donovan gave the order to surround the house and jam any outgoing signals—Wi-Fi, cell phone, even the landline got shut off. Local police quietly and systematically evacuated homes nearby.

Sweat poured down Donovan's back. Every minute he spent here was time Tammie could be using to escape. He couldn't justify abandoning a giant fertilizer bomb in the middle of Gloucester to pursue his grudge against one suspect though, even if she had taken Luis hostage.

Luis would never forgive him if he did.

A local judge was more than happy to sign a warrant. Donovan didn't necessarily think he needed one—they had probable cause thanks to Tammie, and then of course they had the fertilizer and the bomb. It was better to err on the side of caution though, especially when they could do so while evacuating civilians. Once everything was in place, a process that took far more time than Donovan would have liked, he donned more body armor than he would normally prefer and approached the front door.

Kevin was with him, right by his side.

An older man in sweats that had at best a casual relationship with the washing machine answered the door. His beard was stained with orange dust, likely from some kind of snack food. Donovan almost fell for the surprised innocence in his expression, but the hardness in his eyes gave everything away.

"What seems to be the problem, Officers?" Joseph Hatch had been born in Chelsea, just like Tammie. He'd gotten a job on a fishing boat and relocated to Gloucester. An accident involving a cruise ship yielded him a better living than the fishing industry ever would, and now, he spent most of his days causing trouble at one North Shore bar or another.

Having family in local law enforcement all over New England had its advantages. If all Donovan had to go by was a police record, he'd only see a string of drunk and disorderly charges and a revoked driver's license.

"Please step out of the house." Donovan wasn't in the mood to play games.

"I don't feel comfortable going outside. It's cold out there." Hatch scratched at his belly. "I'm an old man. We like to stay nice and warm."

Donovan grabbed him by the arm and pulled him out onto the porch. "We have a warrant to search the premises, as well as a warrant for your arrest. You have the right to remain silent. Anything you say can and will be used against you in a court of law. You have the right to an attorney and to have that attorney present during questioning. If you cannot afford an attorney one will be provided for you."

As Donovan spoke, he secured Hatch's hands behind his back. Kevin patted him down. If the look on Kevin's face was anything to go by, it was an unpleasant experience.

"You've got nothing on me. No reason to arrest me and you know it." The sweet old man act disappeared once the cuffs were on, but Hatch didn't resist arrest. He just smirked. "This is America. You can't just arrest people because you don't like their relatives."

"Actually, you're under arrest for the weapon of mass destruction in your barn. We'll file charges about harboring a fugitive after we find evidence, sport." Donovan faked a grin. "That's how it works. This is America."

Hatch paled and glanced toward the barn. "A man has a right to have fertilizer."

"Give the bomb squad some credit, buddy." Kevin rolled his eyes. "You really think they don't know what they're looking at in there? Please. I don't even work terrorism cases, and I can see you're not *just* storing fertilizer. And I know I can't get that stuff down at the garden center either."

"If you want to talk to Tammie, you're going to have to go in there and get her." Hatch wrinkled his nose.

Donovan handed Hatch off to a pair of state

troopers in full armor. "Get him out of here. And make sure he's someplace good and quiet. At his age, I worry about his heart."

The troopers nodded and hauled Hatch away. The old man tried to needle them, but they ignored him.

Donovan turned to Kevin as the bomb squad got ready to examine the house. "I've got to know. Why's a guy like this ready to blow up everyone in a two-block radius for Tammie? My dad's my dad, sure, but he's still a murderer. I'm not about to go killing people for him."

"You wouldn't cross the street for him at this point, Donovan, because the man is trash." Kevin snorted and pulled out his phone.

"Fair enough." A small part of him thought he should stick up for Fred, but the rest of him knew Kevin was right. "But seriously—Tammie abducted and shot a federal agent. She did it in an attempt to help a rapist and murderer escape. Why in the name of all that's holy would he want to kill for her?"

"Maybe he thinks we've got the wrong person. Maybe he doesn't care. Maybe he's a Gelens supporter. Who gives a shit?" Kevin stuffed his phone back into his pocket. "For a guy who lost his license three years ago, our boy here has been pretty careful to keep his registration renewed."

Donovan scratched his chin just as one of the bomb squad members detailed to go into the house strode out.

"Lieutenant Carey? Agent Rourke?" He glanced between them.

Donovan remembered his name at the last second. "Sergeant Bannicker. How can I help?"

Bannicker wasn't the kind of guy to mess around. "You can get to a minimum safe distance. This place is wired for sound. Be careful where you step."

"Christ." Donovan didn't need to be told twice. He picked his way back up the short walkway to the street. "Thank you!"

"Thank you, sir." Bannicker waved and headed back inside. More bomb squad people followed him. The rest of the team followed Donovan across the street.

"What happens now?" This from Scott, Donovan's brother.

Donovan ran his tongue against the back of his teeth. "We know she's capable of hiding out for a while, at least, in the rough. Kevin, what's the old man's vehicle?"

"Ninety-three Cadillac DeVille, blue." Kevin spouted off a tag number. "Last spotted up by Cherry Street."

A local officer snapped his fingers. "She's

going to Dogtown."

Donovan recoiled. "She's going to go torture puppies?"

"I wouldn't put it past her." The local snorted. "I've been following the Gelens case. But Dogtown used to be a separate village. It's a ghost town now, more of a park or a wildlife preserve. There's nothing left of the buildings but a few cellar holes. It's called Dogtown Common because people slowly left the village until there was nothing left but abandoned feral dogs."

"Well, that's Tammie, all right." Donovan tried not to think about the abandoned dogs. It had been centuries. They'd long since stopped looking for their humans. "How big is it?"

"Massive. If we have to, we'll cordon it off and wait until daylight." Kevin was already jogging back toward their cars.

Donovan wasn't willing to take that risk. For one thing, Tammie was smarter than that. If they tried to wait until daylight to get to her, she'd have slipped away long before now.

Donovan's GPS got him to Dogtown Common quickly. Local police and troopers from the area found less obvious parking areas to seal off, while Donovan, and the other "out-of-towners" blocked the other exits in search of Hatch's car. It was Kevin who found the car abandoned on the street not far from an entrance, but Donovan was sure she was on-site.

Gloucester police called for their K-9 unit, a dog by the name of Bruce. Bruce was able to get a scent from the car, which he immediately followed into the woods. Donovan had some reservations about heading into the woods after dark after a dangerous suspect—he'd done that back when he and Luis first reconnected, and both of them wound up injured. Still, he couldn't see another way around it.

He followed Bruce's handler for about a mile down a bumpy trail when a shot rang out. Donovan dove for Bruce and the handler, knocking them to the ground.

The bullet buried itself harmlessly in a tree.

Donovan fumbled for his night vision goggles. He hadn't trained with them much, but he vaguely knew how they worked. He reached for his gun as his eyes adjusted to the weird greenish-yellow tint.

Tammie was in a tree. She wore sweats that were too big for her, and held a large handgun. That eerie smile she could never drop flashed weirdly in the light.

She aimed her gun. This time, she aimed for the dog.

Donovan fired.

Tammie fell from the tree, screaming obscenities.

Donovan was on her in less than a second. He kicked her gun away and put the cuffs on her. "Where are you hit?"

"My leg, you fucking psycho!" She sobbed and thrashed as she fought the cuffs. "You shot me in my leg!"

He grabbed his flashlight and recited her Miranda rights as he searched for the wound. It didn't look bad, but looks could be deceiving. He radioed back to the others. "I've got the suspect in custody. Suspect is injured with a GSW to the right upper leg. Request backup."

Bruce's handler approached, making Tammie scream and fight even harder. Bruce gave her a look of utter disdain and turned his back on her.

"I've got some gauze pads here." The handler passed a packet over to Donovan. He opened it and applied first aid to Tammie, who howled.

He met her eyes. "Do you think Agent Gomes screamed like this when you shot him in the leg? Or when he drove himself to the hospital?"

She stared at him, shocked into silence. "Who—that pig? You're mad about that pig? Crunch all you want, buddy. It's not like they're not going to make more. Besides, the way I see it, it's an eye for an eye. He's the one who sent Santo to jail. If he's dead, who cares? We're even now."

Donovan grabbed her by the arm and hauled her to her feet. He didn't try to make her walk on her injured leg. He could have. He could have done a lot. He could have slapped her, punched her, shot her.

He wasn't his father.

"He's not dead, lady. He's very much alive. And he's even got his gun back." He gave her a thin smile. "And today, he finished his testimony against Santo Gelens. All this? Your whole big stunt of kidnapping him, hurting him, all of it? You going to jail, your uncle going to jail? It might have bought your boy a couple of extra days. That's it."

Kevin came jogging down the trail just in time to see Tammie's eyes fill with tears. Her face couldn't fall. She could only smile as she screamed and tried to fight against Donovan, the dirt on her face becoming streaked.

"Wow, man." Kevin grinned at Donovan. "If words could kill you'd be looking at a lawsuit."

CHAPTER SEVENTEEN

Luis almost sobbed with relief when Donovan sent him a picture of Hyena Lady—er, Tammie Hatch—in custody. He hadn't anticipated the scope of the fertilizer bomb, and he itched to get in and interview Tammie's uncle. Maybe they'd let him, after the surgery.

The most important thing, though, was Donovan. He was safe. Tammie hadn't gotten to him. He still had work to do, he couldn't just leave the crime scene, but he'd make it back to Luis in one piece. That was all Luis needed to hear. He would be able to get to sleep now.

Okay, he might be sleeping a little more fitfully than usual, but that was only to be expected.

The doctors did the next surgery on Luis' bad leg, kept him for another day, and then sent him home. He'd need more surgery, but he didn't need to lurk in a hospital while waiting for it. At first, he would receive physical therapy at home. Then he'd get to go to a proper therapy provider.

Luis was feeling enthusiastic about finally getting to go back to the town house he shared with Donovan. The stairs inside were another matter, but he'd figure it out.

Tria was so happy to see him when he got home she didn't even pretend to be mad. She sniffed at his crutches, tried to climb them, and then when Luis was properly settled onto the couch she seated herself right on the wound and started purring.

Cats are cats, and will act like cats no matter what.

The ghosts left them alone for Luis' first night home. At least, Luis thought they were leaving him alone. Getting home and getting settled in took a lot more out of him than he'd expected, and he spent a good amount of time dozing on the couch he and Donovan had picked out. Then he spent more time, once he'd made his slow and painful way up the stairs, sleeping on comfortable and clean sheets surrounded by the scent of his fiancé.

The therapist who arrived the next day admitted she was shocked to see he'd made it up and down the stairs.

Donovan, who'd taken the day off to help Luis get adjusted, just laughed at her. "Ma'am, this is a guy who managed to escape from a kidnapper and *rescue her from a burning building* even after she put a bullet in his leg. There's nothing he can't do, eventually, if he decides he's going to do it."

Luis blushed, but rested his head against Donovan's shoulder. He didn't deserve that kind of praise, but he'd bask in it all the same.

The therapist, a woman by the name of Karina, grinned. "Then I can see we'll have some fun. First though, we've got to get the leg ready."

Getting the leg "ready" wasn't as bad as Luis thought it might be. Karina had a portable TENS unit that she used to stimulate muscles he couldn't move on his own yet, and it actually felt kind of nice. He let himself enjoy it for a little while, while she outlined what she intended to do.

"After a few weeks we'll reevaluate with your doctor, and we'll move you over to the office. You might be cleared to do some nonimpact physical activity by then, like swimming. I get the impression that's going to be important for you." She grinned again, just a little, and he was able to laugh at himself.

"You're not wrong."

She didn't pat him on the shoulder or anything, but she gave him a confident nod. "Well, I won't make any promises. There are a lot of possible complications, and sometimes, our bodies just don't do what we want them to do. But even if we have some setbacks, we'll work through them. Okay?"

Luis didn't like feeling like the victim here one little bit. But he smiled and nodded anyway. Karina was a professional, and he had full confidence in her ability to get him back to full strength.

Captain Lightfoot showed up maybe half an hour after Karina left, with Millie in tow. "I'm just checking in with ye, lawman." Lightfoot looked Luis over. "Seems the hospital didn't mess ye up too badly. Ye've still got yer leg, at least. In my day, that wasn't bloody likely."

Luis snickered. "Yeah, well. We can do amazing things with antibiotics these days. Although, apparently, the leg's always going to be held together with plates and screws." He tried not to shrug. He didn't mind if he had a bit of metal in there, as long as the burning sensation stopped.

"What, like actual metal inside yer leg? The future is amazing. I'm glad I stuck around to see it." Lightfoot nudged Millie, who seemed fascinated by the flat-screen TV. "Miracles will never cease, eh, my dear?"

"It does seem that way, darling." She turned to face Luis and now Donovan, who'd just walked into the room. "Oh, it's that nice man. He looks much better than he did the last time we saw him."

Luis blushed. "I'm sure he was a bit of a wreck the last time. He'd been through a lot."

Donovan grinned in the direction Luis was looking. "I can't thank you enough. If it hadn't been for you, we'd never have known where to start looking."

Luis took Donovan's hand. "And if it weren't for you—and Mike and Boom-Boom—I'd have died there on the floor. Thank you so much for everything."

Neither Millie nor Lightfoot blushed. They couldn't. They had no blood. Millie did duck her head and try to hide her face in Lightfoot's coat though. Lightfoot waved a hand. "Think nothing of it, my friends. You've done plenty of good for me and others like me. And you'll do more, I know it. I do have a question for you."

Luis tried to straighten up. "Sure. What is it?"

"Would you be at home for Mike or Boom-Boom?"

Luis didn't hesitate. "Of course."

Donovan nodded his agreement. "Absolutely." He looked down at Luis. "What did I just agree to?"

Luis chuckled. Donovan was getting so good at pretending to know what Lightfoot was saying Luis could forget he couldn't actually see or hear him. "Visits from the other ghosts who helped me. We might just want to keep a fire extinguisher on hand. You know. Reasons."

Millie laughed. It was a beautiful sound, in spite of her deceased condition, and Luis found himself relaxing. "You're a joy to be around, Agent Gomes." Millie smiled at him. "I hope you don't mind if we don't move on, but stay here and enjoy the world a little longer."

Donovan sat gingerly beside Luis, and Luis leaned into him.

"It's not my place to object." Luis smiled up at Millie. "You were already forced into a bad situation, and then you were stuck—trapped in the hospital. Captain Lightfoot here helped break that chain. As long as you're choosing to be here, and you're not out there causing havoc or anything, I'm the last person who gets to tell you no."

She beamed at him. So did Lightfoot.

"And the same goes for Mike and Boom-Boom, when they come to visit. I want to help them, but I feel like enough choices have been taken away, if you know what I mean. I don't want people to be trapped. If you want to be here, then I'm sure not going to stop you." Luis took a breath. "Even if I were the kind of guy to say all ghosts had to move on—and I'm not—I owe all of you more than I could ever repay."

Donovan nodded. "We both do. You're family. Even if I can't see or hear you, you're still welcome here."

Lightfoot seemed to glow a bit, and not the malevolent glow he usually carried with him. "Thank ye," he said in a gruff tone. Then he and Millie disappeared.

Luis couldn't move around much, so he had plenty of time to research cases that might be connected to Boom-Boom. It wasn't easy. Not all of the records were digitized, and even after all this time, privacy laws still applied. Fortunately, Alex Morales was equally bored, and before he'd become an agent, he'd served the Bureau with his computer skills.

Luis wasn't above networking, when the situation called for it.

Mike was the first one to show up, arriving the next day at around noon. He was still dressed in his 1930s or '40s suit, complete with a hat, but he seemed a little more comfortable with the modern technology and layout than Millie was. "Nice place you've got here." He glanced around. "I'm glad they finally let you out of the joint. I wanted to come up and check in on you, but I couldn't."

"I can't imagine why not." Luis laughed a bit. "If I'd been stuck in a hospital for eighty years, I'd have a hard time setting foot in one again myself. They treated me well though. No priests, no problems. Just really good care for my leg." He winked. "And hey—I'd probably have lost the leg if it weren't for you and the others. Thank you for that."

Mike beamed. "Hey, anything for my buddy." He sat down on the other end of the couch. "I've been thinking, an awful lot. I looked up my son, but he passed a few years ago."

"I'm so sorry."

"He had a good life. Three sons of his own. And *they* had kids. Except for what happened, you know, my boy lived pretty well. I feel bad that I wasn't there for him. But I can still help other kids." He glanced out the window. "I've still got work to do. But I feel better now, you know? I feel like I can see better who I need to go after. Who's hurting kids and who isn't."

Luis nodded. "That seems to be pretty normal, after death. I'm not an expert, but from what I'm told, that's part of the healing process."

"I want to stay and keep working. Do you— do you think that's okay?"

Luis took a breath. "The federal agent side of me is supposed to say no one is supposed to take the law into their own hands. The rest of me knows I couldn't stop you if I wanted to. And, frankly, you can see better than I can exactly what you're dealing with. You're my friend, Mike. And I'd love for you to keep experiencing the world. There's so much out there to see and do. And if you happen to find someone who's hurting kids, well, I'm not going to object."

Mike grinned. "So you're okay if I come visit every once in a while?"

"I'd be sad if you didn't!" Luis reached out to shake Mike's hand.

"Thanks, Gabe."

"Thank you, Mike."

Boom-Boom showed up that night. Donovan was home. He'd brought an extra fire extinguisher, just in case.

Boom-Boom had found some pants. It was the first indication that he was starting to heal. He still wasn't well. Anyone could see that. If nothing else, the flies were a big clue, buzzing around his spectral form like he still had something to offer them. He sidled into the living room and lurked in the corner, muttering to himself.

"Hey." Luis kept his voice soft. "Thanks for coming by. I wanted to say thank you for helping me. I wouldn't have made it out of there without your help."

Boom-Boom stilled.

"I took the liberty of looking up your case. Is that okay with you?" Luis' mouth went a little dry.

To say Boom-Boom could be volatile was putting it mildly. Still, he had to try.

Boom-Boom edged closer to Luis.

"You were placed in the custody of the Department of Mental Health when you were ten, after your father died and your mother was incarcerated. You weren't verbal. They didn't have a diagnosis that fit you at the time, and it would be difficult to give you one now. But I did find a name that fit.

"Arthur Kingston."

Boom-Boom closed his eyes and stood stock-still in the middle of the room.

"I read your file, such as it was. You were in overcrowded conditions, and your condition deteriorated. You defended yourself against some of the other patients, who were violent. This got you labeled as violent in turn. And you developed a fondness for fire—not because you were looking to be destructive, but because resources weren't enough and you were cold."

Boom-Boom nodded and looked down at the floor.

"You died in isolation and neglect. But, my friend, you still helped me. A hundred years after your death, you still reached out and helped."

Boom-Boom opened his eyes and nodded.

"I don't care what people told you at the

time, Boom-Boom. They didn't spend enough time with you to know you. I did. Captain Lightfoot did. Mike did. Millie did. We all know the truth. You're a good man. You deserve to be known and cared for and to be warm."

Donovan couldn't see Boom-Boom, and he didn't know anything about the guy other than what Luis had told him. He still spontaneously got up and grabbed a throw from the back of the couch. He pressed it into Luis' hands.

"Christ, Luis. If he's cold, give him a blanket." He was blinking furiously, like he had something in his eye.

Luis held the blanket out to Boom-Boom.

The ghost took it. "Thank you."

Nothing burned that night.

If Donovan were still just a detective, he could have taken family leave to stay home with Luis and help him around the house until he was able to be better on his feet. Technically, that was still an option. Unfortunately, there was still a cop killer on the loose in the western part of the state, someone who'd killed one of Donovan's own men, and he couldn't just hole up at home and expect the case to solve itself.

Even if he wanted to—which he mostly didn't—Luis would never respect him again.

Fortunately, they had Jose. Donovan still didn't feel like he knew Jose well. They hadn't met while Donovan was in college, and Donovan had made excuses after he and Luis got back together. Now he had an opportunity.

He also had a wedding to plan.

Donovan's colleagues and subordinates had plenty of advice to give. Some left copies of wedding magazines on his desk. He tried to read them, he really did. He even shared them with Luis and, occasionally, with Jose or Patricia, when they were around. The only problem was that most of those magazines were geared toward brides.

"I mean this dress would definitely hide the cast." Luis peered at a floor-length chiffon thing with a crinoline. "The garter's going to be a bit of an issue, but we can figure it out, I guess. The article on updos is wasted, but I can definitely figure something out with the veil—but wait. Where's a guy supposed to put his gun in this number?"

At first, Jose had turned scarlet when Luis started in about the dress. Then he burst out laughing. "You're too hairy to make it work anyway." He ruffled Luis' hair.

"Oh, but I'd wax. It's a special occasion." He fluttered his eyelashes, and then he joined in the laughter. "I've done drag for a case, but it's not a look that's ever really worked for me, I'm afraid. Although it might be fun to watch certain people's heads explode, that's not what this is about."

Donovan laughed and settled in. At least Luis could keep his sense of humor about the whole thing.

He didn't know how long *he'd* be able to keep it up. Patricia had been delighted when Donovan told her about his intentions. She'd been eager to start the planning process. Of course, for Patricia, who'd been raised in a strictly Catholic family, that started with booking a church. And while the Church had made great strides since Donovan's childhood on the subject of homosexuality and those experiencing same-sex attraction, Patricia was unlikely to find a Catholic church in the greater Boston area willing to marry two men.

She tried. Donovan and Luis whispered about her efforts, which were heroic. She even denied one church a police detail at a funeral, which tied up traffic for eight hours as a result and got a phone call from the governor himself.

Donovan cocooned himself in the bedroom with Luis that night, hiding from news reports of traffic *still* being snarled in South Boston. "I know she means well. I do. It's just . . . I don't think she's ever found a problem she couldn't bulldoze her way through before."

Luis chuckled. "Patricia is a force of nature. In her head, a wedding means a church, a priest, flowers, people in uncomfortable clothes, and a drunken uncle trying to steal the beer from an open bar."

"You mean it's not?" Donovan rolled over to look Luis in the eye. "Don't get me wrong. The wedding is one day. I want to be your husband, and that one day is only important to me because it's the day that makes it all official." He rolled back over and stared at the ceiling. "I know it's . . . it's kind of trivial in the bigger scheme of things. There's a lot we need beyond just marriage. But I honestly never thought I'd have the opportunity to think about getting married, so I didn't sit around planning my wedding, you know?"

Luis molded himself into Donovan's side. It was such a comforting gesture, one Luis had been doing for as long as Donovan knew him. "I think young girls get encouraged to think of a wedding as the end-all, be-all because traditionally it's kind of the end of their lives. They're Mrs. So-and-So after that, and then just *Mom*. It's getting better, but that's still the expectation. Men of every orientation are less trained to focus on that day.

"But also, marriage isn't just about the

wedding. It's about having the right to be my health care proxy, if something terrible happens. It's about your dad not having the right to chase me out of your hospital room under the same circumstances. It's about having the same rights to survivorship benefits after we've built a life together as everyone else.

"The actual ceremony, the actual date? They don't mean much, not to me. What do you actually want from the wedding?"

Donovan thought about it. "I mean, I want to celebrate us. I do. But I also don't need that to happen in a big blowout kind of way. You're still hurt so there's not going to be a lot of dancing. We can postpone the reception, maybe?"

"I do like to dance." It was dark, so Donovan couldn't see anything on Luis' face to indicate how he felt one way or another.

"I know you do." Donovan kissed Luis' forehead. "And you'll get back to it. I know you will. Maybe we could do a quiet small thing? And have a nice dinner somewhere after because I do think we're something to celebrate. And then maybe in the spring or summer we can do a real reception, like a party with a bunch of family and friends and stuff."

Donovan could hear the smile in Luis' voice. "That sounds nice. It would be good to have the important part taken care of, you know?" He cleared his throat. "As it happens, I might know a judge."

Donovan couldn't help but laugh. "Let me guess, the subject has already come up."

"Well, he did come to the hospital and everything." Luis cleared his throat. "I might have been feeling a little anxious. You know, getting the important part over with, like you said." He swallowed, hard enough that Donovan could feel it. "I was scared, in that place. I mean, sure, I could have sat back and waited for rescue, but since when does anything work out right in a hostage situation? I had the ring and everything. I just didn't know when to say it.

"And then I was holed up in that place, and there were all these people who never got the chance. And I knew damn well I didn't want to wait anymore. Even if you said no, you were going to know how I felt. I don't want to hold anything back. Who does that benefit?"

Donovan blinked back tears. He couldn't imagine what it had been like in that place, in the dark. Luis had been able to put himself on friendly terms with all the ghosts he encountered, or so it seemed, but it had to have been terrifying. And of course he wouldn't just sit there and wait to be saved. Donovan wouldn't have either.

"I don't really want to wait and do some fancy thing." Donovan's mouth felt dry suddenly, but he pushed past it. "I don't need the church part. It might be nice to give my mom that comfort, but let's face it. I can't change who I am, and while it would be great if I could change attitudes at the Vatican, I don't see it happening. And I ain't waiting until it happens."

Luis chuckled a little. "I'm a little worried about giving Patricia a stroke. I love her. I really don't want to see her get hurt about this."

"Right?" Donovan winced. "How soon do you think you'll feel up to going to the courthouse?"

"They voted to convict Gelens. His sentencing is Friday. What if you and I grabbed Patricia and Jose, and they were our witnesses? It gives us time to deal with the paperwork and everything, and then it's done and over with." Luis hesitated a little bit over his words, like he wasn't sure how Donovan would react.

Donovan didn't hesitate at all. "Perfect. All we have to do is figure out how we're going to tell our folks."

Luis laughed. "I think Jose will be thrilled I don't scare him with another threat to wear the white dress."

"My mom might be kind of disappointed

you don't. She's still dreaming of her fairy-tale wedding."

"Notice how I didn't make that joke in front of her." Luis wrapped his arm around Donovan's middle. "For one thing, the dress costs extra if you're over five foot six."

"Really?"

"Mmm-hmm. Another agent from the BAU got married. I learned all kinds of things. Two thousand dollars on top of the regular price if you're over five six, and another two grand if you're over a size eight. What a racket!" He scoffed. "Although I might be able to find some of the underpinnings in my size . . ."

Donovan frowned. "What, the hoopskirts?"

"Er, no."

Donovan's tired brain caught up with him. "That might be interesting." He laughed.

Jose, as it turned out, was perfectly content with the idea of letting the judge marry them and doing a party later on. "Eduardo and I did something similar. We're both older, obviously, but we're long past the point when we might need to go showing off or anything. I'm as religious as the cat, and Eduardo left the seminary in disgust thirtysomething years ago. So I don't think either of us would have considered a church wedding to begin with.

"Is that something your mom is going to be a stickler about though?"

Donovan winced. "Yeah, well, I mean she's from a pretty religious background. So she has her feelings. And I don't want to stomp on them, but I want to be realistic here."

Jose patted him on the back. "I'll talk to her. It will probably go down easier coming from someone who isn't her son." He winked. "And someone who's been through it before."

Donovan could have kissed him, but it would have been weird.

Before he could take steps toward damage control, Donovan and his team made some progress in the Southwick case. He and Agent Holcombe both expected the killer to leave the state because, even though the FBI was involved, tracking murderers across state lines was more difficult by several orders of magnitude.

Instead, an alert security guard at a construction site near Worcester caught two young men trying to dispose of something in a cement mixer. He apprehended them and alerted police.

The item turned out to be a gun, which upon ballistic examination turned out to be the same gun that murdered Fitch, maimed Nguyen, and wounded Alex.

Donovan got to Worcester faster than he'd driven at any time other than when he'd gone to supposedly rescue Luis. He brought Alex Morales with him, to hopefully identify the suspect.

And identify Alex did. With one arm in a sling, he pointed directly at the sullen young white man with bad hair and bloodshot eyes and said, "Yeah. That's the guy who shot me."

Because Donovan never did get to meet the smart criminals, said cop killer shouted, "And I'll do it again, pig!" Then he dove for Alex.

Alex had his gun, but it was secured. Alex used his good hand to grab the suspect by the hair and drag his face down to his knee, which he brought up to meet it.

The suspect collapsed onto the floor, unconscious and with a bloody nose.

The constant hum of adrenaline that had buzzed under Donovan's skin left him. It was over.

CHAPTER EIGHTEEN

Luis had never sat through a sentencing and twitched so much. He had to force himself to keep a somber face during the victim impact statements. It had never been a problem for him before, no matter what else was going on in his life. The victims, and the people they left behind, came first every time.

Today was different, but Luis was going to do his damnedest to not let them know.

Morello had somehow talked Sullivan into allowing a statement from Gelens. Luis wondered who had thought that would ever be a good idea, but he guessed it wasn't his call to make. He suspected Gelens had lied about his own contrition to get Morello to ask.

And when Gelens took the stand, he proved Luis right. He pretended to read from a piece of paper Morello handed him, and then he crumbled it into a ball and tossed it to the side. "Who are we kidding here? You'll put me away. So what? It doesn't give you your kids back. Not the ones I killed and not the ones I just used on camera for entertainment. Yeah, I know they're kind of screwed up right now. I didn't need any of you whining up here, shaking your fingers at me to tell me that. The thing is, I don't care. No one cares.

"Okay. Sure. That guy in the suit." Gelens pointed to Luis. "He might care, just a little. But you know what? He's so weak he got taken out by a tiny woman and a glass of water. You think he can save you or your kids? Please. Someone else is going to come along and do it all over again. And while the stupid bitch couldn't manage to take him out entirely, this guy can't even walk anymore."

Luis' father's voice cackled from deep inside its cell in Luis' brain.

Morello, back in his seat at the defense table, buried his face in his hands. Donovan, beside Luis, flushed scarlet. Jose, on Luis' other side, growled as the rest of the crowd muttered. Luis just stared Gelens down. Maybe another day he would have been more affected.

But now, he reached out and took Donovan's hand. When he did, their rings connected. It was a tiny sound, more felt than heard, but Luis took all the strength he needed from it. He could keep his back straight and his

2

head high as Sullivan banged his gavel on the bench.

"Order in the court. Bailiff, remove Mr. Gelens from the stand and put him in his seat. Agent Gomes, this is highly unusual. But since you were specifically cited in his . . . outburst . . . I'd like to give you the opportunity to respond."

Luis took a deep breath. Gelens didn't deserve acknowledgment. Still, he squeezed Donovan's hand, grabbed his crutches, and approached the microphone that had been set up for the victim impact statements. "Thank you, Your Honor. I, um, I don't need defending. I honestly don't care what a guy like Santo Gelens thinks of me. I don't. I've been called worse by much more interesting and important people.

"I do want to address part of his statement. I testified in this trial because I was the lead investigator on this case. I was the lead because I've worked with the Child Pornography Task Force in the past. Yeah, I know that my agency has gotten some negative press lately. So has all of law enforcement. Some of it has been pretty well deserved, let's face it.

"But do you see those people over there, the people I'm sitting with? You've got a sample of law enforcement officers from Miami, the Massachusetts State Police, and Boston Police.

Every last one of them would do whatever it took to help those kids, to save those kids, and to take down people who hurt kids. Every one of them, and everyone they know or work with, cares.

"I wouldn't be here today if a law enforcement officer hadn't recognized the potential danger I faced as a young child and had taken it upon himself to keep me safe.

"My agency has an entire task force dedicated to fighting the exploitation of children. They work with hundreds of dedicated state and local agencies, along with volunteer organizations, fighting exactly this kind of thing. Yeah, I personally am going to be out of commission for a while.

"But don't think for a minute that means there aren't plenty more where I came from. We're like a hydra. Cut off one head, three more spring up in its place, and they'll be *pissed*. All you families, all you survivors—you all know where to find me. I've still got my phone. I've still got email. If you need anything, I'm still around. And if I can't get to you in person, I'll send someone who can. We are not abandoning you because something happened to me."

Gelens turned around to sneer at Luis, but Luis didn't care. Gelens was going off to the federal high-security penitentiary in Waymart,

4

Pennsylvania. Luis was going back into the judge's chambers to formally commit the rest of his life to the man he lived. Gelens was going to spend the rest of his life watching his back because people who hurt kids the way Gelens did tended to live short and unpleasant lives in prison. Luis was going back to school, keeping his dream job while he did so, and living a family life he never dreamed possible.

While Luis hobbled back to his seat, leg burning and throbbing at the same time, the assembled family and survivors applauded. Luis hadn't looked for that. He'd just wanted to give the families something to counter Gelens' poison. His cheeks burned almost as much as his leg by the time he got back to his place on the bench, and he tried to avoid drawing attention to himself when he got to his seat.

Jose patted him on the back. "I'm proud of you, son."

Luis could have floated off the bench, just from those words.

Sullivan allowed the applause to die down before clearing his throat. "The Commonwealth of Massachusetts does not have a death penalty option, Mr. Gelens, but you were tried under federal laws and convicted under the same. Your murders are considered aggravated and are federal offenses because they occurred during the commission of federal crimes—specifically, production of child pornography.

"The jury did recommend a death sentence for you, Mr. Gelens. And I did consider it—strongly. That said, upon the recommendation of a majority of families, I have decided to give you a sentence of life, without the possibility of parole. You have no remorse for your crimes. You are certain to reoffend, were you to be released. You view people as objects, tools to further your interests, rather than as individuals with their own lives, hopes, and dreams.

"Furthermore, I sentence you to an additional fifty years for the child pornography sentence, to be served consecutively. Mr. Gelens, you will never breathe free air again. Bailiff, take Mr. Gelens into custody, please." Sullivan banged his gavel and then rose. "This court is adjourned."

Everyone rose, Luis included. He couldn't feel anything for Gelens. He hadn't expected a death sentence, not from a Massachusetts jury, and he hadn't wanted one either. Gelens didn't deserve the gift of life, but he didn't deserve the massive outpouring of money spent on a death row inmate either.

The bailiff hustled Gelens out of the courtroom, not into the custody of the sheriff's office but into the waiting arms of federal corrections officials. Sullivan exited to his chambers, and the rest of the observers filed out of the courtroom.

Some family members were crying. Luis could understand that. Sentencing could be a catharsis, and it could be frustrating too. So many families found their feelings of grief and rage and pain unabated after the final gavel pounded, even though they expected to somehow feel better. Luis tried to prepare them, but nothing really could.

A clerk in a gray suit approached Luis and his companions. "Agent Gomes? Judge Sullivan will see you now."

Luis followed, Donovan by his side and Patricia and Jose behind them. Patricia had, predictably, been upset when Jose told her their plans. She'd ultimately given in with good grace though, and today she turned up with as much joy as anyone could wish.

They slipped into Sullivan's chambers. Luis hadn't been back here before. The lawyers were the ones to deal with the judges, unless they were getting warrants, and Luis usually let the higher-ups do that. Sullivan's chambers weren't much more than an elegant office, with some memorabilia from some of the more exciting trials he'd handled and one folded-up American flag in a glass-fronted case in the corner.

The judge himself, out of his robes, rose to meet them. He shook hands with everyone, Luis first. "Thank you for speaking to the families like that, Agent. It's pretty far outside typical protocol, but I couldn't just let those words stand."

He pulled a piece of paper from a file in his drawer. "Shall we get started?"

Luis stared at the paper. He knew what it was, even without looking at the words. That piece of paper was his marriage license. Luis and Donovan, officially and legally a family. This was it. This was forever.

His palms got damp. He wiped them on his pants. "So how do we do this?"

Sullivan chuckled. "All right. How about this? Do you, Luis Gomes, take this man, Donovan Carey, to be your lawfully wedded husband?"

Luis didn't have to think about it. "I do."

"And do you, Donovan Carey, take this man, Luis Gomes, to be your lawfully wedded husband?"

Donovan swallowed hard. "I do."

"All right. If you could each sign here—it doesn't matter which one is Spouse One or Spouse Two. Very good. And if we could get Mom and Dad to sign here and here as witnesses. Fantastic. All right. With the power vested in me by the

8

Commonwealth of Massachusetts, I now pronounce you husband and husband. You may kiss the groom."

Luis leaned on his crutch and pulled Donovan in for a kiss. Kisses for public performance aren't usually satisfying for anyone involved, but it wasn't the first time Luis had put on a show. He kissed Donovan deep and thoroughly, molding his body to Donovan's in promise of what was to come later.

Married life didn't necessarily feel different to Donovan. It would, he knew, especially around tax time. Or the next time Luis got injured and Donovan didn't have to get the FBI's okay to get into his hospital room, regardless of who was listed as his emergency contact. But for now, there weren't any significant changes.

And Donovan was okay with that. He wouldn't have gotten married if he wasn't happy with Luis, and he knew Luis felt the same way.

They would take a honeymoon after Luis' first semester at Harvard ended, when he was (hopefully) in better physical condition and able to enjoy travel a little more. For now, the work continued, and both of them were willing to wait.

The gang member who'd killed Fitch was a twenty-year-old man by the name of Evan Harrison. He'd been born in Chicopee and kind of drifted into a life of crime, following two brothers and his own father. Luis referred to him as the "anti-Donovan," and Donovan could see where that was the case.

Harrison had no remorse at all for what he'd done. He was only annoyed that he'd been caught. Donovan wasn't surprised at that either.

While the Constitution guaranteed the right to a speedy trial, Harrison's case was complicated by the competing jurisdictions involved. Kevin, who'd been a lawyer briefly before deciding the FBI was where it was at, tried to explain it. "The investigation that brought your guys and Morales to his door was a joint investigation, right? State and federal. So there's an actual army of lawyers and a few judges trying to figure out whether or not Fitch's murder is a federal case or state. And if it's federal, it carries a death sentence." He tugged at his tie, as if it had become too tight.

Donovan sat back and tried to process Kevin's words. "I'm not sure how I feel about that. What does Fitch's family think?"

"They'd like to see him fry, even though we don't use the chair anymore. But they're still reeling from the loss. I don't know. It's not like it would bring Fitch back." Kevin heaved a sigh. "It's not much of a deterrent. Everyone knows this. No one sits there and thinks, 'Well, I'd better not shoot this cop because I'll get the death penalty!' They think, 'I'm not going to jail, not today.' And that's that."

Donovan looked out the window. "You're not wrong. To be honest, if people started using their brains, we could probably lay off ninety percent of our workforces. I'm not going to lie. I mostly agree. I'm not a fan. There's still a part of me, the part of me that sent Fitch out there, that chose him for that assignment, that wants to get revenge. And I ain't proud of it."

Kevin huffed out a little laugh. "It's understandable, Donovan. It's not your fault, obviously. Harrison would have made his choices no matter what, and no matter who. We're certainly not going to go ignoring major drug trafficking and even human trafficking just because they might get violent. We took the appropriate precautions. Sometimes shit happens, and we have to roll up our sleeves, get a mop, and deal with it."

"Yeah. I know." Donovan sucked in his cheeks. "Luis said almost the same thing."

"Well, I'm not about to hug you to make it feel better—"

Donovan had to laugh. "Yeah, still

newlywed here. Let's not."

"But he is getting his doctorate in feelings and brains and stuff. So maybe listen to him." Kevin winked. "At least when he's not pretending to deal with his own shit."

"He's getting better about that. At least he admits when he's not dealing well." Donovan shrugged. "He's doing better than I expected with that honestly. He's talking with Father Geoffrey, he's not trying to push past where his body will allow, and he's actually talking when he needs to."

"Will wonders never cease?" Kevin snorted. "It's good that he's taking care of himself though. We'll see how he's doing once the trial starts."

Nguyen's road to recovery was going to be even longer than Luis'. She'd lost her leg entirely, and it was going to be a while before she could be fitted for a prosthesis. She opted to retire on disability rather than let the department try to create a position for her. "I don't think I could handle seeing everyone else get to leave the office and have to sit behind a desk." She shuddered. "Even if I eventually got so good with the prosthetic that I could go back out into the field, getting there would be more than I could handle. I'm actually going to take a page out of Agent Gomes' book."

Donovan blinked at her for a second.

12

"You're . . . getting a cat?"

She scoffed at him. "I'm going to go back to school. Pursue academia. I've got a good amount saved, and I'll have money coming in from retirement. Maybe I can go on to teach at the academy, or even in the criminal justice department at a college or university. It doesn't have to be a lot, but at least I'll still be using my training and my brain."

Donovan shook her hand and smiled, even though he had to blink back tears. "I won't say I'm not going to miss you. You're a damn fine detective."

"Yes, I am. And I'm going to miss the work. But I know myself, Lieutenant. I'd rather focus on building something new than have something I worked so hard to achieve right there in front of me, just out of my grasp."

"I can't fault that decision. You always did have a good head on your shoulders. I genuinely hope you'll keep in touch, as a friend at the very least."

"That's a promise." Nguyen's smile was radiant as Donovan left her side. He noticed she already had graduate school sites open on her laptop.

Jose had taken a decent amount of family leave, so he was still in Boston when Tammie Hatch had her first pretrial hearing. Unlike Evan Harrison, there was no confusion about jurisdiction for Tammie. She'd interfered with a federal trial, she'd assaulted (and tried to kill) a federal law enforcement officer, and she and her uncles had tried to bomb a town. An entire town. That was federal.

She had the temerity to ask Morello to defend her. Morello laughed in her face. "Everyone has the right to representation, Ms. Hatch, but I literally cannot defend you. I've already been subpoenaed by the prosecution—seeing as how you involved me in your abduction."

No other private attorneys would take the case either, so Hatch was forced to make do with a public defender. Luis was twitchy about that. Apparently, the Justice Department had decided to seek the death penalty in Tammie's case, both because she'd tried to kill a federal agent and because of the whole terrorism thing. Donovan once again found himself ambivalent.

She initially pled not guilty. Donovan had no idea how that was supposed to work, but she had the right to lie he guessed.

Prosecutors asked to meet with her, her attorneys, and Judge Sullivan. After a moment's thought, Sullivan invited Luis to be part of the meeting. "I wouldn't normally do this," he advised everyone, "but in this case, I think it's important."

And so Luis and Donovan got dressed up for court. They drove down to Boston and went back to the very chambers in which they'd been married, where they sat down at a table with Fahey, Sullivan, Hatch, and her defender.

"It's not my fault." Tammie's permanent grin seemed especially vile when she looked Luis up and down. "My uncle's pissed at you, by the way. You wrecked artwork that had lasted forty years."

"He can die mad." Luis flashed her an insincere grin and turned his attention back to the situation at hand.

"Ms. Hatch." Fahey cleared her throat. "I'm aware that you insist the abduction was not your fault."

"It wasn't. Santo put me up to it."

"The power to say no was still yours, or it would have been had you been telling the truth. But you're not." Fahey gave her a thin smile. "Surely, you know every conversation in prison is recorded."

Tammie's smile never faltered. Her eyes didn't widen. She couldn't make either expression. The color did drain from her face.

"You suggested the scheme. Gelens went along with it, of course. He gave you pointers. But you were the one to initiate the crime. And the bombs were your brainchild too. Your uncle told us so. He definitely didn't mind blowing up the town he'd been living in for fifty years, but he wouldn't have done so on his own. You're the one who set that whole thing in motion." Fahey leaned forward just a little. "No one's coming to save you, Tammie. I'm going to offer you a deal—one time only. You plead guilty and take life."

Tammie swallowed, hard. "And if I don't?"

Luis cleared his throat and reached out. He put his hand over Tammie's. "I didn't ask them to seek the death penalty. I don't like you, and I think you're dangerous, but I'm not a fan of that particular punishment. I might be able to get you out of a death sentence for what you did to me because you didn't actually kill me.

"The bombs are a different story. The fact that no one died is just coincidence. The administration wants to look tough on crime. They want to look tough on terror, and they're desperate enough for a win that they'll overlook every mitigating factor. They'll find a way to loop Gelens in. You did everything you did to try to save him. Do you really want to be the one to get him killed?"

Tammie tried to stare Luis down, but she couldn't do it. Not when she didn't have any power over him. "Fine. I'll plead guilty if the death
16

penalty is off the table."

"The people accept." Fahey quickly turned to Sullivan.

"I approve of this arrangement." Judge Sullivan passed the plea agreement document to Tammie, who signed it and handed it to Fahey. "I'll go tell the jury the good news." Sullivan returned to the courtroom, and the bailiff returned to bring Tammie to face the rest of her life.

Fahey shook Luis' hand before leaving with the public defender. Donovan was alone with Luis now.

"You actually intervened to save the person who did all that to you?" Donovan only glanced down at Luis' leg once. He didn't have to do more.

"Not so much. I mean it was Fahey's idea, but she did feel me out on the subject before approaching anyone else about it." Luis moistened his lips. "I . . . I mean, you already know how I feel about capital punishment. Especially given the other stuff." He glanced around, and Donovan knew he meant seeing ghosts. "But it's more than that. If I let her, and what she did, change who I am, then she wins and I lose.

"My whole reason for going into law enforcement, as someone from a background that doesn't have great relationships with the cops, has always been to help. To save lives. I'm not always able to do that, but I have to take every opportunity given to me. I don't have a choice, you know? It's part of who I am. Tammie's gone through a lot. She let it become an excuse for why she did some really bad shit. But she can still change. She can do some good, even if it's behind bars. I don't want to be part of taking lives. I want to save lives."

Donovan wrapped his arms around Luis. "And that's why you're here."

Luis chuckled. "I'm here because I found someone who makes me feel like I *can* save lives." And then he kissed him.

ALSO BY J. V. SPEYER

Prodigal
Hollywood Lighting
Faith
See Ya, Space Cowboy
Under His Skin
Rites of Spring
All This Could Be Yours
Nine Cocktails
Building Up To Love
Absolution
Paper Hearts
Snowed In – Ross and Ashton
Professional Courtesy
Hunter
Whirlwind
Carriage House
The Dented Crown
Starlit
Midnight

ABOUT THE AUTHOR

J. V. Speyer has lived in upstate New York and rural Catalonia before making the greater Boston, Massachusetts, area her permanent home. She has worked in archaeology, security, accountancy, finance, and nonprofit management. She currently lives just south of Boston in a house old enough to remember when her town was a tavern community with a farming problem.

J. V. finds most of her inspiration from music. Her tastes run the gamut from traditional to industrial and back again. When not writing, she can usually be found enjoying a baseball game or avoiding direct sunlight. She's learning to crochet so she can make blankets to fortify herself against the cold.

J. V. can be found at www.jvspeyer.com, on Twitter or Instagram at @JVSpeyer, or on Facebook at https://www.facebook.com/JVSpeyerAuthor. You can get exclusive updates, cocktail recipes, and other notes here: http://eepurl.com/dtlwBH